Roots of Hope

Saber

Book One

Monica Red

 Formatted with Vellum

To my whole world, Josephine

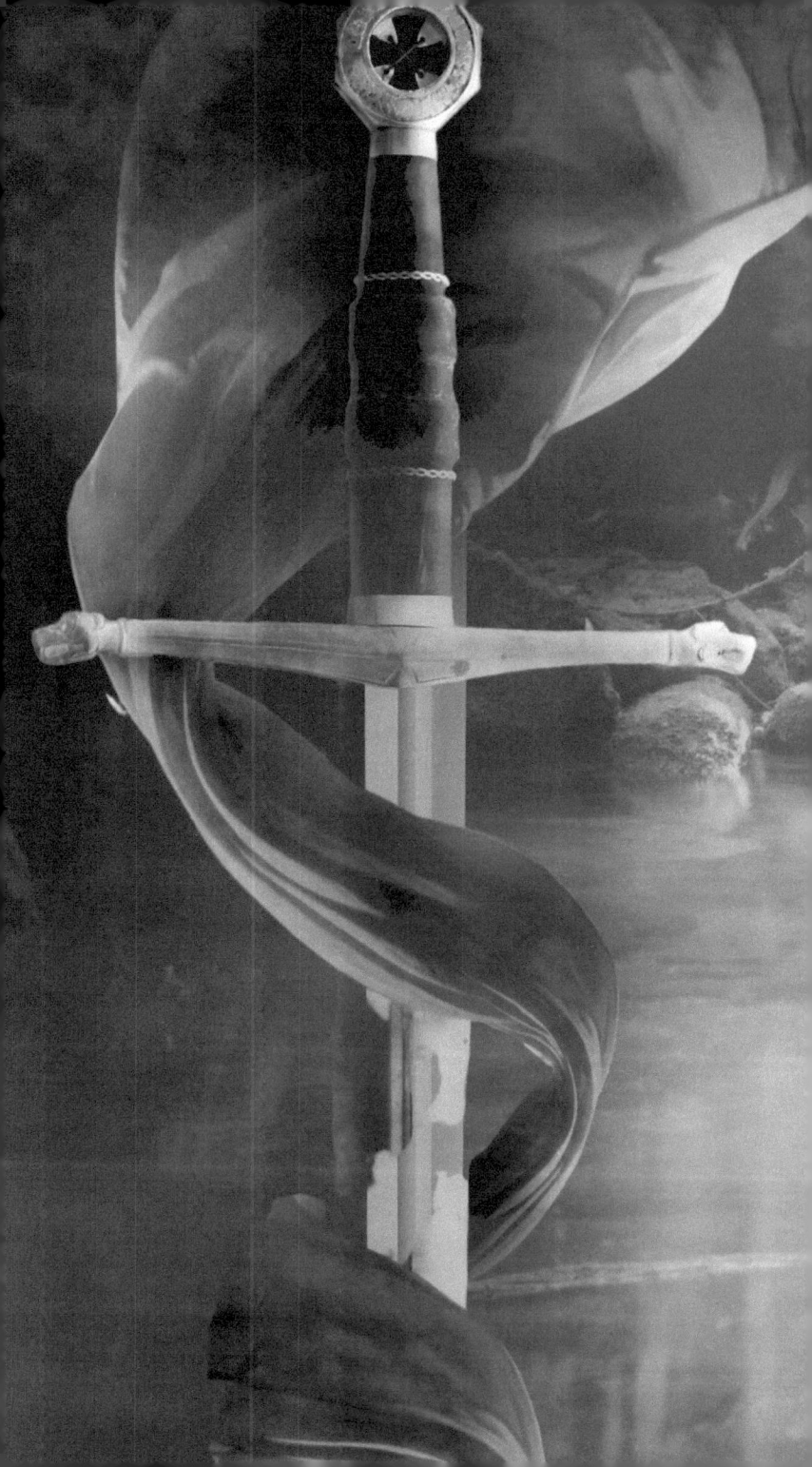

CHAPTER ONE
BEFORE THE WAR

The only reason she was alive was because her captors wanted her to be. For weeks she had tried to escape, but the birth of her baby had left her body weak and frail. Now, lying on the cold, wet street, she had lost all hope. She knew she would not live to see her daughter grow—and there was no one left to care for the child. Her little girl would never know how fiercely her mother loved her.

It was his fault. The father—her husband—was a man bound to greatness, a destiny he had once abandoned for her. But when the world fell apart, he returned to it, too late to save them. The life she treasured died with him, or so she was told, when soldiers brought back the unrecognizable body that wore his medals. He left without ever knowing he had a daughter.

Yet deep in her heart, she had never truly believed him gone. Not until now, when she was about to be murdered. Because only death could have kept him from saving them.

The men's voices carried through the alley. Ignoring the agony burning through her, she curled herself around her baby, shielding her as best she could.

"Let's be done with this," a deep voice growled.

"I told you before," another snapped. "Killing her now will only bring more complications."

The tallest hooded man yanked the baby from her arms. Her daughter's cries filled the night, piercing through her own screams.

"No!" she gasped. "Don't hurt her!"

The deep-voiced man silenced her with a vicious kick to the stomach. Through her sobs she saw him take the baby from his partner and place her down on the street—far from reach, yet close enough for the mother to see her face.

"We keep her alive until we find the saber," the tallest man said coldly. "If she survives, she's yours."

An owl hooted in the distance, its haunting call carrying an eerie weight. Strangely, it calmed her. The sound drew forth a memory—an old prayer her husband had once taught her. With each ragged breath tasting of blood and iron, she forced herself to crawl toward her daughter, whispering the blessing words through her tears.

A third man crouched beside her. He lowered his hood, and her heart froze. She knew that face. A friend. Or so she had believed.

"That is a peculiar blessing," he murmured, moving the baby back within her reach.

At her touch, the infant quieted, nuzzling against her

finger. Her body was failing, her strength slipping away. In despair she lifted her gaze to him, pleading.

"Please... save her."

His eyes narrowed, then softened when the child let out a sudden laugh. For an instant, guilt shadowed his features, and something almost human stirred in his expression.

"What the hell are you doing?" the tallest man barked.

But the hooded man ignored him, staring at the baby with hesitation, doubt, and something that almost looked like sorrow.

"Please," she whispered again, her voice nearly gone.

The baby's laughter drew her back. That smile—the same smile she had dreamed of—was enough to warm her broken heart. Once more she prayed, and this time the air seemed easier to breathe. A faint scent of flowers drifted around her, and she knew, somehow, that her daughter would be safe.

With the last of her strength, she unclasped a silver pendant from her neck and slipped it over her baby's tiny wrist.

"This will guide you home, sweet one." She kissed her child's head, tears falling into the dark curls. "I love you, Sara."

Her daughter's laughter was the final sound she heard as the light of her life slipped away.

CHAPTER TWO

The empty sands of the desert surrounding Tundra, Hune's capital city, mirrored the bleakness of their future. Not long ago, the sound of ocean waves had filled the air. Prairies brimming with colorful flowers and wild grasses had circled the city. People had come and gone freely, unaware of the enemy waiting in the shadows.

Chris had longed to see his hometown for years. He had imagined it marking the end of the war. The fighting would be over, they'd no longer need him, and he could begin again. But the war hadn't ended. It had only grown more violent, and his future was sealed.

Like his father, Colonel Alexander Riddley, Chris had become a decorated soldier and earned command at a young age. His guard ranked just below his father's and the king's armament—something to be proud of. But pride didn't stop him from wishing for something better, for all of them.

In all the years he'd fought, he'd never battled near

Tundra—until now. The reisers had won the last battle. That third race of Hune, once dismissed as grotesque and weak, living in hiding, had become the architects of their destruction. The reisers had torn through their world. No one fully understood their reasons, but their hatred was undeniable.

His father never made it back to the city. Chris returned home only to bring dreadful news—and to find a sick mother and an arranged marriage to a stranger.

Tundra no longer felt like home. It was a broken shell, just like the future. Logic whispered that they were next to fall.

There was still hope among the people—Hune was a land steeped in magic, after all—but Chris had seen too much. He had never encountered a sorcerer, and didn't want to. He hated them. They had cost him too many men. They had cost him his father.

In the last battle, the reisers had become indestructible. He assumed they'd received help from a higher power. He had never believed in the prophecy that claimed humans were doomed, not until the day he struck a reiser and his sword bounced off like it had hit stone.

Since returning to Tundra, the days had blurred together in misery. That evening promised more of the same. Commander Christopher Riddley had just received a second royal order. The king wanted to relocate Chris's men—the last remnants of Hune's army—and hinted that the High Council supported the decision.

A lie. The High Council hadn't been seen since

before the war began. Rumors claimed they'd been murdered, but Chris and his men knew better. The council had vanished before the reisers' first strike.

The king was using them as leverage, hoping to manipulate Chris into abandoning the last human city. Chris feared that anger might cloud his own judgment.

"Any sign of them, Lieutenant?" Chris asked as John Monder returned from scouting.

"No, sir," the soldier replied.

They moved a few paces away from the others.

"Anything else from His Highness-less?" John said.

Chris shook his head but offered a half-smile as he held out the letter.

"That freaking coward."

"You should be careful, John; he is our king."

John's face hardened at the word. His disdain for the king was no secret, and Chris didn't feel much like defending him either.

"If that's so," John said, "why are we still here?"

Chris had asked himself the same. It was the first time he'd ignored a direct order long enough to receive a second. And still, he hadn't decided. Leaving Tundra defenseless felt wrong. King Leonard III was a cold leader, but this command was unusually bold.

Moving the army to the Soto Forest to "preserve humanity's secrets" made no tactical sense. The zhortas —holy men devoted to the gods and keepers of Hune's prophecies—didn't deserve protection. They had disappeared after delivering the prophecy that damned them all.

The soldiers blamed the zhortas for the war, and Chris couldn't disagree.

"You've got first watch, Lieutenant," Chris said.

"Oh, come on! I just got back."

"Next time, watch your tongue."

Chris chuckled and left John grumbling with the scouts.

LATELY, CHRIS PREFERRED WALKING AT NIGHT. Fewer people recognized him. His family name was legendary in Tundra—government figures for generations. His grandfather had poured his life into turning Tundra into a shining gem, even more beautiful than Laconia, their former rival. Before the war, their biggest concern had been how many flowers to plant in the city boulevards.

Chris reminded people of those days. Tall and striking like his father, with his mother's pale gray eyes, he stirred old memories of peace. But like the city, he only resembled better times—faded and eroded. The war had carved lines into his face and left him cold. Command had hardened him, and compassion had become a luxury.

He kept his head down as he walked. His mind turned over the king's order again. If he obeyed, Tundra might fall. But his plan—to hide what remained of humanity in scattered settlements—was no better. If the reisers found them, it would be over. But at least hidden, they had a chance.

Chris believed they weren't losing because of magic, but because of arrogance. They had underestimated the reisers. Assumed they were weak. That mistake had cost them everything.

When he reached the tavern, the sound of laughter and badly played instruments spilled out onto the street. A part of him longed for that easy denial of reality.

"Christopher. I'm so glad I found you."

He flinched. The tavern door was so close. He considered stepping inside and pretending not to hear.

Jean Walker wouldn't follow him into a place like that.

"Jean," he said, forcing a smile and crossing his arms. "What can I do for you?"

She glanced around, shaking her head with an exasperated sigh. "Your mother and I prepared the special dinner she told you about. Our guests will be arriving soon. You're expected."

Chris frowned. "Goddamn it."

"You forgot." Her voice tightened.

For a moment, he saw a flash of the girl she used to be —shy, sweet, always bringing him little gifts. That girl was long gone. Now she was elegant, beautiful, and demanding. Her assertiveness reminded him of a royal girl from his past, and the hard lesson she'd taught him.

"Oh well." Jean lifted her heavy skirts and motioned for him to follow. "It'll be all right. I won't tell your mom, and you can pretend you had something important to do."

"Pretend I had something important to do?" Chris echoed. "I've got an army to run and a city on the brink."

"Really? And that involves loitering outside a tavern?"

Chris took her arm and moved her out of the main path. He wasn't about to argue in front of his men. The only reason he tolerated Jean was the old arrangement between their families—an agreement he had no time or patience for.

"What I'm doing doesn't concern you," he said.

"It does, Christopher," she snapped. "You may think you're above us all, but I belong to Tundra, to these people... and to you. You're my fiancé, and your behavior makes a mockery of me!"

Chris sighed, glancing up at the darkening sky.

He was about to walk away when he noticed her tears. A flicker of guilt caught him. Jean had been there for his mother during the war. She was like a daughter to her. He had hurt that woman enough already.

"You've heard about the king's order?" he asked. "I need to talk with my soldiers, and they happen to be here."

Her expression softened. "Right. Our last chance."

"What did you say?"

She looked hopeful—dangerously so.

"Your mother explained it to me," Jean said. "If the king wants you somewhere else, it must be important. Maybe it's our way out. Maybe it's how we survive."

Chris didn't like what that hope stirred in him. Hope was dangerous.

"I was angry when I heard you were leaving again," she continued. "But I trust you. I know you wouldn't abandon your mother unless it truly mattered."

Chris hadn't considered that angle. Since losing his father, he hadn't felt hope. Alexander Riddley had been the best of Hune, and his death had destroyed what was left of Chris's optimism. But maybe... maybe Jean and his mother were right. Maybe this strange order *was* the only chance left.

"Go home, Jean," he said with a tired smile.

He'd barely taken two steps before she blocked him again.

"Chris, we have to go now. Dinner. The visitors—your mother will be furious. We can't postpone this, not if you're leaving."

"Right," he said, sighing. "I'll be there soon."

He turned back toward the tavern. From behind him, he heard a soldier chuckle and call out, "Don't wait up!"

As he turned from the tavern, Chris's thoughts drifted—not to Jean or the king's order—but to a strange dream he'd had the night before.

He rarely remembered his dreams anymore. But this one lingered like smoke.

A woman's voice had whispered his name, gentle but urgent, calling to him through silver light. He couldn't see her face, only a silhouette surrounded by the scent of wildflowers—flowers that hadn't bloomed in Tundra since the war began. Her presence had felt... familiar, though he was certain he'd never met her.

He'd dismissed it then, a trick of exhaustion. But even now, it tugged at the edges of his mind—soft and impossible to forget.

CHAPTER THREE

The tavern was packed with off-duty soldiers. Like Chris, they didn't enjoy being surrounded by the hopeful gazes of civilians. They knew better. Their kingdom was crumbling.

Major Charles Abbott was the exception.

Chris had met him the first day he arrived at training camp. He'd been demonstrating sword techniques when someone in the back dared to laugh.

"You look like a girl pretending to use a magic wand."

By the time three other trainees separated them, both looked like they'd lost the fight. The major in charge hadn't cared that Chris was Colonel Riddley's son. He threw them in a tiny isolation cell, tied back-to-back.

They'd been best friends ever since.

Charlie was a walking contradiction. His dark skin made his bright green eyes even more striking, and his playful nature belied the deadly precision he fought with.

He was sharp, lethal—and the first to crack a joke when the fighting stopped.

The only time Chris had seen him quiet and shaken was the day Colonel Riddley died. The brutality of it had scarred them all. It was worse than anything they'd seen in years of war.

"Attention!" Charlie's voice rang from inside the tavern.

Chairs scraped the floor as the soldiers stood abruptly. The noise cut off, replaced by heavy silence as everyone turned toward Chris, waiting for his command.

He blinked, caught off guard, then gave a small nod. "At ease."

They relaxed, though not completely. Most bore fresh wounds—some on their bodies, others deeper. They were Hune's last defense: a weary collection of brave, broken young people.

Chris made his way through the room toward Charlie, who was grinning.

"Well, I had to make sure they greeted you according to protocol, Commander," Charlie said. "But I can see you weren't expecting it."

"Shut up." Chris punched him lightly on the arm. "Now everyone thinks you're jealous of my rank."

Charlie smirked. They both knew that wasn't true. Chris had volunteered for the war. Charlie had been pushed into it by his parents. Still, he'd never complained —just found ways to see the bigger picture. That perspective had often helped Chris find balance when making hard decisions. And it was part of why he'd already chosen Charlie to lead the troops in his absence.

They took a table in the corner. While Chris waited for his drink, Charlie filled him in on the latest gossip.

Before Charlie could finish his thought, two soldiers bumped into their table—one tall and stoic, the other lean and twitchy with boyish energy.

"Evening, sirs," the younger one said, offering an exaggerated salute. "Mind if we join for a moment?"

Charlie groaned. "Gods help me. Lowd, if you're trying to impress us again, I swear I'll have Fred tie you to the stables."

"I'm *not* trying to impress anyone," Terry said. "I'm just being personable. Social bonding is crucial to morale in wartime."

Fred rolled his eyes. "He read that in a pamphlet once and now thinks he's the morale officer."

Chris smirked. "You do talk a lot for someone who hasn't been in that many battles."

"I've been in *enough*," Terry said, puffing his chest. "And I've survived them all. That counts for something, doesn't it?"

"It does," Chris said. "Especially since your first mission involved falling off your horse and nearly stabbing your own foot."

"That was tactical misdirection!" Terry protested. "I distracted the enemy with chaos."

Charlie choked on his ale. "By 'enemy,' do you mean the mule tied to the post?"

Fred snorted. "Let the kid dream, Charlie. He's got heart."

Terry beamed as if that were the highest praise he could receive.

Chris leaned forward, his tone turning a touch more serious. "You still stationed with the scouts under Lieutenant Monder orders?"

"Just reassigned this week," Fred said. "Rear watch with Lowd here."

Charlie raised an eyebrow. "John is lucky. Terry can spot a dust trail half a mile out."

"Yeah, and then run straight into it," Fred added dryly.

Chris chuckled. "Well, try not to get killed. I'll need you both when this mess is over."

Terry saluted again. "Sir, we plan to be legends."

Fred gave a lazy half-salute. "We plan to survive."

Charlie pointed his mug at both of them. "That's all I ask."

The pair wandered off to find drinks, and Chris watched them for a moment, a strange tightness settling in his chest. It was rare, in these times, to see young soldiers still trying to joke and dream like that.

"They remind me of us," Charlie muttered.

Chris nodded. "Yeah. That's what worries me."

"The big event's got the town buzzing," he said.

"What event?"

Charlie stared. "Your wedding, idiot. What did you think—reiser welcoming party?"

Chris snorted. Both options sounded equally dreadful.

"No event," he said, brushing it off and pulling out the king's letter. "But I do have news from our glorious leaders."

Charlie groaned and took the parchment. "This better be about vacation."

Chris didn't laugh.

Commander Christopher Riddley,
As your king, I am pleased to reward you for saving
my life. As such, you are now tasked with
protecting the zhortas. Your high swordsman
skills, along with your clarity to make decisions
during a battle, have made us believe you are the
best candidate to go forth to the Soto Forest to keep
our heritage and holiness safe from evil hands.
It is the command of this government to keep our
past safe in order to assure our future. You
may find your time and company in the abbey
enjoyable and instructional.
Since this is your second notice, I am forced to
remind you I will take any disobedience as
high treason and won't hesitate to punish it.
Your Magnificent Grace and Ruler,
King Leonard the III and the High Council
of Hune

Charlie threw the letter back onto the table.

"'Your Magnificent Grace and Ruler'? Really? What a jerk." He laughed. "What's he going to do—pop out of his hiding hole and cut your head off himself?"

Chris didn't smile. He read the letter again, Jean's words echoing in his mind. Her belief that this order might hold something more... something worth risking.

"Come on, Charlie," Chris said. "Aren't you the one always preaching hope? Don't you think this might be... a chance?"

Charlie laughed between sips of ale. Chris stared into his drink, blinking away the ghost of that strange dream that still clung to the back of his mind.

If Charlie noticed his silence, he didn't comment. They sat in companionable quiet for a moment, until Chris finally spoke.

"Tundra needs protection, right?"

Charlie lifted his glass in agreement.

"Good," Chris said. "So, I'm going to the Soto Forest. Alone."

Charlie choked on his drink.

"What the hell? Are you out of your freaking mind?" He shot up from the table. "That's bullshit! You're seriously going to do what that idiot king and his imaginary council ordered? By yourself?"

The tavern fell silent again. The soldiers nearby stopped laughing.

Charlie looked around, his voice rising. "We need you here, Chris. Not that pompous coward in a crown."

Chris offered a crooked grin. "See? You do need me."

But Charlie wasn't in the mood for jokes. He sat back down, voice low. "Are you trying to get yourself killed?"

Chris let out a rough laugh.

Charlie stood again, barking at the crowd. "Get the hell out of here! This is now an official conversation, and it concerns none of you."

Some soldiers turned to look at Chris, who nodded apologetically, conscious of ruining their night.

Charlie waited until the tavern was empty and quiet.

"Chris, this is suicide. We only know rumors about the Soto Forest—and none of them are good."

"Rumors are like campfire stories. A lot of fantasy, not much fact."

"Even if you survive the desert, you have to find the damned place."

"Abbey," Chris corrected. "It's an abbey. Whatever that means."

Charlie sat down again, barely keeping his voice level. "Is this your way out?"

Chris's jaw clenched. He didn't answer.

"As my second," he said, "you'll take command here."

Charlie exploded. He shouted, swore, paced. He called the zhortas cowards and traitors, and swore they didn't deserve protection.

Eventually, his energy drained, and he dropped onto a stool.

"What about Jean?" he asked. "Are you going to leave her again? She's expecting you to be here. With her. To fulfill your promise."

Chris stiffened. That conversation had already cost him enough. His father knew he'd never intended to marry Jean, but apparently hadn't passed that message on. Now Jean—and everyone else—believed something that had never been real.

He'd always suspected Charlie had feelings for her. Now, he was sure. And oddly, he didn't care.

"Jean," Chris said. "It was her idea... more or less. I guess my mom had a hand in it too."

"What? When did you even—"

Chris waved it off. "Listen. I won't risk our people. But if there's even a sliver of a chance this could change something, I have to try. If I stay... it's only a matter of time."

Charlie stared. "Why you and not me?"

"Because if it fails, it fails under my command. Not yours. I'll take the blame."

Charlie didn't respond.

They spent the next few hours planning. Discussing the escape routes, the danger, the defenses for Tundra. They avoided the topic of the zhortas. Chris had no intention of treating them gently. If they had magic that could save Hune, he'd make them use it.

A long time ago, a superior officer had warned Chris that this war would never be won in a traditional way. He'd never doubted it.

Now he'd test the theory.

ALLETA RIDDLEY HAD ONCE BEEN THE STRONG, sharp-witted woman who ruled their household with humor and fierce love. But the years had changed her. Her red hair had faded to white. Her laughter was rare. Her strength had withered with her husband's death.

Chris found her seated near the window, a formal dinner half-eaten behind her. The room smelled of roasted meat and old memories.

"I'm sorry, Mom," he said quietly. "Something came up, and I had to—"

"I understand," she said, not looking up. "But Chris... I can't bear to see you like this. So heavy. So hopeless. This war—whatever it's done to you—it isn't your fault."

He braced himself. She meant well, but her words always scraped at wounds he couldn't heal.

"You've given up," she continued. "I can't even imagine what you've seen. But you're alive. And that means something. Don't forget that."

He knelt beside her. "Mom... I'm leaving tomorrow. Charlie will check in on you. And Jean."

She pulled him into an embrace before he could finish. He held her tightly, steadying his breath so he wouldn't break with her.

When she finally pulled back, her smile was weary but proud.

"My poor boy," she whispered. "You've changed. You're stronger now. But it's hurt you."

He kissed her hand, but said nothing.

"I'll miss you with all my soul," she said. "But if there's anything out there that can help us... I believe only you can find it."

He lowered his head to hide the guilt. He didn't believe in miracles anymore. Only desperation.

"Could you stay just one more day?" she asked. "Jean would agree. It doesn't have to be a big deal."

"What deal?"

Alleta stood, folding her arms in that familiar, motherly way.

"Your promise," she said. "To marry Jean."

Chris rolled his eyes.

"Christopher Riddley, I never thought you a coward."

That stung more than it should have.

"A coward?" he snapped. "I can prove to you I'm not—"

"Oh no," she interrupted. "You're brave enough to face a reiser, but not your own word? Not the heart of a girl who waited for you?"

He turned away, frustrated and raw.

"Mom," he said, "I'm not the one who's going to break her heart."

"Good," she said, calm again. "I'll make sure you two—"

"Goddamn it, Mother! That's not what I meant. She doesn't like me. And I don't give a damn about the wedding."

The disappointment in her eyes gutted him more than her words ever could.

"You know this isn't the time to build a family," he said, voice low. "You, of all people, should understand that."

Before she could reply, he turned and walked out.

EVEN AS SLEEP CAME, HE REPLAYED HIS mother's wishes and their argument in his mind. He couldn't understand people anymore. All he could see was a future buried beneath dust and ruin.

To him, the only plan ahead was finding a hiding place—or building a tomb.

And yet...

That memory returned again, hazy and persistent.

A woman's voice had whispered his name in a dream —calm, familiar, and strange all at once. He hadn't seen her face, just a shadow wrapped in silver light and the scent of wildflowers long vanished from the earth. It hadn't felt like an ordinary dream. It had felt like hope.

He clenched his jaw and forced the thought away.

Dreams were dreams. He had a war to lose.

CHAPTER FOUR

As he expected, sleep didn't come easy that night. The thought of never seeing his mother again haunted him as he lay in the familiar comfort of his old bed. Before the first rays of sunlight broke over the horizon, Chris was up, quietly packing his things.

He tiptoed downstairs to prepare his horse, only to find his mother already in the kitchen. The warmth of the oven wrapped around him, and the smell of fresh bread made his stomach growl. The simple scent carried years of memories—meals, laughter, love. For a fleeting moment, he wished he could stay.

"Mom, I'm really sorry," he said. "I didn't mean to yell. I didn't want to miss dinner."

Alleta turned, and the look in her eyes told him her night had been just as long as his. She stepped forward and hugged him tightly.

"I just want you to be happy," she whispered.

He smiled and kissed her forehead.

"Could you have breakfast with me?" she said.

"Absolutely. I'll get my horse ready and be right back." He stole a piece of bread from the table on his way out.

The family stables were small compared to the barracks, but the quiet and simplicity brought comfort. It wasn't just the better bed or food that made him stay home—it was the extra time with her.

From behind, footsteps crunched across the yard. Chris instinctively reached for the hilt of his sword.

"Good morning, Christopher," Jean said coldly. "I hope you had a good night."

She stomped toward him with clenched fists and a stormy glare. Oddly, he found it more genuine than her usual careful smiles.

"I was busy," he muttered, turning to check his saddle.

"I heard you're leaving today."

He wasn't sure which was more concerning—how quickly news traveled through Tundra or the fury in Jean's eyes. Her deliberate stride reminded him too much of someone on the verge of drawing a blade.

"Jean, I'm sorry I was—"

"Stop." She exhaled, folding her arms. "I don't need your fake apologies or empty promises. What are you expecting from me?"

Chris looked down. Like always, she seemed frustrated and disappointed. And he couldn't really blame her.

"I don't expect—" he began.

"Good." She stepped back and took a steadying

breath. "I've honored our parents' wishes, and my promise to you. But I'm not naïve. I know you haven't."

He opened his mouth to protest, but she wasn't done.

"I don't care anymore, Christopher. But you should be ashamed of yourself—not of me."

"What? How am I ashamed of you?" he asked, arms crossed. "Why would I—?"

"Don't deny it! You fumble your words every time you introduce me to your soldiers. Or 'conveniently' forget who I am. You avoid me—everywhere."

Chris had enough.

"So what?" he said sharply. "I don't like you, and I've been a jerk. But I'm not stupid. You don't like me either. You've never wanted to be around me."

Jean stepped closer, and for a second, he saw the girl she used to be—the friend who gave him wildflowers and chased him around the gardens. The one who once felt like a sister.

"I just want you to understand this," she said. "I'm done waiting for kings, councils, or you to decide my life. And I'll handle talking to your mom and the others. You owe me at least that."

Without waiting for a reply, she turned and walked away.

Chris kicked the dirt—but as she disappeared down the path, a surprising sense of relief crept in.

CHRIS WAS ALMOST DONE LOADING HIS GEAR when Terry and Fred appeared, dragging a large sack between them with more noise than necessary.

"I brought you something, sir," Terry said, face flushed from effort. "Survival essentials."

Fred snorted. "It's junk. Kid packed three socks, a dented flask, and a brick of cheese so old it's developing its own military rank."

Chris raised an eyebrow. "Why am I not surprised?"

"It's good cheese," Terry mumbled, trying to adjust the crate with some dignity. "Aged. Like strategy."

Fred leaned against the wall, arms crossed. "You know, Commander, you could just tell the king you got lost. Turn back around, pretend you fought a squirrel bear or something terrifying."

Chris gave a dry smile. "Not a bad idea. Got one I can borrow?"

"Only if you want to die with dignity," Fred said. "Those things are vicious."

Terry sat down on the crate with a thud. "Honestly, sir... are you sure you want to do this alone? I'd volunteer to go."

Chris paused, surprised by the genuine concern behind the question and offer.

"Thanks for the offer," he said. "I don't like it either. But someone's got to go. Might as well be the guy the king already wants dead."

"That's fair," Fred said. "At least you're taking the scenic route to your doom."

Terry stood and offered a slightly-too-serious salute. "Just... promise you'll remember, sir."

Chris tilted his head. "Isn't that what I told you, Terry?"

"It's a great advise," Terry said, then added, "I thought you may need it."

Chris nodded, and had to swallow before adding. "You have my word, soldier."

Fred grunted and turned to leave. "Come on, Lowd. If we hang around any longer, you'll start hugging people."

Chris watched them walked away between proud and afraid for them. For all his soldiers.

THE DESERT STRETCHED ENDLESSLY AHEAD. Chris's days bled together in blistering heat and silence. He had never liked this journey, and traveling alone made it worse. It was hard to believe the wasteland had once been ocean—cool, blue, teeming with life. As a child, he'd watched the waves from his bedroom window. Now it was all dust and memory.

The last time he left Tundra, the land had been green with fields and flowering orchards. Now, it was a graveyard.

Two blurry figures appeared on the horizon. Chris tensed. He recognized their posture, their shape. He drew his sword.

Reisers.

The cursed race. Some said the gods had punished them for their cruelty. Whether it was true or not, there was no denying their danger. Their armor—stitched from layers of dead skin—reeked of decay and death. It wasn't just for protection; it was meant to terrify.

Worse than their appearance were their tactics. The reisers fought as one. If a few died to give others the upper hand, they didn't hesitate.

Chris's odds weren't good. If these two were magically enhanced, he was as good as dead.

He turned toward his horse, calculating the distance. He had seconds—maybe less.

The wind howled.

Sand lifted violently, whipping across the dunes. Chris barely had time to react. Grains stung his skin as the storm swallowed everything. He was sure the reisers had seen him before the winds hit.

One desperate idea took hold. Dangerous, but better than nothing. He veered several meters off course, pushing his horse into a full gallop. Every second counted.

Sliding to a halt, he dismounted, pulled the tent from his saddle, and dove underneath, guiding the horse into a lying position beside him. The fabric beat against his back, shielding him from the storm.

Over the howling wind, he thought he heard voices. But they passed. Nothing touched him.

When the storm finally quieted, he crawled out. Sword in hand, he scanned the area. No enemies. Just endless dunes—and an unexpected scent on the breeze.

Flowers.

The air held a soft, floral sweetness, impossible in the desert. He froze.

A memory unfurled in his mind.

Not a memory—

A dream.

The whisper of his name, warm and soft. Silver light. A woman's silhouette framed in brightness. Her voice had echoed in the hollow place inside him where hope used to live.

He blinked. Was this another hallucination? Or had she... somehow... come again?

The light shimmered off the dunes, bending into a mirage. Chris had seen plenty before—but none so vivid.

It was a woman. Tall, elegant, with flowing hair and regal robes. A valsing.

Her beauty was otherworldly, as their kind always was, but her expression was different—distressed. Sad. She didn't radiate the usual smugness of her race.

Legends said the desert of Tundra was full of supernatural happenings. Chris had never cared to believe them. But the storm, the scent, the vision... it was too much to ignore.

For the first time in years, magic didn't feel like an enemy.

It felt like it had just saved him.

He didn't waste the chance.

Before more reisers arrived, he removed the saddle and let his horse go. If the reisers found it, they'd assume its rider was dead. Maybe—just maybe—the horse would make it back to Tundra. Charlie would understand the message. Chris couldn't risk hiding a note. The reisers were thorough. Too thorough.

He slung his sack over his shoulder and turned toward the horizon.

One last glance back.

Just sand.

Just dreams.

And a scent he couldn't forget.

CHAPTER FIVE

Charlie stood just outside the command tent, boots buried in sand, a map half-folded in his hand. The camp buzzed behind him—orders being barked, tents being rolled up, armor being buckled with weary fingers.

It had only been two days since Chris left, and already the weight of command felt heavier than the sword at his hip.

"Commander Abbott," a voice called behind him.

Terry Lowd approached, posture mostly upright, but the grin on his face couldn't quite be hidden.

"We're ready for inspection, sir. Fred's complaining that if you don't come soon, he'll start making up new ranks just so someone has to listen to him."

Charlie snorted, folding the map completely. "If he ever promotes himself to anything above 'professional nuisance,' tell him I'm revoking his rations."

"I did, and he said he'll just eat mine."

"Then I'll revoke yours too."

Terry gave a mock gasp. "Savage leadership already. Hune is in good hands."

Before Charlie could respond, John joined them, arms crossed, gaze steady. "You two done playing officer and idiot?"

"Depends who's who," Terry muttered.

Charlie waved them both toward the center of camp, where a small unit of soldiers waited. Most had been together for as long as Charlie could remember. Still, all looked too young to have seen what they had.

Fred stood at the front, arms folded, chin up. He gave Charlie a proper salute. "Commander."

"I see the troops haven't burned the camp down yet," Charlie said.

"Tempting as it was," Fred replied, "they're still standing. Mostly because of the fear of Terry's singing."

Terry held up a hand. "You wound me. Art is resistance."

"It's not art if it offends the gods," Fred muttered.

John cleared his throat, sharp enough to pull the focus back to Charlie.

Charlie took a moment before speaking. The air was still. The soldiers quieted.

"I'm not going to make a speech," Charlie said. "We've all had enough of those. You know what we're facing. You've all seen more than anyone your age should."

He looked at each of them. Tired eyes. Scars that hadn't fully healed.

"But we're still here. We still have a line to hold. And

I'm not Chris. I'm not here to replace him. I'm here because he trusted me—and I intend to earn that."

He paused. The silence didn't press on him this time. It steadied him.

"I'm not going to promise we'll make it out of this untouched," he said. "But I will promise you this: we will not fall easily. We will fight for our people."

Charlie stepped back and gave a final order. "Check your weapons. Remain prepared for immediate departure."

The soldiers dispersed, quieter now. Focused.

John lingered, hands behind his back. "You did well."

Charlie's expression softened. "It's different without Chris here. You feel it too, right?"

John hesitated. "Yeah. He left big shoes behind."

Charlie glanced down at his boots, half-buried in the dust. "I just hope mine are big enough."

John clapped a hand on his shoulder. "They are. You're not here to be him. You're here to be you. And that's what they need."

CHARLIE HAD BEEN BORN IN ANDROMEDA, a small town at the edge of the Southern Forest of Hune. It wasn't much compared to Tundra, but it had once been full of life. Now, as he walked the capital's dusty streets, he couldn't help but feel like the city had lost its soul. It was nothing like the grand place he'd heard about as a child.

The citizens' anxiety over Chris's sudden departure only made things worse. Now that Chris had promoted him to Commander and left him in charge, everyone wanted answers Charlie didn't have, and their pointed questions left him feeling incompetent—like an outsider playing soldier. He now envied Chris for escaping it all, even if he'd gone on a fool's mission. Sometimes, Charlie imagined following him.

Across the street, he spotted Jean exiting a house, struggling with two heavy baskets. Even from a distance, her smile stood out—warm, luminous. He should've kept walking. Pretended not to see. But he didn't.

No one had ever held his attention the way she did.

The day he met Jean had been both wonderful and terrible. She was the most stunning woman he'd ever seen. Graceful, kind, persuasive. He'd wanted to draw her into his arms on sight.

Then Chris had introduced her as his fiancée.

From that moment on, she became the one woman Charlie could never hope for.

He watched her shift the baskets in her arms, clearly struggling.

"Good afternoon, Major—sorry, I mean Commander," Jean called out as she spotted him.

He crossed the street and smiled. "Hello, Jean. Let me help you with those."

"Thank you, Commander."

They walked together in silence for a while. Charlie, usually quick with words, found himself stumbling inwardly. This wasn't like him. Conversations with women used to be easy.

"I have to ask," Jean said suddenly. "How could you let Chris go? Aren't you supposed to be his friend?"

The question hit harder than expected. He knew Tundra's people would judge him—but he hadn't expected it from Jean. He stayed quiet.

She stopped and turned toward him.

"Please forgive me," she said quickly. "It's not my place to question you."

Their eyes met for a beat too long. A faint smile touched his lips, and to his surprise, she blushed.

"I'm just... worried about him," she said softly.

"I understand," Charlie said. "I tried to tie him to a chair, but the bastard was too sneaky."

She laughed, the sound as sweet as spring.

"So where are we taking these?" he asked.

"To Chris's house."

Charlie flinched. Of all the places he'd hoped to avoid, that was number one. He met Alleta the same day he met Jean, and he was fairly certain she could see right through him.

"Chris's house?" he said carefully.

Jean raised a brow. "So, it's true. He never mentioned me."

"No, he didn't," Charlie admitted. "But he's not the brightest."

She groaned but smiled again. "I suppose he isn't. Let me rephrase: we're taking the baskets to my house."

"Your house? As in... you live with—wait, what?"

Jean giggled. "Don't worry. I don't live with Chris."

"Of course not. I mean... even if you did... it's not like I think—I mean, I wasn't implying—"

Her laughter rang louder.

"No wonder Alleta kept me away while Chris was here," she teased. "People love to invent stories."

Charlie rubbed the back of his neck. "Honestly, I just figured if you lived with him, you might have killed him by now."

They walked a little slower after that.

"Wait," he said, frowning. "Chris also made you move from your home?"

"Not exactly." Jean looked down. "I doubt he cared either way. It was Alleta who asked me to leave. She wanted to wait until we were married."

Her voice dimmed. "My parents were killed by reisers when I was one."

Charlie's chest tightened. The war had stolen people from everyone, but somehow, it still hit him hard every time.

"I'm sorry, Jean."

She nodded. "My mother and Alleta were close. That's why she raised me. That's also why... the engagement."

Charlie hesitated. "And that never bothered you? Being told who to marry?"

Jean's expression cooled instantly. "No, it didn't, Commander."

He regretted asking.

"You don't understand," she went on. "An engagement like mine is an honor for a girl in Tundra—especially with Chris's family. It would be stupid not to want him. He's brave, responsible, well-mannered... tall."

The words should have sounded like praise, but her tone made them feel like accusations.

"But Jean, you don't—"

"It doesn't matter now," she interrupted. "And I don't want to talk about him. Not in front of Alleta."

Only then did Charlie realize they'd arrived.

Just like the first time he'd seen it, the Riddley house surprised him. For a colonel, he'd imagined something grand—ornamental, stately. Instead, it looked like his childhood home. Simple. Human. That made it worse.

He shouldn't be there. Jean was engaged to his best friend, even if it wasn't her choice. And he... he had no place in her life.

Charlie set the baskets down and stepped back.

But her eyes, suddenly glossy with tears, froze him.

"Jean? What is it?"

"I want... I wish you—"

The door opened.

"Commander Abbott," Alleta said, her voice calm and unreadable. "I wasn't expecting you."

"Mrs. Riddley," Charlie said with a nod. "Just helping Jean with the baskets."

"How kind of you. Please, come in."

Alleta smiled gently, leaving him no room to argue. He picked up the baskets and followed them inside.

FROM THE WINDOW, ALLETA WATCHED THE PAIR walking together and sighed. Jean's smile had returned—something Alleta hadn't seen in days.

She shook her head. For all her plans, for all her insistence, she'd failed to see what was right in front of her.

She had taken Jean in after the girl's mother died. It was supposed to be temporary. A simple favor for a friend visiting the barracks. But the reisers had changed everything.

She still had nightmares about that night—about the box of remains brought home. The soldiers swore it was Jean's mother. The rounded abdomen, the untouched face. But her expression—that frozen look of terror—haunted Alleta more than anything else.

That night had shattered everything.

It wasn't long before she clung to the idea of Jean and Chris together. The match had made sense. It honored her promise. It gave meaning to their losses. For years, she'd crafted an image of a bright future for them both.

But now, she saw it for what it was—her dream, not theirs.

And now, someone else had given Jean back her smile.

"Commander," Alleta said as she poured hot water into three cups. "I understand you've been quite busy these past few days. Chris's departure came as a shock to us all."

Jean stiffened.

"But it's not as though I sent him away," Charlie said, his tone even. "I didn't encourage him to go, Mrs. Riddley."

"Of course not," she replied. "Chris was a symbol of

hope here. If his father hadn't... well, Chris would have been in your place now."

She paused, taking a deep breath.

"I'm sorry for your loss," Charlie said softly.

"Thank you. And I don't doubt he left us in capable hands. He spoke highly of you."

Charlie smiled. Alleta suddenly understood why Jean was drawn to him.

"I like myself too," he said. "Though some days I'm not sure why."

Alleta chuckled, and even Jean seemed to relax again.

"Commander, where are you from?" Jean asked.

"Andromeda," Charlie said. "My family tried to reach one of the camps after the reisers took our town."

"I'm sorry," Jean said gently.

"Everyone's lost someone these days."

Jean's eyes softened. Charlie's gaze lingered.

Alleta watched them. Maybe Chris had noticed too. Maybe that was his real reason for walking away—not cowardice, but loyalty. A way of letting his friend step in.

The city bells rang—three sharp chimes. Galloping hooves echoed outside.

Charlie stood instantly, all lightness gone from his expression.

"Gods be damned!" John called out. "There you are —Commander Abbott, we need you!"

Another soldier handed Charlie the reins of a horse. He mounted in one fluid motion.

"Mrs. Riddley. Jean." He nodded once, then rode off.

It didn't matter that it was already dark —half of Tundra had gathered in the park. Panic and fear clouded the faces around them as Alleta and Jean wove through the crowd.

What terrified Alleta most was the silence that fell when people recognized them.

She quickened her pace, pushing past the murmuring mass toward the center of the commotion.

"Tundra is no longer safe," Charlie said. "We have to evacuate."

A man shouted back, "If you were a real man, you'd protect us, not make us run!"

"Where are we supposed to go?" someone else demanded.

Alleta's gaze fell on a familiar black horse—a soldier struggling to calm it. Jean gasped behind her.

Desperate, Alleta pushed through the last of the crowd and ran to the animal. She knew that horse. Chris had ridden it the day he returned to Tundra. She'd fed it in her own stables. There was no mistaking it.

Her heart sank.

"If you can't defend us inside the city walls," a woman cried, "why should we trust you outside them?"

A soldier reached for Alleta's arm. "Mrs. Riddley, please come this—"

"No!" she snapped, yanking away. "What happened to Chris? Tell me now!"

Jean stepped beside her and gently touched her shoulder at the same moment Charlie approached.

"It's all right, John," Charlie said to the soldier, then turned to Alleta. "Mrs. Riddley, I can't be certain. But my gut tells me he's alive."

Alleta inhaled deeply, hope blooming where despair had been. Her shoulders shook as tears spilled down her cheeks. She pressed her forehead gently to the horse's flank, grateful for the warmth.

"All right?" Jean said. "How can—"

Charlie didn't answer her. The shouting resumed around them, louder this time—questions, protests, confusion.

He raised his voice over the crowd.

"Does anyone remember what happened to Laconia?"

The name struck like a thunderclap. Conversations died.

"If not," Charlie said, "let me remind you: Laconia's people also thought they could defend their homes. They believed they were strong enough. But they died. The city burned with most of its citizens still inside. The reisers will come for Tundra. And they will destroy it like every other city in Hune."

A heavy silence settled.

"I won't let that happen here," Charlie said. "We leave at sunrise."

He turned back to Alleta and spoke softly. "Like I said... I think this is Chris's way of warning us that the reisers are near."

Jean stepped forward, her voice rising. "How can you possibly know that?"

Charlie nodded toward the horse. "He let it go. There's no sign of struggle. The saddle's in perfect condition. The horse is tired, yes—but unharmed."

Jean's face contorted. She grabbed Charlie's arm, pulling him down to her eye level. "Why would he release his horse in the middle of the desert? Chris is not stupid. It doesn't make sense. You're lying!"

Charlie didn't pull away. He met her eyes steadily, placing his hand gently over hers.

"I don't lie, Jean."

The soldiers around them, and several civilians, had stopped to watch. The air was thick with tension.

John stepped closer to Alleta and placed a hand on her shoulder. "Chris is all right. He cares more about us than himself. You know that."

The relief that had briefly taken root inside Alleta vanished. Her chest tightened painfully.

Of course he would do this. He would sacrifice everything.

Her knees buckled. John caught her before she fell.

"Lieutenant," Charlie said, his tone firm, "see to it that Mrs. Riddley and her daughter are safely prepared to leave."

Alleta didn't remember getting home. Somehow, she found herself seated at her table, watching Jean and John rush around the house, packing bags and gathering supplies.

She sat in silence, the image of Chris's horse burned into her thoughts.

CHAPTER SIX

The stars blazed across the night sky—one of the few things the reisers hadn't destroyed. Chris closed his eyes for a moment, letting the silence wrap around him like a blanket.

It had been years since he camped alone. Back then, he was still a scout, sometimes a messenger. No command. No responsibilities beyond himself.

He'd forgotten how easy it was to sleep without an army depending on him. The reisers near Tundra still troubled him. So did the long, uncertain road ahead. But if something went wrong tonight, at least only he would suffer the consequences.

As he worked to start a fire, Chris felt a flicker of self-pity. Maybe his mother had been right about his lack of expectations. His greatest hope was simply to die alone—and not take anyone with him. Hardly the dream of a hopeful man.

Stillness settled around him, and for the first time in a long while, he let his thoughts wander.

Years ago, during one of the worst punishments he'd ever endured, he had started seeing a woman in his dreams—if she was a woman at all. Maybe just a hallucination, something born of pain and silence. Her voice had been soft, steadying. Her presence kept him sane when everything else seemed to be slipping away.

He could still remember her bright blue eyes, glowing like starlight, and the way her dark hair framed her face in waves that shimmered under some dream light he could never explain.

She had seemed real. Too real.

And that had terrified him.

So when the punishment ended, he buried the memory. He forced himself to forget her. Soldiers didn't have the luxury of illusions—especially not ones that felt like hope.

He shook his head and tried to focus on the other occurrence in the desert. The mirage of the valsing woman.

The valsings—the third race of Hune. Arrogant. Nomadic. Beautiful. Short.

They believed all of Hune belonged to them, and that everyone else was inferior. Chris knew better than to underestimate them.

He'd met them once. And it had cost him more than pride.

It was years ago, when the war began to turn. He'd just been named captain under Commander Daniel Madeck. Their mission: convince the valsings to join the fight.

It didn't go well.

King Orson, the valsing monarch, had humiliated them in front of his court.

"Inspect this dirty, desperate group," the king had said. "This is what stupidity looks like. An appearance we will never share."

Chris had burned with rage. Orson's condescension, his refusal to help, had shattered their morale.

"You deserve death at the hands of those monsters," Orson had spat. "Keep destroying each other—perhaps the land will finally be cleansed."

Back then, Chris had been arrogant. Impulsive.

His reckless choices led him to Princess Cassandra—and she changed everything.

In the end, maybe it made him stronger.

But it came at a price. One he was still paying.

Orson's fury had landed Chris in a vault—a cramped hole underground where he'd been left for nearly three weeks. No standing room. Barely enough space to kneel. Light and food trickled through a slit in the ceiling. When he emerged, his perception of life had changed, and had to deal with the consequences of his decisions.

Over time, the story twisted. His friends said the valsings were weak. That Chris had broken free from their guards, half-drunk and shirtless, and knocked them out cold.

He preferred that version.

Still, as he stared into the fire, he smiled faintly. No one would call this current mission "orthodox." Which meant, maybe, it had a chance.

A flicker of movement caught his eye.

He turned quickly, sword drawn. Something struck the fire, sending the flames roaring higher.

"Hey, you!" a voice called behind him.

Chris spun, slashing through the air—but there was no target. A blow slammed into the back of his head.

And everything went dark.

HIS MIND DRIFTED IN AND OUT OF STRANGE, disjointed dreams. He felt sand dragging beneath his body. The sun and stars danced above, chasing each other across the sky.

Time passed. Maybe days.

When he finally managed to open his eyes, the sun was high—but the heat wasn't what it should be.

That's not good, he thought.

He tried to sit up, but nausea slammed into him, and he vomited into the sand. His arms shook. His vision blurred. His thoughts marched like soldiers out of step.

Later—how much later, he couldn't say—he realized the desert was gone. He lay near the edge of a forest unlike any he'd ever seen.

Towering trees loomed above, their twisted trunks like giant spirals reaching into the sky. At the base, dark wood curved into arches that supported the canopy, casting deep shadows across the ground.

"Well, you're a heavy sleeper," a voice said nearby.

Chris flinched and tried to rise. His legs gave out, and he collapsed to his knees.

"Oof. That looked painful."

He groaned and looked up—only to curse under his breath.

A valsing.

The last thing he wanted.

"Listen," the valsing said. "I had to sedate you. You were twitchy. Also, dragging you across the sand on that ridiculous rag wasn't ideal. I assure you, you won't be sprinting anytime soon."

Chris scanned the area. No one else in sight.

"How are you alone out here?" His voice rasped.

The valsing's smile vanished. "Alone? Who said I'm alone? Valsings are *never* alone."

Chris narrowed his eyes. "Who the hell are you?"

"Commander, where are your manners?"

Chris didn't reply.

"I suppose my name is of little value to you," the valsing continued, offering a tin cup of water. "But I'm Donald Terrance."

The water looked like heaven. Chris's hands trembled, but he didn't trust the man—or whatever he'd given him before.

Donald looked like a storybook royal: curled brown hair, elegant suit, wide brown eyes. He was radiant, charming—and exhausted.

Something about him was off.

The tent nearby was large, but plain. Practical. The setup lacked the luxury most valsings obsessed over.

Chris stared at the cup.

"Are you going to drink that?" Donald asked.

"Hell no. You drugged me."

Donald laughed—a disarming sound. "Overdosed,

perhaps. But not poisoned. I was honestly worried about you."

Chris snorted. "Touching."

"You humans are heavy," Donald added. "Especially with all your weapons and primitive stuff."

Chris was considering hurling the cup at him when the ground around them shifted. Whispers filled the air.

He looked up.

Hundreds of valsings were approaching, their movements graceful and unified. A woman led them.

Chris stiffened. She was the one he'd seen in the mirage.

Donald's face fell. He dropped the cup.

"My Queen," he murmured, bowing deeply. "I have completed the task—"

Vanessa Nord raised her hand. Donald fell silent.

She stared at Chris. Her dark eyes were piercing. Familiar.

He'd never met the valsing queen before, but she looked just like her daughter.

The same gaze. The same calculating strength.

"Commander," she said. "I apologize for the way you've been treated. This was not my wish."

Chris didn't reply.

She turned to Donald, her voice laced with disappointment. "I did not order you to sedate him. What did I command you to do?"

"My Queen, I—"

She lifted her hand again. Silence fell.

"Tell me the exact command."

Donald shifted uneasily. "To bring the human to you."

She tilted her head.

He sighed. "You told me to *convince* Commander Riddley to speak with you. With an open mind."

She smiled and turned to Chris, as if that explained everything.

Chris wasn't impressed.

"Your Highness," Donald said, voice tense. "As I told you, I didn't think he'd come willingly. You gave me too little to work with. He distrusts our race. I wasn't about to end up like Gale."

A hush swept through the gathering. Whispers rippled outward.

"Enough!" the queen snapped. "If he refuses to listen now, that will be on you, Donald. Along with the consequences."

She stepped closer, her voice rising.

"Perhaps if you controlled your charm—and didn't rely on your perfect features—you would not have been disciplined."

Donald clenched his fists, but bowed his head.

Chris, despite himself, felt a flicker of sympathy. He'd stood in that position too many times—powerless, outvoted, shamed in public.

The queen turned back to him, still seething.

"Commander, I regret this incident deeply. The gods know how important our relationship may become. I will reprimand him for what he's done."

She looked around, and without a word, the

surrounding valsings dispersed. The hum of movement resumed as the camp buzzed with renewed activity.

"Let me start again," she said. "I am Vanessa Nord, Queen of the valsings."

She waited for Chris to speak.

He didn't.

"Excellency," he said at last. "I think we're well beyond introductions. I'm wasting time, and so are you."

Vanessa raised an eyebrow—and then smirked.

"You do not look well. Let's find somewhere better to talk."

CHAPTER SEVEN

The last valsing settlement Chris had visited years ago had opened his eyes to a very different life-style. Their tents were massive, made of an unbelievably smooth, silky material that danced in the breeze. Inside, furniture was buried in cushions, all color-coordinated with meticulous elegance. Every table, every lamp, every flower pot followed a strict aesthetic. The settlement had structured streets, ambient lighting, and blooming gardens—nothing like the rugged sprawl of human camps.

But even that had nothing on what rose before him now.

In a matter of seconds, the valsings built a village out of the sands. Structures seemed to grow from the earth, unfolding like origami until a city appeared before his eyes. It wasn't magic—it was engineering, architecture, and packaging at its finest. Their brilliance was undeniable.

Chris had gone from baking in the desert to reclining

on a soft cushioned chair inside a cottage with wide windows and quiet fans. The once-hostile dunes were now part of a scenic vista.

In that short time, he'd recovered enough strength that when the queen reentered, he rose out of habit.

"Oh my!" Queen Vanessa placed a hand over her heart, eyes wide with surprise. "I'm glad to see you feeling better, Commander. Please—sit."

"After you," Chris said politely.

Vanessa gave a tight smile and took her seat.

"Commander, have you ever heard of the High Council of Hune?"

He arched an eyebrow. Everyone had heard of it. Strange, though—this was the second time in a matter of days that someone in power had brought up the long-forgotten council.

"The High Council is just a comforting legend, Your Majesty."

She took her time observing him, not bothering to hide the judgment in her eyes—assessing not just his answer, but his posture, his tone, and his armor.

"We valsings have a vast understanding of Hune's history," she said.

Chris held back a smirk. There it was—arrogance and condescension wrapped in silk. She sounded exactly like her daughter. The last thing he needed right now was a history lecture.

"Your Majesty, I'm in the middle of a mission. I need to—"

"This is difficult for me," she interrupted, leaning forward. The mask of superiority slipped from her face, replaced by something rawer. "I understand you have a mission, but this is critical. I wouldn't involve you otherwise. This may be the only way to save Hune."

One of her guards entered and placed a jeweled box on the table. Chris noted the intricate engravings and fine craftsmanship. It hummed with importance.

"May I call you Chris?" Vanessa asked, her voice softening. "This isn't a political conversation. What I'm about to share has nothing to do with our roles."

Chris crossed his arms. "Go ahead."

"At the beginning," she said, "the reisers were cursed by a god for their lack of empathy. That's the story you know."

"I do," Chris said. "We're not as naïve as you think. We've been fighting them for years."

Vanessa paced to the window. Her voice turned distant.

"I know the history between our races. I can't look at you without thinking of my daughter... and what you two—" Her voice caught. "I've often wished it had been me you reached out to instead of Orson. I'm sorry for what my husband did. His refusal cost so many lives... so many regrets."

Chris didn't respond immediately. He knew she didn't want the truth—that what happened between him and Cassandra had been fueled by mutual revenge. Better to let her believe whatever gave her peace.

"Your daughter is a difficult memory to forget, Your Highness," he said, the lie bitter in his mouth. But her brief smile—relieved and maternal—made it worth it.

"After that, I started searching for answers," she said.

"The members of the High Council had disappeared, yes—but not all were dead. I believe the war started within that council."

Chris narrowed his eyes. "You think they betrayed Hune?"

"No. But the reisers' power is unnatural. It must have come from a council member. I suspected their leader—the Great Wizard—but learned he died. Our own representative did, too. I don't know what happened to the human one. But the zhortas... I had to find out."

"Did you?"

"Only a few weeks ago."

She opened the box, revealing a scroll sealed in blue wax. The emblem of Hune was pressed into it—surrounded by the words *Wisdom and Justice*.

Her hands trembled slightly as she held it out. "This is for you."

Chris hesitated. He took the scroll and broke the seal.

The parchment was cold—unnaturally cold. Like ice in his hands. The engraved letters shimmered with magic.

Chris had seen magic used by reisers on the battlefield—but never held it. Its power made him shiver.

Commander Christopher Riddley,

> *The High Council of Hune has appointed you to protect the Great Wizard's descendant and legacy.*
>
> *Your strength in battle, your loyalty to Hune, and your wisdom in action have revealed the true light within you. Trust it—it will guide you.*

*King Leonard I once uncovered the secret to
 defeating your true enemy. You must now find
 his journal.*

*Enclosed is a map to help you. Once you retrieve the
 journal, seek one of magic to translate it.*

*We cannot say more. This message is too dangerous
 if intercepted.*

*Your choices alone will determine the fate of
 us all.*
— The High Council of Hune

Chris read it twice. Then again. He wanted to believe it—but it sounded too much like the beginning of a bedtime story.

He hadn't even realized the queen was beside him until her hand touched his shoulder.

"I know it's a lot to take in," she said softly. "But I'm begging you—take this mission."

"Is this all you found?"

She nodded, eyes glistening. "It's our only option. If the reisers win, my people will fall—just like yours."

He lifted the map from the box. It was more artwork than chart—every region of Hune rendered in rich detail. He could see cities he had marched through, now marked in ruin. He didn't understand the language written on it, but the message was clear.

Too much of Hune had already fallen.

"There's no choice," Chris muttered. "I don't believe in this High Council fairy tale, but... I'll go."

"I know," Vanessa said. "It's all we have left."

Night had fallen again, but Chris didn't notice.

He stood alone, thinking about the letter and the strange convergence of fates. The king's order had sent him to the Soto Forest. Now the Council had as well. Coincidence? Or something larger?

He didn't like what he couldn't see.

The map was precise—but unfamiliar. Many parts of Hune he'd never set foot in. And the writing...

He'd need a translator.

The queen had left earlier, and he was glad. He didn't want to talk about their history. Too many ghosts.

He was heading toward the door when two soldiers shoved someone inside.

Donald.

They dragged him across the cottage and tossed him like garbage.

"Let me go, cowards!" Donald shouted.

"Gladly," one muttered. The other aimed a kick at his ribs—then stopped when he saw Chris standing there.

"Enjoy your new company," he sneered, and the two left.

Donald groaned, blood smeared across his mouth. His shirt had been ripped open, bruises spreading across his chest and ribs. His hands were bound.

"You doing all right over there?" Donald wheezed. "Or still dizzy?"

Chris helped him into a chair and cut the rope.

"At least they didn't break your nose."

Donald winced. "You're right. Could've been worse. Could've ruined my perfect face."

Chris snorted and propped his feet on the side table.

"You'll find me a bit harder to knock out now."

"Fair." Donald grinned—then groaned and held his side.

He spotted the map on the table.

"Is that... the First Map of Hune?"

He leaned forward, awestruck.

"This is a treasure. The High Council created it. The Great Wizard enchanted it to update with Hune's changes automatically!"

Chris raised an eyebrow. "Automatically?"

"Yes! It's alive, in a way. It's a miracle you have it."

Chris chuckled. "And I suppose the Great Magician—"

"Wizard," Donald corrected, dead serious. "Show some respect."

Chris was still laughing when the door slammed open.

Vanessa entered, fuming.

"Donald Terrance," she snapped. "What were you thinking?"

They both stood.

"Your Excellency," Donald said, falling to one knee. "I had to talk to her. I needed to know if she—"

"You are forbidden from speaking to her again," the queen said coldly. "Never."

Pain flickered across her face as she turned away. Her voice trembled.

"If you want to die, Donald... I cannot protect you from your own foolishness. I should not even try."

Her gaze flickered across Chris, and with a sharp intake of breath, she stiffened, her tone hardening.

"Chris. I know this task is difficult. You need help."

Chris started to object, but she raised her hand.

"You've met Sir Terrance. I know it was under complicated circumstances, but trust me—he is the most intelligent member of my congress. A trained medic. A decorated knight."

Donald groaned. "My Queen, please—"

"He's had his... conflicts with our society," she continued. "But I trust he will not disappoint you."

Chris sighed. "You're serious."

Donald looked horrified. "Your Majesty, this is a death sentence! I cannot work for a human!"

Two guards grabbed him before he could throw himself at the queen's feet.

Vanessa's gaze didn't waver.

"It's the only way I can save your life, Donald."

Then she turned to Chris, eyes full of something he hadn't expected.

Not command.

But hope.

And mercy.

He nodded.

It wasn't an order.

But he'd accepted it all the same.

As soon as the queen left, silence filled the room like a fog.

Chris closed his eyes, hoping for silence—but silence never came easy.

The stillness of the valsing cottage unsettled him. The cool air, the way the curtains danced like silk, the faint scent of flowers—everything was too familiar. Too close to something he'd worked hard to forget.

The dream came back before he could stop it.

It had visited him once, years ago, when he was locked in the vault—days underground, half-starved and on the edge of madness. He hadn't spoken about it. Not even to Charlie. He'd buried it like everything else that made him feel too much.

But now, it stirred.

He remembered the dream like it had happened yesterday.

The pounding in his head. The sour smell of stone and blood. Then—salt. A breeze that didn't belong in a prison. And light, blue and silver, pouring through cracks in the stone that weren't there before.

Suddenly, he was standing barefoot in the sand.

The ocean stretched wide before him, waves lapping at the shore with a slow, calming rhythm. Behind him, his childhood home stood proud against the cliffs. The windows glowed like lanterns. The world was quiet, soft, impossibly still.

And she was there.

A woman—no, a vision—walking along the edge of the sea.

Her hair was long and dark, wild in the breeze, her

white dress clinging to her figure like foam. Her arms were crossed tightly over her chest as if bracing against more than the cold. She didn't see him at first.

Chris remembered how his throat had burned. He'd forgotten how to speak. But somehow, the words had come anyway.

"Gods," he'd whispered. "You're so beautiful."

She turned, startled by the sound. Her eyes were the clearest blue he'd ever seen—almost too bright, too unnatural. For a heartbeat, she looked afraid.

Then she saw him properly.

And something in her gaze changed.

"You're not supposed to be here," she'd said, her voice cautious, almost sad.

"I know," he'd murmured. "Neither are you."

She stepped forward.

He remembered thinking she must be a valsing. What else could explain the way she moved, the glow in her eyes, the impossible comfort in her voice?

"Are you..." he'd asked, "valsing?"

And she'd laughed. Really laughed.

It was the most human sound he'd heard in weeks.

"No," she'd said, her smile soft and a little broken. "Not even close."

She knelt beside him as he collapsed in the sand. Her hand had touched his forehead, and it felt like water in the desert. Real. Impossible.

"Are you real?" he'd asked.

She didn't answer.

Not directly.

But the way she looked at him—it stayed with him longer than it should have.

Even now, lying on valsing silk in a strange desert cottage, that same warmth pulsed faintly under his skin.

He squeezed his eyes shut, trying to bury it again.

It was just a dream.

A delusion.

He had convinced himself of that for years.

But tonight, for the first time since the vault, the memory refused to let go.

CHAPTER EIGHT

The Abbey's kitchen was quiet this late. Most of the pots were stacked, the fires banked low. Sara White stood against the counter, watching her dear friend pour out her heart.

"I told Donald not to talk to that stupid princess," Lily said. Even with her face streaked in tears and her eyes red and tired, her valsing features still shone through.

They had met when both were younger, after Lily's community settled near the Abbey. Lily had become the sister Sara never had—and though Lily, being a valsing, would never say it aloud, Sara knew she felt the same.

Lily pressed her palms against her eyes, sitting at the small kitchen table. "Of course the Queen listened to her daughter. Even though she should know better. We all know what that spoiled brat did before."

Her voice broke, and between sobs, she continued.

"The valsings started shouting *traitor* at him, and I couldn't—I had to do something. I turned back and went to the Queen. I couldn't let him die for me. I begged and begged. I offered my life for his."

Sara had never been in love. She was sure of that. But as Lily spoke, her own heart pulsed in strange sympathy —like it somehow knew what it felt to fear for someone that deeply.

She sat across from Lily. "What happened?"

Lily didn't look up. "The Queen spared Donald's life."

The knot in Sara's chest loosened—just slightly. "That's good, isn't it?"

A bitter laugh escaped Lily's lips. "Not really. She sent him to find the human—the same one who humiliated King Orson and plotted with Cassandra. Apparently, he's the human leader now, and Queen Vanessa wants Donald to convince him to let her join the war."

Sara leaned closer. "She wants to fight the reisers?"

Lily nodded once, her mouth pressed tight.

Sara frowned. "But... that's—"

"Stupid?" Lily cut in. "I know. And the worst part? You know humans. They're full of prejudices and stubbornness. After what happened with Princess Cassandra, they'll see Donald as a spy and kill him on sight."

Sara reached across the table, gently taking Lily's hand. "He's the royal medic and part of the Congress. He must be incredibly smart, Lily. Don't give up hope just yet."

Lily nodded, wiping her eyes. Only when she seemed a little more composed did Sara ask the question she feared most.

"What about you, Lily? What did the Queen—?"

Lily sat straighter, the innate confidence of her race lighting her features. "She had to send me back to the King. I'm not under her command, and if she tries anything... well, Orson will use it as an excuse to fight her. I'm not worried about myself. It's Donald I'm afraid for."

Though impossible, Sara had the distinct sense that she'd felt Lily's despair before—that feeling when what you care about most is slipping away, and begging isn't enough to stop it.

Sara took a steadying breath. "Then let's protect him."

Lily stared. "How? I don't think either of us should try to reach the humans. You're not exactly welcome in their world, Sara."

"Of course not." A shiver ran down Sara's spine at the thought. The image of soldiers flickered in her mind, waking a deep pain in the scar on her shoulder. "But you're being sent back to King Orson, right?"

"Yes, but I don't think he'll be pleased. I failed my mission."

"Maybe," Sara said. "Or maybe you'll remind him how much he hates his ex-wife."

Lily blinked. "What?"

"Queen Vanessa cast you aside. Publicly. Cruelly. Like a humiliation."

A glimmer of interest lit Lily's tear-streaked eyes.

"You think... I could use his hate for her?"

Sara nodded. "Tell him what happened. Make sure he knows she sent Donald on a suicide mission—and blamed you for it."

Lily hesitated. "And then what?"

"Then tell him how important Donald is—how he could benefit Orson's own Congress. If Orson hates Vanessa enough, he'll protect Donald just to spite her."

Lily exhaled, the idea blooming behind her cautious gaze. "You think he'll listen?"

"I think Orson wants to win." Sara gave a small shrug. "And if helping you costs Vanessa something, he'll find a way to enjoy it."

A long pause stretched between them. Then Lily whispered, "I'll leave at dawn."

Sara sighed. "I'll miss you."

Lily reached out and pulled her into a hug. "Me too. But I have to go."

The fire crackled. Lily's shoulders sagged again, but the trembling in her hands had stopped.

"I don't understand how love can hurt like this," she murmured.

Sara opened her mouth—then closed it again. Because she didn't know either. Not really. And yet something inside her was quietly unraveling, a soft ache that didn't belong to Lily.

She looked at her own hands, suddenly unsure of the weight in her chest.

"Me neither," she said softly.

AFTER LILY LEFT, THE ABBEY'S QUIET RETURNED —but it felt different. Stillness had settled over the corridors like dust, the kind that refused to be swept away.

Sara walked quietly, her steps soft as usual against the cold stone floor, the echo of Lily's words still heavy in her chest.

She found Zhorta Willson where she always did when the world grew too heavy—on the south terrace, gazing at the stars like they were old friends.

"I thought you might come tonight," he said without turning. "Lily. Is she feeling better?"

Sara hesitated in the archway. "I hope so. I'm glad you are here."

He looked back, and a gentle smile creased his weathered face. He wasn't really old, but something about Willson made people trust him like a grandfather. Maybe it was the quiet way he listened. Maybe it was the eyes—sharp and deep and full of things he rarely said.

He motioned her over, and she sat beside him on the stone bench, curling her knees beneath her. The breeze was cool, but familiar.

"I need to ask you something," she said.

Willson nodded, letting her speak when she was ready.

"Lily is heartbroken." Her voice came out quieter than she expected. "I could feel it... like it was happening inside me.

Willson said nothing, but his brows dipped slightly in thought.

"At first I thought it was just empathy. But... it didn't go away. It's still here." She pressed a hand to her chest. "Like a thread pulling on me. Or like I'm forgetting something I shouldn't."

"Something—or someone?" he asked gently.

Sara looked at him, startled. "I don't know. There's no memory. Just... this ache. Like something was torn away."

Willson studied her for a long moment, then exhaled. "You've always been intuitive, Sara. Special. And though you aren't zhorta by blood, you were raised as one. Maybe your dreams, your feelings, are starting to catch pieces of what lives ahead."

"But I'm not like you," she said. "I can't see visions or read signs. I can't *know* things the way you and the elders do."

"No," he agreed. "But prophecy isn't the only path to truth." He paused, his voice soft. "Your mind might not see the future, but your soul remembers the past. The heart is a powerful witness—even when memory fails."

She looked down at her hands, pale in the moonlight. "You think it's just... empathy. For my doomed people?"

He smiled gently. "It could be. There's no denying that humans are losing. The valsings trying to join the war is a significant shift—politically, spiritually. Your heritage might be responding to that. Even without connection to them, your blood still listens."

Sara nodded slowly, letting his words settle inside her.

"But," he said, "you already believe it's more than that, don't you?"

Her breath caught. She looked at him sharply, then gave a small, sad nod. "Yes. I do. It feels too personal. Too... familiar. Like I'm grieving someone I don't even know."

Willson placed a hand on her shoulder. "Then trust

it. Don't chase answers, not yet. Just follow the ache. Let it lead you. When the time is right, the truth will come."

A breeze swept through the terrace, and Sara tilted her head back, looking at the stars.

"I just wish I understood why it hurts so much," she whispered.

"Because something in you remembers being loved," he said.

And for a moment, she felt like she could almost hear the echo of laughter in the distance—someone's voice she didn't recognize but missed all the same.

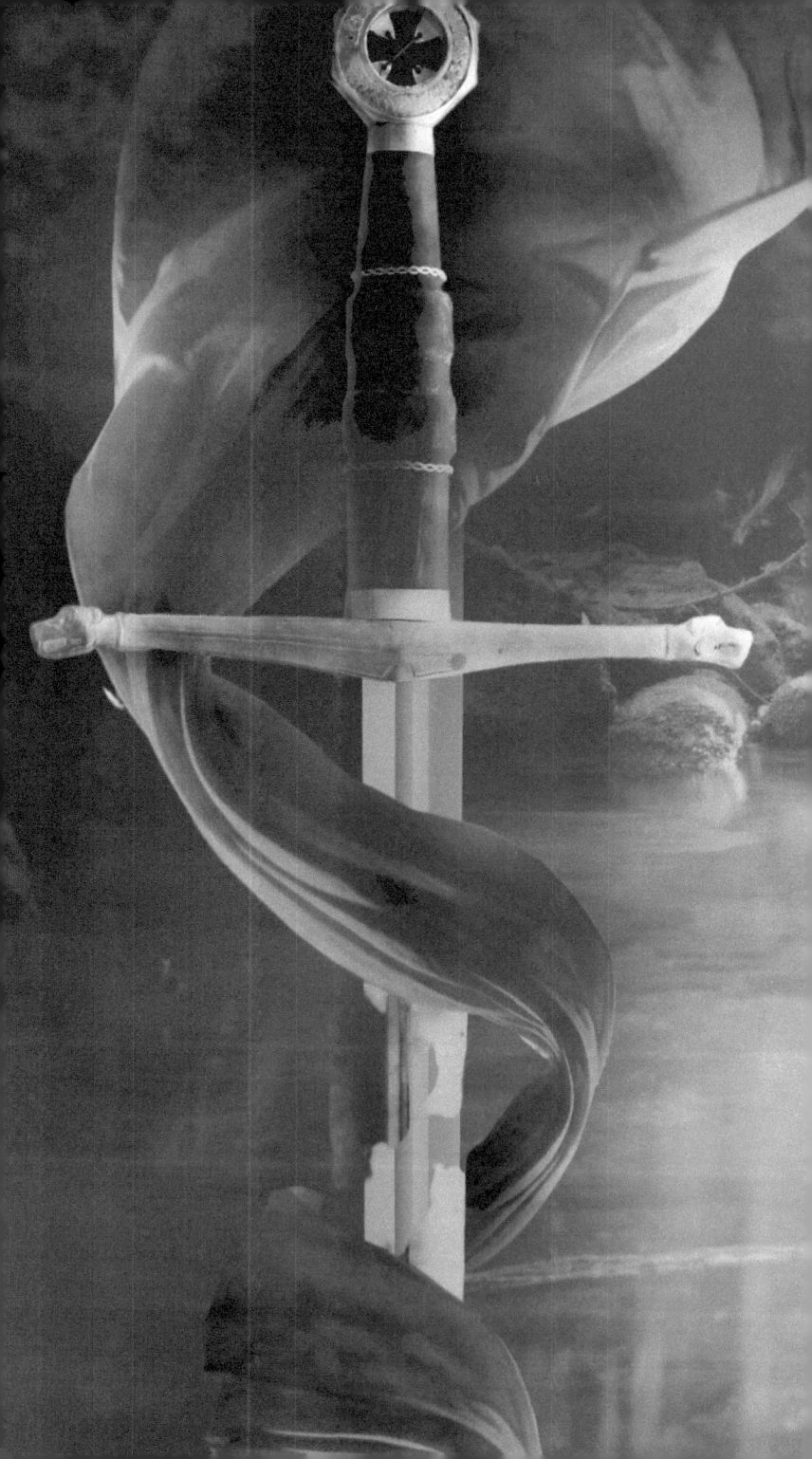

CHAPTER NINE

The sun was setting behind the ragged stone ridge, casting long shadows over the makeshift camp. Soldiers moved like ghosts, checking weapons, tightening saddles, bracing for the road ahead. Terry sat on a boulder just outside the outer ring, fidgeting with the leather strap on his forearm. His sword lay across his lap, clean but nicked—like him.

John found him there, gaze turned toward the hills where Tundra had once stood proud.

"You should be sleeping," John said, crouching beside him. "Or eating. Or at least pretending to do one of those things."

Terry didn't look at him. "Do you think they're scared?"

"The civilians?" John followed his gaze. "Terrified."

Terry nodded slowly. "I can hear it in the way the kids don't cry anymore. It's like they don't want to draw attention to themselves."

John studied him for a moment. "You're not wrong.

But they're still moving. Still walking. That counts for something."

Terry looked down at his hands, his fingers curling around the scuffed grip of his sword. "I never thought I'd be doing this. Standing between them and death. I always imagined someone older. Better."

"You're good enough, Lowd."

Terry smiled faintly. "That's what Chris used to say."

John leaned forward, elbows on his knees. "You care about them. That's what makes the difference."

"I don't care if I die," Terry said softly. "Not really. Not if it means they get out. The kids. The old ones. The moms carrying both their bags and their babies."

He looked at John now, eyes steady.

"But if I fall, I want it to matter. I don't want it to be another pointless name on a list of 'what we lost.'"

John was quiet for a moment, then reached out and gave Terry's shoulder a firm squeeze.

"If it comes to that, it'll matter. I'll make damn sure of it."

Terry stood and slung the sword over his back. "Let's just make sure they don't have to find out."

John smiled faintly and stood beside him. "Spoken like a soldier."

Terry nodded, hoping John was right.

JEAN'S LAST MEMORY OF TUNDRA FELT LIKE A bad dream stitched together with real moments: empty homes with doors left wide open, silent streets crowded with people marching out of their city. In a heartbeat, the capital of Hune had been abandoned. Now, everyone prepared to fight—not for victory, but for survival.

They moved in a slow, ragged caravan. Most of the people were children, women, and older men. There were few wagons and fewer horses. The soldiers hated the pace as much as forcing this group through such a brutal journey—but their resources were limited.

It amazed Jean how quickly her life had unraveled. She wasn't blind to the dangers; the war had killed her parents. Still, she clung to the fantasy that Tundra's walls would always protect her—that the woman who raised her would always be there.

But days ago, she saw Alleta slumped at their kitchen table, hands pressed to her heart, barely able to breathe.

"He's all right," Jean had whispered, helping her up. And she'd said it again—countless times since.

Each day of travel grew quieter, heavier. Fear threaded through hushed voices. Jean began to believe they wouldn't make it. That they would die.

She hated herself for it, but she was angry at the soldiers. They were supposed to protect, not retreat.

"We'll keep walking for just another hour," Charlie called out.

Despite herself, Jean smiled. She couldn't stay angry at **him**.

From the beginning, Charlie had kept her and Alleta near the front with the rest of the soldiers. He said Chris's rank—and their connection to him—made them targets. Jean never argued. It was easier to believe Charlie wanted them nearby. Easier to pretend he chose to walk beside her because he wanted to.

She didn't know when it started, but at some point, Charlie became the only reason she could keep moving. His glance could stop her breath. His presence made her feel safer, seen.

She feared for his life in a way she never had with Chris.

Still, she said nothing. The engagement was over—but Alleta didn't know. Not while Chris was gone, not while she was sick.

Sudden hooves cut through her thoughts—riders galloping back toward the front. Jean's stomach clenched. For days, Charlie had pushed the group hard. Stopping now couldn't be good.

"What happened?" Alleta asked.

Jean scanned the line, trying to spot Charlie.

New faces emerged, covered in dust and dread—soldiers she hadn't seen in days.

It wasn't until hours later that Charlie and John returned, still arguing as they dismounted.

"There's no freaking way we'll make it!" John snapped.

"Don't you think I know that?" Charlie bit back. "But we don't have another option."

Charlie reached for the bowl Jean held out, and her skin tingled when his fingers brushed hers. She smiled.

"It's not ideal," he said, "but it's what we've got."

"Commander," Alleta called, "what's going on?"

John didn't wait for Charlie's response. He moved toward the fire and snatched a bowl from beside it.

Startled, Jean stepped forward. "I was going to—"

"No worries." John's smile didn't reach his eyes. "I can get it myself."

Jean flushed, looking down at the fire.

"Our scouts found reiser tracks on the eastern trail," Charlie said. "Chris and I had agreed to head for the Eastern Refuges, but—"

"But something happened," Jean cut in. "You both knew the reisers might attack—and he left anyway?"

She didn't mean it as an accusation, but it came out sharp.

"He followed the king's orders," John said coldly.

"You mean our king." Jean stared him down.

Charlie raised a hand to defuse the tension.

"Chris didn't want to leave. He hated the order. Believe me."

The silence that followed was heavy.

"Now the safest route is gone," Charlie said. "We'll have to go north."

Gasps and murmurs spread. Everyone knew what that meant.

The northern route was harsher—deadlier. The desert there was unforgiving, with scarce shade, little water, and violent storms.

"What about Andromeda?" Jean asked.

"The reisers took it," Charlie said gently. "We can't go there."

Jean bit her lip, hesitating. Then she said, "The king banned it, but... people have still been going. For years."

Charlie's expression turned serious. "We need to talk somewhere private."

She led him into the shadows beyond the camp.

"Some of the men," she began. "They've been sneaking into Andromeda. It started with supplies—wood, cloth, medicines. No one meant to disobey, but we were running out of everything. Please, don't punish them."

Charlie stared at her. "Punish them? Jean, I'm not going to punish anyone."

She blinked. "But... the king's orders..."

He smiled and gently took her hand. "We do what we have to, to survive. That includes listening to you."

JEAN FELT LIGHTER THE NEXT MORNING, DESPITE the cramps in her legs and the blisters on her feet. She'd spent hours working alongside Charlie, speaking with the men who'd been quietly traveling to Andromeda for supplies.

To her surprise, one of the first to do so had been Daniel Madeck—Chris and Charlie's old commander. Though he'd vanished years ago, many believed he'd died on a journey outside the city. Charlie, however, didn't seem shocked to learn his former superior had come up with the plan. He said Madeck had always had his own ideas about the war—and the king.

Jean also noticed a shift in the camp. The people of Tundra, who had once whispered their disapproval of Charlie, were now watching him with a little more respect. They still loved Alleta—and by extension, Chris—but their frustration had always been clear. Now, for the first time, Jean saw some of that tension begin to ease.

"Good morning, Jean," John called as he passed.

"Morning."

Her smile grew when she spotted Charlie behind him, but it faded quickly. He didn't stop. He barely looked at her.

John, on the other hand, glanced back—and Jean flinched at the coldness in his expression.

Something had changed.

All morning, she tried to catch Charlie's eye, but he stayed near the back of the caravan. By midday, when he didn't come forward to eat, Jean was sure of it: he was avoiding her.

"What's wrong, Jean?" Alleta asked. "If I didn't know better, I'd think you and our commander had a fight."

"What? No," Jean said quickly. "I just... misunderstood something."

Alleta caught her by the arm and pulled her aside.

"If you ask me, you hurt him."

Jean stopped walking. "I didn't do anything to him."

Alleta folded her arms. "Don't look at me like that. I may be sick, but I'm not blind. I see more than you think."

Before Jean could reply, the ground began to tremble with the sound of galloping hooves.

Dark smoke painted the sky behind them.

A city was burning.

It didn't take long for Jean to realize—it was **Tundra**.

The home she'd known her whole life was gone. Flames reached toward the heavens, and though she couldn't smell the smoke, her mind conjured the scent anyway. She could picture the gardens, the old stone streets, the markets—and all of it reduced to ash.

The caravan surged forward. Jean helped Alleta onto a wagon, but as she climbed up, a child's cry pulled her attention back.

A little boy was stumbling after the crowd, tripping on his too-big sandals, his parents too far ahead to notice.

Jean jumped down and ran to him. She scooped him up, placed him in the wagon, and turned back to help the next one.

All day, Jean moved through the exhausted, terrified masses. She coaxed children into wagons. She convinced elders to leave behind their bundles of possessions. Over and over, she repeated the same promise:

"It's going to be all right. Just keep moving. We'll find a safe place soon."

She didn't know if it was true—but that lie was her only comfort.

For the first time, Jean understood what Chris had carried. How heavy it must have been to lead people who looked to him for salvation, even when he had none to give.

That night, the camp was tense. People whispered about the flames, about how far the reisers had come. Sleep was out of the question.

Jean stayed behind to light fires, organize food, and check on the children. When she finally returned to Alleta, the older woman pulled her into a fierce hug.

"Where have you been?" she asked.

"Helping," Jean whispered. "I'm fine."

A soldier nearby shook his head before walking off with his horse.

Alleta pulled her aside. "They've been searching for you. Charlie's been yelling orders all day."

Jean's heart fluttered. Then she remembered his cold shoulder that morning, and her expression soured.

"They weren't exactly trying hard to find me."

Alleta raised a brow. "Were you hiding?"

"No! I mean... maybe. They were ignoring everyone who needed help, and I didn't want to—" She paused, guilt blooming. "I'm sorry."

The older woman's expression softened. "He was worried about you."

"I doubt that."

"He likes you as much as you like him."

Jean's eyes widened. "Alleta, no—I don't—"

"You don't what?" she said gently. "Care about him? Please. I've seen the way you look at him."

Jean covered her face with her hands. "I feel awful. Because of Chris. I never meant to hurt you."

Alleta kissed the top of her head.

"You're my daughter, too. I want your happiness as much as I want Chris's."

"I broke the engagement," Jean admitted softly. "I told Chris the morning he left, in the stables. I couldn't let him go without knowing. I was so angry with him for abandoning you."

"He didn't have a choice," Alleta said, her voice sad but steady.

"I know. I just... I couldn't pretend anymore. It wasn't fair to him. Or to me."

"You did the right thing."

Jean hesitated. "Do you think my parents would be angry?"

"Not at all. They loved you. They would've understood."

Tears welled again, but they didn't fall.

"You need to tell him," Alleta said.

Jean blinked. "Tell who what? I already told Chris."

"No, dear. Tell Charlie."

Jean recoiled. "Alleta, he's been avoiding me! He was awful earlier. Cold and short. Even John—"

"He's Chris's best friend. He probably thinks he's doing the noble thing by staying away. But he won't, not if you tell him the truth." Alleta smiled. "I'm sure John will like you more after that too."

Alleta took a deep breath and looked at the sky.

"As for Chris...my son lost all hope. He can't see a reason to live. I can only wish he finds something that will bring him back to us...wherever he is now."

CHARLIE RUSHED BACK TO THE FRONT OF THE camp as soon as he heard Jean was there. He felt a mix of anger and relief, and she was going to hear about it. As soon as he spotted her sitting by the fire, he leaped from his horse and walked over.

"Where the hell have you been?" he barked.

Jean blinked at him, stunned. "I was helping—"

"Helping?" he snapped. "You think this is a game? These soldiers aren't your personal guards. We're trying to survive out here!"

Jean took a step back. "I'm sorry I troubled—"

"Troubled? We've been searching for hours. While you were off playing hero?"

Alleta stepped between them.

"Enough, Commander."

"I'm sorry," Jean said, her voice shaking. "But I wasn't hiding. I was helping children. Elders. People who were falling behind. I promised them things would get better, even if I didn't believe it. I'm sorry I didn't ask permission."

She turned and walked away.

Charlie froze. He hadn't expected that. He pushed through the others and caught up to her.

"Jean—wait."

She turned, and he flinched at the tears in her eyes.

"I'm sorry," he said. "I didn't mean to—look, I've just had a terrible day. I think I'm turning into a real commander."

She didn't laugh. She didn't even smile.

"Jean, please."

He jogged to keep up with her and couldn't help noticing how kind and innocent she seemed to be. John talked to him the night before and warned him about her. He insinuated that Chris's hesitation toward her could be because of who she really was, how she had been flirting with him while being engaged. It was time to learn the truth.

"Do you have any idea what would happen if the

reisers got to you? Don't you think you should act like someone Chris might actually want to marry?"

Her eyes narrowed. "Wants to marry me?" she said. "What is that supposed to mean?"

"I don't know, Jean. How about you tell me why Chris left you? Why you seem to enjoy my company when you know—"

"When what?" Her voice rose. "When I'm engaged?"

She raised an eyebrow and tilted her head. Charlie thought about leaving things like that. Move on and leave her alone, just like Chris did. But he'd had a horrible day avoiding her and a worse night looking for her.

"Are you going to deny that you are playing with me? Because I'm not an idiot. I can tell you like me."

She turned to move away, but he held her arm before she could leave.

"If you tell me I'm wrong, I'll apologize and leave you alone. Hell, I'll beg for your forgiveness on my knees."

Charlie felt worse when she avoided his gaze.

He sneered at her. "Now I understand why Chris never talked about you. I'm sorry for him."

"You are such a hypocrite!" Jean pushed him back. "I'm not one of those girls you and Chris fool around with. I stayed true to my word until I broke up the engagement. I don't owe Chris anything."

Jean pulled her arm free and walked away.

It took Charlie a moment to grasp her meaning. As he chased after her, he cursed the moment he listened to John and felt like a jerk. He could only hope she would forgive him. Later, he would kill John.

"Jean," he said as he touched her arm, but she pulled away from him.

"Leave me alone!"

Her foot caught in her skirt, and she stumbled.

He caught her.

And without thinking, he brushed her curls from her face and kissed her.

She stiffened—then melted into his arms, pulling him closer.

But even as he held her close, the sky behind them still burned—and somewhere ahead, the desert waited.

CHAPTER TEN

The sun shone through the narrow window of the Prime Zhorta's office—a rare and welcome sight in the Soto Forest, where fog usually swallowed the light. On another day, Rafael might have enjoyed the warmth. But troubling news from the king—and his unexpected ally—kept the zhorta restless.

The letter had come weeks ago, sealed by Leonard III and signed, disturbingly, by the High Council. Rafael didn't trust their so-called "only living member." What troubled him most was the silence that followed. The letter stated the First Guard of the human army was on its way to the abbey, yet gave no reason for the visit. And now, they were late.

That alone was reason to worry. But Rafael had other reasons not to trust the king's intent. Decades ago, they had once been close, even friends. But that had been before war and duty had changed them both. Now Rafael knew his concerns would not be heard—Leonard had long stopped listening.

He was alone in this burden. Alone, and increasingly tempted to disobey his king.

The delay gnawed at him. He feared he wasn't the only one doubting the king's command.

The zhortas had been the first to uncover the prophecy—one that painted a grim future for Hune. Once rumors spread, panic followed. In the eyes of the people, fear turned to blame. Soon, hatred for the zhortas burned hotter than their hatred for the reisers.

The humans accused them of betrayal. The soldiers hunted them like traitors. At the end, the truth was simpler, more tragic.

They had fled to the Soto Forest not to escape the enemy—but to escape those they once served.

"Zhorta Rafael," a voice called from the door. "Did you send for me?"

Rafael turned as Stuart stepped into the room.

"Yes, Stuart," Rafael said, moving from the window to the desk. "Any word from the king's men? Did anyone spot scouts during this morning's harvest?"

For weeks now, he'd posted zhortas near the forest's edge, hoping to catch sight of the approaching Guard.

Stuart's face gave the answer before he spoke.

"Are they even looking? How far out are they going?" Rafael sighed and rubbed his brow. "They should be here by now."

"Rafael, you need patience," Stuart said. "This is the First Guard we're talking about. The best soldiers in Hune. I'm sure they'll arrive, safe and sound."

The last thing Rafael needed was Stuart's optimism.

Without a word, he grabbed a stack of books from his desk and headed out into the corridor.

"Wait!" Stuart caught up beside him. "I do have news. Something... different."

They walked together through the ancient stone halls of Saint Peter's Abbey. Once a place of grandeur, time had turned it to ruin. Still, Rafael was proud of the improvements they'd made. Scholars, not builders, the zhortas had kept the abbey standing through sheer will and effort.

"Is it about the Guard?" Rafael asked.

"No," Stuart said. "Well—no, not directly. It's about Sara."

Rafael's steps slowed. "Is she all right? Did something happen?"

"No, no. She's fine," Stuart said, waving his hand. "But she's... worried."

They continued walking.

"It's her friend. The valsing girl."

Rafael stopped. "What? She's back? Are the others with her?"

"I don't think so," Stuart replied, more cautiously. "But would that be a problem?"

Rafael exhaled sharply. It was more than a problem. The involvement of the High Council was troubling enough—the last thing they needed was valsing drama at the abbey.

"You know how they treated Sara," he said. "You remember what she went through?"

"I know," Stuart said, his voice quieter. He looked just as uneasy. Sara was their shared weakness.

Years ago, Rafael had arrived at the abbey as a reluctant leader under royal command. The zhortas resented him—called him a power-hungry outsider. But he had not come alone. He brought with him a small child, no older than three. Sara. Her bright eyes and sweet voice had melted the coldest hearts. The zhortas might not have accepted him—but they had embraced her.

Especially Stuart. And himself.

"So," Rafael said, his voice cooler, "what's the valsing girl doing here?"

"She's heartbroken," Stuart replied with a sheepish shrug.

"That tends to happen when they chase real love before they're old enough to recognize it."

Stuart laughed behind him. "Rafael, those girls are closer to starting families than playing with dolls."

Rafael smiled despite himself, memories rising unbidden—Sara's first words, first questions, her strong will. He'd never imagined himself a father, but sometimes...

"Has it really been that long?" he murmured.

They entered the abbey's library—a vast, secretive chamber containing the knowledge of a civilization. The zhortas had brought thousands of books from their lost city of Laconia. Within these walls, the full history of Hune lived on, accessible only to them.

The dome above gleamed in the sunlight. It rivaled any palace in grandeur. But it remained quiet today. Everyone was outside, enjoying the unusually warm weather.

"So." Rafael took a seat near the fire. "This girl with the broken heart—what's her name?"

"Lily," Stuart said, then added with a frown, "And her heartbreak may matter more than you think."

"Oh?"

"She fell in love with a valsing who—unfortunately —was already engaged. To the princess."

Rafael straightened in his seat.

"Yes," Stuart said gravely. "The queen was furious. She punished him... by commanding him to find a human soldier."

Rafael blinked. "You mean to say...?"

"Yes. The valsings have joined the war effort. They're on our side now."

Silence fell.

When the zhortas had first arrived at the abbey, Rafael had tasked them with searching for a way to escape the prophecy. They scoured ancient texts for signs. Most had yielded little.

But some suggested that when the races of Hune united, the end would come—and be decided.

Rafael had hoped for unity years ago, when the humans first begged the valsings for help and were denied.

But now...

"This isn't hearsay?" he asked.

"No. I checked myself. Lily isn't confused. Sara knows more. Talk to her."

Rafael nodded, thoughts racing. Only three people in Hune knew the truth of what Sara meant to this war. If the valsings were truly involved—if the prophecy was unfolding now—then time was running out.

"Yes," he said quietly. "Let's go talk to our sweet girl."

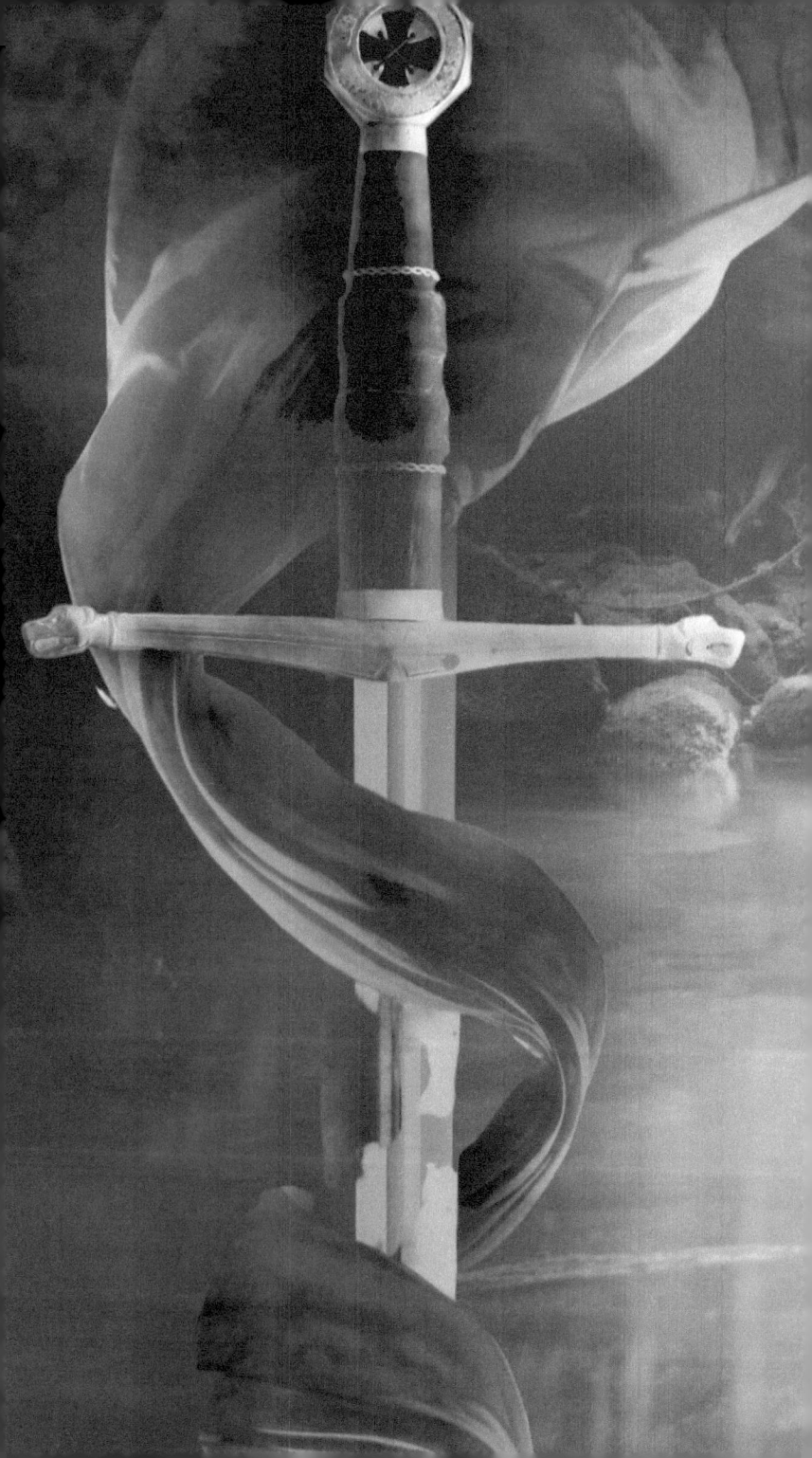

CHAPTER ELEVEN

Morning arrived, and it was the sunlight that woke Chris—a small miracle. That hadn't happened in years. A peaceful night, filled with no dreams and deep rest, left him feeling lighter. For the first time since his father's death, he dared believe they might have a chance.

In contrast, Donald looked like a storm cloud. He sat stiff in the cushioned chair, staring into space, fists clenching and unclenching with restrained fury.

"Are you going to sit there brooding all day?" Chris asked.

Donald leaned over the map between them. "For someone so important to your people, you sleep too much. No wonder your race is losing the war."

Chris sat up and stared at him. "That's a lot of talk from a delicate flower the queen had to save."

Donald's shoulders dropped and he sighed. The jab wasn't meant to mock him, but the valsing took it in stride.

"Let's call it even," he said. "We're in this together now. Might as well make it livable."

Chris wasn't sure he'd call them even. The guy *had* drugged him and dragged him across the desert.

But when he stood, his complaints evaporated. A wave of pleasant aromas surrounded him—fresh fruits, warm bread, melted cheese, meats, and dishes he didn't even recognize. It felt more like a royal banquet than breakfast.

"Is that...?"

"Yes," Donald said. "I told the queen you'd be starving. She sent it."

"All this? For me?"

"Well, no. For both of us."

Chris didn't hesitate. He grabbed a plate and piled it high.

"Is this how you eat every day?"

Donald blinked at the mountain of food. "Ah... not in *that* amount, but yes. This is typical."

"Don't worry," Chris said with a grin, "I'll go back for more."

As Donald shook his head and returned to studying the map, he added, "You *don't* eat like this daily?"

Chris nearly choked. "Of course not. Back in Tundra, we have food, but this? This is special-occasion stuff."

Donald's confusion only deepened. "Because of the war?"

Chris kept eating. "Let's just say I understand the true value of soft bread and fresh fruit."

When he stepped outside, the world had changed

again. The valsings were folding up their city—entire homes collapsing like origami into wagons. Chris spotted their hut, still standing amid the vanishing village.

He raised an eyebrow. "Why is *this* one still up? Don't tell me they were waiting on me to sleep in and stuff my face."

Donald replied without looking up. "They respect the queen's wishes. She gave *us* this hut."

Chris turned to him. "Oh no. I'm not hauling this thing through the forest."

Donald waved him off. "Don't be ridiculous. We're only taking *my* old one."

Chris sighed. "Look, this mission has no room for luxury. If you're traveling with me, it's with what I approve—no exceptions. Got it?"

Donald frowned. "We'll face hardships, you know."

Chris didn't argue. He knew that already.

"Fine," Donald said. "Then tell me—what *is* this mission, anyway? What's so important?"

"Didn't the queen explain it to you?"

"She doesn't trust me," Donald said, bitterness creeping into his voice.

Chris didn't respond right away. Whatever Donald had done to fall from grace, it wasn't his problem. At least not yet.

He dug out the parchment the queen had given him the night before.

"The High Council wants the journal of King Leonard I."

Donald raised an eyebrow. "Shouldn't that be in a vault somewhere in your palace?"

Chris shot him a look. "That's what you ask? Not *why* the High Council suddenly reappeared? The Council that disappeared decades ago? What's next, a dragon guarding it?"

Donald grinned. "Hey, it *could* happen."

Chris wasn't laughing.

"We humans have a tradition," he continued. "We bury our kings with all their belongings. Wherever Leonard chose to rest, the journal should be there."

Donald's eyes narrowed. "Then use the map."

He slid his hand over the map. The symbols shimmered, shifting before Chris's eyes. Suddenly, everything was readable. Names. Locations. Labels in perfect human script.

Chris gawked. "What the hell?"

"You're welcome," Donald muttered. "Whoever gave you this forgot that you don't read valsing."

Chris leaned closer. "You've got to be kidding..."

He scanned the map, now fully legible. Right there, in the middle of the Soto Forest: *King Leonard's Sepulcher.*

"No," Donald said, backing away. "We are *not* going to that cursed place."

Chris smirked. "Afraid of legends?"

"My people don't make up stories, Chris. That place is damned."

Chris straightened. "You can stay behind if you want. But I'm going."

Just then, a too-familiar voice stopped him cold.

"There you are, handsome."

Princess Cassandra stood in the entrance—perfect as

ever, dripping with charm and contempt. She was stunning. Impeccable. And Chris wanted nothing more than to forget she existed.

Donald stood. "Your Grace, I don't think your mother would approve—"

Cassandra's smile turned sharp. "Since when do you care about *her* opinion? I remember you being quite the disappointment."

Donald flinched. "What do you want?"

She ignored him, locking eyes with Chris. "You look older. And sad. Not at all how I remember you."

Chris didn't blink. "Funny. I barely remember you at all."

Her smile faltered for a breath, but then returned. She strutted in, pretending to admire the tent.

"Donald, I need water. The heat is making me faint."

Chris rolled his eyes. "Cut the act, Cassie. What do you want?"

Her mask dropped. "Is the Soto Forest still standing? Are the zhortas safe?"

Chris blinked. "You care about *them*?"

"They're in danger," she snapped. "You have to help them."

Chris crossed his arms. "Why should I? The zhortas abandoned us when we needed them most."

Cassandra's voice broke. "Because no one else will. Not even your king. You're the only one who—"

She stopped herself.

"You'll regret it if you don't," she whispered. "I know guilt. You do too."

Then she turned and left.

Chris said nothing.

The tent was silent for a long time.

AFTER CASSANDRA LEFT, CHRIS'S OPTIMISM went with her. Doubts now gnawed at him—about the abbey, about the zhortas, and about the king's silence. His orders had seemed questionable before, but now...

He stepped into the tent again, fuming. "Donald! Let's go!"

Donald was struggling to pack an impossible amount of clothing into a tiny bag.

"You were giving me crap about sleeping in, and now you're trying to fit a castle into a sack?"

Chris sighed.

"All right, fine—just tell me. Were you the queen's lover?"

"What?! No!"

"I mean," Chris added," she's mature, but... you know, cute—if you're into that."

"Stop talking."

Chris leaned against the doorframe. "So what's your story then? Everyone knows it around here. You might as well tell *me*."

Donald was quiet for a beat too long. Then, softly:

"Princess Cassandra. The queen betrothed us."

Chris froze.

Donald looked away. "She offered me the highest

honor. I was loyal. Trusted. I would've been Prince Consort."

He chuckled bitterly. "But then I met *her*. The most astonishing valsing in Hune. Lily. And nothing else mattered."

"You broke off the engagement?"

"No. I tried to handle it with dignity. But Cassandra made it public. She wanted vengeance."

Chris winced. "Sounds like her."

Donald clenched his fists. "Vanessa spared me. She exiled me—sent me to find *you*. I don't know what happened to Lily. I told her to run. I just... I need to know."

His voice cracked. He threw his bag across the room.

"I lost everything. And everyone. All because I loved someone who wasn't part of the plan."

Chris wished he could say something—anything—that would help. But there was no time. And no easy fix.

When Donald stepped out to join him, the other valsings whispered and stared.

Chris raised his voice. "Hey, Donald—remind me again how your *super-intelligent* people think babysitting a spoiled princess is a leadership role?"

The whispers stopped.

"I mean, come on. Let's be honest—*no one* can control Cassandra. You dodged a spear, not a crown."

Donald looked stunned. Then... relieved.

Chris swung onto his horse. "I swear, your people may be brilliant—but they're blind if they let you go."

The camp fell silent.

Donald smiled as he climbed into the saddle. "You didn't have to say that."

Chris shrugged. "Yeah, well. You wouldn't *believe* how much pleasure I get making your people feel stupid."

CHAPTER TWELVE

S oto Forest's name came from its vegetation, where the trees were so tall and wide that, at a human scale, the only visible part were the roots. Their height was beyond perception from the ground. The thickness of the top blocked most of the sunlight, making the soil humid and filled with mushrooms and decaying leaves.

The unbelievable part was the roots. They formed tunnels and bridges with their organic arcs. They didn't grow straight up, but twisted as they searched for food on the ground.

Although the Soto Forest was a dark place, Donald learned the difference between day and night soon enough. Once the sun set somewhere among the thick roots of the woods, the cold turned bitter, almost painful, and the silence was profound and unrealistic.

Starting a fire had been close to impossible, and keeping it going was an unexpected full-time task.

After the first night, Donald could appreciate the

dim light and the slight warmth from the humid air during the day.

"I never thought I'd miss the desert," Donald said. "Do you think it will take long to reach the mountain?"

The silence in Chris's answer was enough, and Donald laughed at himself. One night was already too long in that damn place.

Chris finished reading the map and passed it to him.

The details on the parchment were impressive, but in this place, they were close to useless. The covered ground and the blocked sun were a problem. Donald stopped believing these were normal woods. There was something off about it. The magic of Hune was present and did not have their best intentions at heart.

He was a great navigator though. As a child he feared getting lost. He learned at a young age how to find the right direction and how to calculate distances.

"Hey," Chris said, "I'm leaving the horses here before we get too deep inside this hell."

"What!" Donald said. "Are you out of your freaking mind? Those horses are the fastest way—"

Chris's exasperated expression stopped him.

"Is this friendly ground for riding?" Chris said. "Because if you want to take your chances and have to kill your horse after it breaks a leg, be my guest."

Donald felt his hate for the Soto Forest grow while his hopes of finishing the mission in a couple of days withered.

"Fine." Donald pulled his bag from the saddle and threw it at Chris's feet. "But you take that one. I will share my tent, but—"

He stopped himself. Threatening Chris with leaving the comfort of his tent wasn't a good idea. Most likely the soldier wouldn't care about sleeping on the cold and wet ground.

It wasn't just the place; the walk wasn't easy either. Just like the previous day, it involved too much climbing and crawling through the roots. The worst part was there was no sign of improvement.

At the beginning, Donald had hoped they entered the forest at a wild edge and that a path would open at some point. However, after a day in that maze, he was certain that time and lack of use had allowed the foliage to cover any path.

"Do you think we could stop for lunch soon?"

Donald hated having to ask, but he was having trouble keeping up with Chris.

Chris rolled his eyes but stopped.

Donald's disheveled look and unusual posture must have shocked the soldier. He felt sweat dripping around his face and body. His hair had to be all messed up from having to pull himself from root to root.

"Haven't you ever hiked?" Chris said. "I thought your people moved everywhere all the time."

When he reached Chris, he let himself fall to the ground and lie down there. He didn't care about the disgusting mushrooms he had smashed with his back or the stain they would imbed on his shirt.

"To start, this is not a hike," he said, short of breath. "And yes, we walked a lot but never at your speed, idiot! If you have not noticed, I am not as tall as you. It is taking me twice the effort to move at your comfortable pace."

Chris laughed and sat against a root.

"Maybe it is true that the air is thinner at your height." Donald rested on his elbows to look at Chris. "Your brain suffers from a lack of oxygen. That would explain your lack of understanding."

Chris took a sip of water that looked very appealing to Donald. "Or maybe I'm just more intelligent, taller, and stronger than you."

"Taller, maybe sort of smart." Donald took the water when Chris offered it and gulped half. "But never as handsome!"

Something behind Donald got Chris's attention, and he turned, ready to jump.

"This is impossible, but—" Chris said. He walked to the other side and took a close look. "Have you seen this place before?"

Donald held his breath and looked around. Only when he was certain nothing was familiar did he exhale.

Chris took out the map, and Donald pushed him out of his way to check the parchment.

"We are going in the right direction," he said.

"How can you be so sure?" Chris said. "There is nothing here that can be—"

"Because, little human, I have a great sense of direction, excellent speed calculation, and the Map of Hune. How can I be wrong?"

Although surprised at his own tone of security, he continued. "I think your calculations are wrong. Close, but not perfect. We are almost half a mile farther ahead.

Nothing to be troubled though. It is understandable from a human."

Chris pulled the map away and rolled it up. Without another word they walked once more.

Donald was sure the reason their pace slowed was that Chris doubted their direction. He confirmed it when, less than an hour later, Chris stopped again.

"I'll be damned!" Chris said.

Without asking, Chris pulled his sack from Donald's shoulder and almost made him fall down.

"Hey! What is your problem?"

Chris didn't reply and kept throwing things out of the bag. "We are moving in circles."

Donald shook his head and controlled his breathing, preventing a panic attack.

"I told you. I am sure we are walking—"

He forgot what he was saying. Chris took out an old compass from the bottom of his sack.

"Gua!" He kneeled and stared at the metal object. "That is a treasure, Chris."

The soldier sat back and looked at the compass.

"It is a unique piece in all Hune," Donald said. "It must be worth a fortune."

Chris's eyes darted at him, and the pain was palpable in them. "It belonged to my father."

Donald went quiet. He knew what that meant, even when he never met Colonel Xander Riddley.

Chris didn't stand up or open the compass. So, after a while Donald asked, "What is the problem then? Come on. It is just fair you tell me. I talked to you about—"

"Fair?" Chris's hands shook with hate. "I tell you what is not fair. That I'm alive and he is not."

Donald didn't know what to say. The darkness of the Soto Forest deepened.

CHRIS SAT BACK AGAINST A MASSIVE ROOT, THE compass still resting in his hand. Its lid was closed now, but the weight of it felt heavier than anything else he carried. Donald was silent beside him, giving him the space he needed.

"My father was the last colonel of our army," Chris said finally. "Not like the armament. Never like those bastards. He fought the reisers until the end."

Donald listened carefully, nodding once.

"I did something, and I hurt my father—" Chris shook his head and exhaled. "Well, you know what happened when I met your freaking king, and for sure my father hated it. After that, we avoided each other. No matter how much I changed or what I achieved, his disappointment was there...always."

Donald thought Chris and Cassandra's strategy was well-calculated and mutually beneficial. She ditched her father, and he boosted the soldiers' spirits. Back then, he only knew his princess' side of the story. After meeting Chris, he understood the remorse a moral person might feel.

"For years, we barely saw each other," Chris said. "And if it wasn't for the war turning for the worse, the king would have never forced us to work together...I enjoyed those times. I didn't think I'd ever have that again—his respect. But I did. For a little while."

He looked at the compass again. It was closed, and Donald could distinguish the engraved initials on it: A.R. Alexander Riddley.

"Do you believe he was better than you?"

To his surprise, Chris nodded.

"The king decided to get back to Laconia." Chris's eyes filled with hate. "He believed there was something important that was worth a suicidal mission. Because of the high risk, my father gathered the last five guards."

"Which was your guard?" Donald asked, excited.

A corner of Chris's mouth lifted. "The second! We met in the desert to prepare to ambush the reisers in the city." He took a deep breath and passed his hand through his hair. "The reisers must have known about it, because the second the last guard arrived, they attacked us. One of the largest brigades of those freaking monsters I have ever seen. To make things harder on us, the reisers had a new inexplicable protection. Nothing got through their armor."

Donald moved forward. He had never seen a reiser, but he knew they were brutal. If they were magically protected, only destiny had saved Chris.

"My father should have taken the king, along with the armament, but instead, he commanded me to do it." He shook his head. "We both knew the war was over. They defeated us. It was our turn to die. He gave me this compass and commanded me to get to Tundra."

Confused, Donald shook his head. "Tundra? Not Laconia?"

"Correct. My mother was in Tundra." Chris looked straight at Donald. "If you have seen what the reisers can do to a person, you would understand. You would make sure your loved ones don't go through that."

Donald swallowed hard. "Did your father send you to kill your mother?"

Chris looked at him for a second and then exhaled.

Donald's concept of humans, war, and Chris changed in that moment. He understood how terribly desperate they had to be to believe that ending their lives would be for the best.

"But you are here." Donald felt stupid for saying that, but he needed to know what Chris did.

"It was a long shot, Donald," he said. "Tundra was too far, and the reisers were right behind us. In half of the time I was hoping for, we saw the dust from their galloping. Flying arrows covered us not too long after. I stopped my men to give the armament more time, but I knew better. My time was up."

Chris closed his fists. "Then, as soon as I made my first strike on one of those monsters, my blade cut it clean. I felt its blood dripping in my hand and I turned just in time to see his head fall and roll to my feet. Whatever the hell had been protecting them before was gone, and the bastards weren't expecting it. We are superb warriors, and that day we were desperate. We killed them all, just like a freaking miracle."

He sighed and shook his head.

"I was one of the first ones to reach what they left of our army. I hoped the same change happened there...such a stupid thought. We found only death and the echoes of torture."

Donald nodded understanding Chris's predicament. Guilt and shame for surviving. Just like he felt about his fate and Lily's.

"As my father wanted, we continued on to Tundra. To our last city—and my mother."

Chris's agony was visible through his eyes.

"I have done terrible things in my life, but the worst was telling my mom she would never see my father again and that he couldn't have a proper funeral."

Chris looked at the ground.

"How was I supposed to tell her he sent me to kill her as proof of his love for her? As an act of mercy? And that she was the reason I wasn't at his side? That he wanted to give me time to reach her, so he took my guard's job? I should have been the one who died. He should have escorted the king to Tundra."

Donald didn't know for how long both remained silent until Chris looked up again. "Gods be damned!"

"I do not know what to say, Chris. I'm sorry."

Chris stood up and nodded. "Thanks, but it's not that. We are lost, Donald."

DONALD'S EYES OPENED WIDE AS HIS BREATH sped up. He fell to his knees and tried to pull open his shirt while he fought his shaking hands. Chris had seen panic attacks before, and they weren't pleasant.

"Hey, hey!" Chris knelt at his side. "Just try to take deep breaths."

"Lost!" Donald's voice squeaked in a high-pitched whisper. "No. I know my way—"

"Listen. You need to count backward."

Donald grabbed Chris's coat and pulled him close. "No! We are not lost."

Chris moved Donald's hands from him and opened the compass in front of the valsing.

The arrow inside bounced a couple of times, pointing to the north, straight ahead from where they had been walking. Reign Mountain was to the west though, the direction Chris thought they had been following.

Donald grabbed the compass from his hands and stood up. He walked in circles, looking at the arrow in his hands and shaking his head faster every time.

"This thing is broken, Chris! I know we have been walking west. You know that too! This is not working. That is all!"

"What number is before eight, Donald?"

Chris took the compass back and used it to find the real west. Without saying a word, he stood there, just observing the distance. Behind him, he felt Donald sit back down, still trying to control his breathing.

"Is it ten, smartass?" Chris said. "Or four?"

"What?" Donald said. "I am not stupid—I can't breathe—"

The compass's arrow moved and pointed to the side. Chris checked the roots, and small, simple differences became clear. He sat down by Donald and tried his best to give him the news.

"So, what is it? Six?" Chris said.

"No, eight. I mean five, seven? What the hell—"

"Good. Now listen and breathe," he said. "For a day and a half, we woke up, we took a bearing with the compass, and we set a target at the farthest root we could see and walked toward it. We didn't consider one small possibility."

Donald looked up at him, and it was clear how hard he was trying to focus.

"This freaking place is moving around us."

A wide smile crossed the valsing's face as a chuckle escaped from his mouth. Without asking, Chris offered him the compass. Hesitating, he took it and stared at the arrow. When this one spun to the right, Donald gave it back to Chris and held his head with both hands.

"Now listen." Chris shook him to get his attention. "Breathe and count backward. Twelve, eleven, then what?"

"This is—" Donald said, "dumb. I can count. Three? Ten? Nine, maybe eight? Se-seven."

"Good. Now think about something else. Anything else."

Donald looked up, and although he still had trouble breathing, the color was coming back to his skin. "Did you go back to Laconia?"

The question took Chris by surprise. "Laconia, really? What about Lily? A nicer thought?"

Donald rubbed his eyes with both hands.

"I was trying to avoid thinking about her because I

can picture her lost somewhere, and that reminds me, we are lost and—"

"All right. Fine," Chris said. "No, we never went to Laconia. The closest we ever got was the gathering point at the desert. After what happened, the king changed his mind."

"What happened with—" Donald said. "You know, the important thing? What was it? Um, sorry, so sorry. The last thing you want to talk about must be this, but—"

"It's all right. The last thing I want is to listen to you scream and whine."

Donald's laugh sounded too enthusiastic and erratic, confirming Chris's point.

"The king took his personal armament to find the rest of the troops around the desert and the forest. He ordered my guard to protect Tundra. Then he sent orders for us to get to the Soto Forest."

"You...mean you?" Donald lifted an eyebrow. "The king sent *you* to the Soto Forest. Just you, right?"

Chris closed his eyes while he shook his head. He didn't want to trigger Donald's psychosis, but he would not lie to such a straight question. He couldn't.

"Look," he said, noticing Donald's incriminating look, "I couldn't leave Tundra unprotected. It is our last city. Because of that, it is their next target." He didn't let Donald talk. "And now I'm not following his orders thanks to your people, right?"

After Chris started a fire, he left Donald and walked with a torch to find water. He wondered how to find anything in this place, where he couldn't see more than a couple of steps ahead of him. Now he was supposed to account for the foliage's movement. He had no idea how lost they were, and Donald's panic wasn't going to help them.

His boots slid on the damp earth, but it wasn't just the terrain that wore him down—it was the weight of command, of decisions he couldn't undo.

The sound of running water caught his attention, and he turned to follow it. He lowered the torch to pass under a root but missed the uneven ground. He slid down until he stopped at the edge of a tiny creek.

"Freaking place."

In the fall, he lost the torch, so he stood still, waiting for his eyes to adjust to the lack of light. The glow from their campfire in the distance was easy to find. At least in such darkness, a small fire became so bright.

He took out his bottle and filled it with water as fast as he could. Although he was certain that nothing would attack him—because nothing lived there—the roots around weren't appealing.

A twinkle nearby caught his attention.

He brushed the ground around and found what seemed to be a flower. He covered his hand with his sleeve and picked it up.

The blossom was more like a strange mushroom than a flower. It was the size of a rose and reminded him of a snowflake, with its delicate symmetry and icy white color. But it was sharp—its petals like tiny blades of steel. He moved it closer, and the same floral essence he had perceived in the desert, and in dreams washed over him, strangely comforting and familiar.

It didn't belong in a place like this. Or maybe it was the only thing that did.

He wrapped it in his handkerchief and slipped it into his pocket, not realizing yet why he felt compelled to keep it.

The walk back was more complicated without a torch, and while he watched his step, he forgot all about the blossom.

He found Donald sitting close to the fire, wrapped in a blanket and staring at the roots. He reminded Chris of some of his soldiers after a battle—exhausted but unable to rest.

"We'll figure it out, Donald," Chris said. "We have a map, a compass, and a great sense of direction. Right?"

Chris took out the map and placed it on the ground.

"What are we doing?"

"Well, I'm going to figure out where Reign Mountain is from here—"

"No, idiot!" Donald said. "What were we thinking? You're a deserter and I'm an exile. Nothing good can come from that!"

Chris walked closer to the fire and felt the warmth seep through his wet clothes.

"You're being dramatic."

Donald walked toward the tent. Halfway there, he turned and pointed at Chris, who didn't let him speak.

"I'm not a deserter," Chris said. "I have every intention of helping the stupid zhortas. And anyway, if this is a

High Council order, we're following a higher command."

"Ha! Well, that's convenient."

Chris didn't reply. He knew he was lying to himself. It was true he never liked his king, and it was true that during the war, he complained and criticized his ruler's orders, but he had never disobeyed him.

Now, he wondered if he was a traitor.

The orders made it seem like the king wanted to leave his people at the reisers' mercy, and that weighed on Chris's mind. It made him wonder if Leonard III was fighting for Hune at all.

His behavior during the last battle added to that doubt. Chris would never forget the king's expression when he saw his soldiers massacred on the field. He seemed surprised, but not filled with horror. It was more like admiration.

During the war, they learned at great cost how cruel the reisers' nature was. Still, Chris had seen nothing close to what those monsters did to his father and his men. He didn't regret witnessing what happened—now he knew what his enemy was capable of.

But there were images in his mind that would haunt him the rest of his life.

He remembered how the desert sands turned darker and soaked with blood at least a mile before they reached the camp. The smell of death mixed with metal and rotting flesh extended even farther.

Most of the soldiers were still alive but couldn't be saved. Missing limbs and wounds beyond healing weren't the only problem. The poison from their enemy's blades had no cure when left in deep punctures. The reisers had made sure to leave those men in torment and agony, where a merciful end was the only option.

Chris gave one of the hardest orders of his life so the dying men could rest in peace. He knew he scarred his own guard by asking them to end their friends' suffering, but it was that or see and listen to their agony. He didn't let them do it alone. When they finished, his hand carried a weight he would bear for the rest of his life.

There was no funeral or ceremony for any of them—including his father. They didn't have time. At the end, they set everything on fire.

Against Chris's best judgment, their king was with them when they did this. He insisted that he needed to see his men. And during all the hours Chris and his guard finished the reisers' work, Leonard sat on his horse, protected by his armament, watching everything.

Charlie tried to tell Chris the king must have been in shock, unable to act—but Chris agreed with John. Leonard hadn't looked stunned.

He looked satisfied.

Chris's most vivid memory was when he found his father. He first saw the unique sword and ran to it. The colonel's hand was still holding it. Nearby, he found who once was the strongest man he had ever known and loved.

There was no doubt the monsters had given his father special treatment.

If there had ever been the slightest desire for revenge in Chris's soul, it died in that moment. He could never inflict so much pain and suffering—not even close.

For the first time in years of fighting, Chris's vision blurred and his eyes stung. He drove his old sword into the ground and picked up the colonel's in tribute. In his nightmares, he could still feel the cold steel of the sword's pommel and see the stains on his uniform shirt when he cleaned its blade.

The king was standing right behind him.

"At least you didn't have to finish him like all the other soldiers," Leonard had said. "Hune lost a great fighter. Tell that to your family."

And then, right there, Leonard had asked Chris to kneel and named him commander of the new First Guard.

Chris hadn't regretted interrupting the ruler, cutting him off before he used the colonel's rank. He would not be a colonel.

No one could ever fill his father's place.

Donald's snores brought him back to the Soto Forest and its unnatural silence. He lay back and tried to see through the darkness above him, but it was impossible. He could wish for a dreamless rest, but he knew better.

Still, he closed his eyes and waited, listening to the quiet creak of the shifting roots and the whisper of his own breath.

Tomorrow, they would walk again. Somehow.

CHAPTER THIRTEEN

Charlie assigned Terry Lowd, along with his superior, Lieutenant Fred Laurence, to the rear watch of the newly reorganized Second Guard. Ever since smoke had begun to rise from the city skyline, the people had grown anxious. To keep order and buy time for the First Guard to protect the caravan, Charlie split the forces.

Terry didn't mind the task itself—it was simple enough. He and Fred had to watch for signs of the reisers and cover the rear. But he *did* mind being transferred to the Second Guard. It was petty, maybe, but the demotion stung.

Less than three years ago, fresh out of training, Terry had joined the Second Guard. Back then, he was desperate to prove himself. He'd been the youngest, but the best in his class, and eager to belong. A few weeks later, he met Major Christopher Riddley—and everything changed.

"If you work so hard, you won't have energy for a real battle, soldier," Chris said. "Follow me."

Terry had seen him before, but Chris hadn't spoken to him until that moment.

The silence as they walked together only fed Terry's anxiety. His hands were slick with sweat, twitching with nervous energy. Chris had a reputation across the army—respected, even feared. Terry didn't want to disappoint him.

"So, Terry Lowd," Chris said once they were inside the headquarters. "That right?"

"Yes, sir."

"It says here you were in training for less than a year before they sent you out. No battles yet, right?"

Chris read from the papers on his desk, not bothering to look up.

"Yes... sir. But I can do it. I'm ready, sir—Major."

Terry braced himself. He expected the next question would be about his age or inexperience—how he was too green, too reckless. That fear of being sent home, of failing before he even began, gripped his stomach.

But Chris surprised him.

He leaned back, smirked, and gestured to the chair across from him. "I can't even imagine fighting during my first year. Not even my fifth. It's not fair to anyone. But war is war, and we're not in a good place."

Then his face turned serious.

"Are you afraid, soldier?"

Terry hesitated, staring at the table. He shook his head. No way would he admit it—not to Chris.

"Do you think I'm not?" Chris asked.

Terry froze, unsure how to respond.

Chris gave a dry chuckle. "You're wrong, soldier. I'm afraid every time I give an order. I'm afraid of making a bad call that costs lives. I'm afraid we'll lose Hune... and everyone will suffer because of it."

His expression darkened.

"I'm afraid because when I fight, I risk everything. And if that's not something to fear, then you don't understand war."

The fear in Terry's chest shifted into something else. It wasn't gone—but now he knew he wasn't alone in it.

"How do you fight through it?" Terry asked. "I mean —sorry, sir. I didn't mean—"

"That's more like it." Chris sat forward. "I remember *why* I'm doing this—and *who* I'm fighting for."

Then he leaned in further.

"But remember this: for the soldier beside you, it's better to quit *before* the battle than during it."

Terry never forgot that moment. During his first fight, it became his anchor. The brutality of combat made training look like child's play. But Chris's words stayed with him.

By the end of that first battle, bloodied and exhausted, Terry understood what it meant to stand between his people and the enemy.

No one would ever replace the father he lost—but Chris had come close.

"What the hell are you daydreaming about, boy?" Fred said, shielding his eyes from the sun as he lay in the sand.

"Not about you, that's for sure," Terry said.

Fred had once served in Laconia's army, alongside Lieutenant John. They'd both been present when the city fell to the reisers. John had left the battle barely alive. Fred had been knocked out cold—saved, supposedly, because the reisers thought he was already dead. He liked to say he'd survived thanks to a puddle of someone else's blood.

"Hey, Fred—aren't you from Andromeda?"

Fred lifted his head. "Why?"

Terry was from a small settlement. Cities fascinated him. Andromeda might be in ruins now, but it had once been a major port. It meant something to him.

"Just wondering what it looks like. Do you think we'll get there soon?"

Fred scoffed. "Sometimes I forget how young you are. It'll be a pile of junk, that's what. Haven't you seen enough wreckage already?"

Terry ignored the jab. It always annoyed him when people made fun of his age. One day, Hune *would* rise again, and he planned to be there to help rebuild it.

"Just because you've lost hope doesn't mean—"

He didn't finish.

In the distance, a faint ripple of movement stirred the sand.

Terry wanted to believe it was just wind—but Fred sat up. That alone told him otherwise.

The ripple grew, fast.

Terry reached for the signal torch.

Fred stood and raised his sword, striking the first reiser that leapt toward them. The blow should have been fatal, but the creature barely flinched.

Terry ran toward Fred—but another reiser slammed into him, flinging him into the air. He hit the ground hard, knocking the wind from his lungs.

Still, he forced himself to his feet and ran to his horse.

If Fred had managed to wound the reiser, he might have stayed. Let the signal warn the others. But the reisers' armor had changed. That changed *everything*. Their orders were clear: if the armor still held, one had to survive to warn the rest.

He climbed into the saddle and turned back just once.

Fred was still fighting, sword heavy in his hand, his uniform already soaked in blood.

"Just go!" Fred shouted.

Terry obeyed.

He kicked his horse and sped across the sand. Behind him, Fred's screams echoed. He hated himself for even thinking about it, but he hoped the reisers would take their time. He needed every second.

A sharp pain bloomed in his side. His fingers fumbled at his ribs. Warm wetness soaked his clothes. He looked down.

Blood.

His own.

He gripped the reins with one hand and pressed the wound with the other, his vision swimming.

The reisers stopped being his immediate threat. Now, his only battle was to stay alive long enough to tell someone.

ANDROMEDA WAS CLOSER THAN THE NORTHERN Refuges, and the caravan was moving faster—but Charlie remained uneasy. Reaching the city would only delay the inevitable.

This time, though, he had a plan.

Before Jean, he hadn't cared what happened to him. He'd lost his family. All his friends were soldiers. He was ready to fight—and die—if needed.

But now?

Now he couldn't imagine leaving Jean at the mercy of the reisers.

His priorities had changed.

He'd use Andromeda as a decoy—a base to mask their real escape. In small groups, they would slip away into the Soto forest and regroup with his former commander, Chirs. There, they could wait, build a future, and maybe... fight again.

Before sunrise, Charlie rode out from the main camp to check on the Second Guard.

He wondered if their fake trail toward the Eastern Refuges had fooled the reisers. If so, they might have enough time to carry out the plan—and give Chris time to persuade the zhortas to find something that could help.

That last thought made him laugh.

The army's only hope resting on Chris's *persuasive skills*? He thought about how Chris's last diplomatic encounter with the valsings had gone and shook his head.

Jean came to mind. He missed her—deeply.

She insisted they keep their relationship quiet. People would talk. The timing of her split from Chris made it too easy for others to judge.

Charlie didn't care what anyone thought. But for her, he kept quiet. He didn't need to start breaking jaws. John was lucky to be his friend; after what he pulled, not many would keep his health intact.

"Commander," a soldier called.

"Soldier." Charlie dismounted. "Any news?"

"No, sir."

They walked toward the guard camp.

Charlie sighed. No children yelling, no crying—just soldiers. There was peace in that, ironic as it was.

"Hey, Charlie!" John said, grinning. "I mean—Commander. To what do we owe the pleasure?"

Charlie had no problem putting John in charge of the Second Guard—John was a great soldier. He remained a lieutenant solely because of his past involvement with the Laconia army. King Leonard III rarely, if ever, promoted those soldiers.

The war brought the cities an alliance, but some ignorant people still made fun of Laconia's army. They even called them cowards.

The reason the waterfall city was destroyed before Tundra was because the war started on that side of Hune. By the time Tundra's army joined the fight, it was too late to save Laconia. Charlie never said it out loud, but he believed the cowards had been his side of the army.

"Look at you!" Charlie said, "I didn't think you'd miss me this much!"

"Miss you?" John laughed. "Camp's been nice and quiet. I was having a great day! Less noisy and calm."

Charlie scowled while he looked around.

"I will say though," John added, "I'd have bet you would have enjoyed the big camp more. You know, your new privileges."

"You would think so...but I can't."

"How come?" John lifted his eyebrow. "I thought— no. You made it pretty clear she was free of her engagement and that you—"

"She is." Charlie sighed. "She's worried people will judge her. Think she only moved on because Chris is gone."

John laughed, too loud.

"You aren't afraid of the reisers, but fear a tiny woman?"

"I'm not afraid, idiot. I'm thinking of her."

John smirked. "She's your new commander."

Charlie looked at the ground, shaking his head and laughing.

"She is just a sweet and innocent girl, right?" John said. "Isn't that what you called her when you almost break my nose?"

"She is sweet and innocent...too innocent. She thinks people's opinions matter," Charlie said.

John's features clouded with sadness. "She knows what she wants."

Charlie got the impression that John wasn't talking about Jean anymore, but he never had the chance to ask.

A horse running toward the camp appeared in the distance.

John beat him to it, mounting his horse and racing out.

Charlie didn't notice the smoke until he was in the saddle, and the short time it took to reach the soldier seemed to last forever.

While John helped the soldier off his horse, a horrifying realization dawned on Charlie.

"Terry?" he said as the wounded soldier collapsed into their arms.

"Commander—they're coming. Protected..."

Charlie froze.

John's grim expression said it all.

The reisers were back.

And their armor still held.

They rode back to the camp, where all the soldiers of the second guard were ready. But Charlie didn't let them attack.

"Fall back," he ordered. "We protect the caravan."

THE CARAVAN WAS ONLY MINUTES AWAY FROM the camp. Not enough distance from the reisers. Fortunately, the first guard's soldiers saw the smoke and were prepared to follow orders.

Within seconds, Charlie spotted a group of sand hills and pointed at them. One of his sergeants took the sign as an order and led the civilians toward the hills. It wasn't an organized march, but at least they listened and followed the instructions.

Then came the reisers.

Charlie rode to the front. Jean flashed in his mind. He hadn't even told her he loved her.

"Listen!" he called to his troops. "Today, we don't fight for some distant future. We fight for the ones behind those hills. We're the First Guard. Their *last* hope."

A roar of voices answered.

He kicked his horse and charged, not waiting.

During the years of war, they had improved their approach to fighting the enemy. When possible, they hit the reisers in waves. Two soldiers per reiser—an old tactic. It gave them a chance.

Luckily, a quick assessment revealed that his soldiers outnumbered the enemy. It might seem unfair to an outsider, but to those involved, it was hardly fair at all. The Reisers' power and assertiveness were unmatched in combat.

Charlie struck first—and was stunned when his blade sliced clean through.

"They're vulnerable!" he shouted.

John was already beside him, decapitating the beast. The soldiers roared, surging forward.

The battle was brutal—but they had momentum. The reisers weren't prepared to be wounded. Or afraid.

By the end, Charlie stood among hundreds of dead monsters.

It was the greatest victory humans had seen in years.

CHAPTER FOURTEEN

Alleta thought time had stopped.

One moment, she was walking with the others toward Andromeda. The next, soldiers were shouting, shoving her aside, forcing everyone to crouch behind a dune.

Panic overtook them.

Like her, people clutched their loved ones and whispered prayers between breaths, trying to remain still. The bravest soldiers formed a line ahead, shielding the civilians as best they could. Around her, Alleta heard weeping, cursing, and the terrifying ring of metal on metal.

Then she saw them.

Two reisers flanked the dunes, their movements too swift, too calculated. Alleta had never seen one before—and she was stunned she didn't scream. Instead, she gripped Jean tighter, shielding her with her body.

What horrified her most wasn't the sight of the enemy—but what it revealed.

For the first time, she truly pictured her husband and

son fighting like this. For years. While she'd stayed home and convinced herself it couldn't be *this* bad. Tears slid down her cheeks as shame bloomed in her chest. She'd been the mother who'd sent her son off to war without question. And when he came back quiet and bitter, she'd blamed him for losing hope.

Now she prayed—desperately—that her son would find a way out of this kind of life.

Then, the desert fell silent.

The quiet lasted only a few heartbeats... before it was broken by soldiers cheering. Cries of victory echoed across the sand. Bodies hugged, laughter broke out, and a wave of cautious relief moved through the crowd.

"It's all right, Jean," Alleta whispered, tears falling freely now. "It's over."

But when she tried to rise, Jean pulled her back down, clutching her arm.

"What if he's—I can't look. I can't handle it if—"

Alleta brushed Jean's hair from her face. She couldn't promise anything, but she could *try*. "I'll go," she said gently. "I'll look for you. Just wait here."

Alleta climbed to the top of the nearest dune—and stopped cold.

The battlefield stretched before her. Dark streaks marred the once pale sand; the air hung heavy with heat, ash, and an unfamiliar but unforgettable scent. Soldiers moved among the fallen, guiding civilians away from the worst of it. But it was impossible to hide. The cost was everywhere.

Then, a voice broke through the haze.

"Jean!"

Charlie's voice.

Alleta's breath caught as she turned to see her daughter running into his arms. He lifted Jean effortlessly, spinning her in a circle as laughter and cheers erupted nearby. Their kiss drew even more noise—but Alleta didn't mind. Her hand pressed to her heart. They were alive.

And that was enough.

CHARLIE'S HEART SURGED THE MOMENT HE SAW Jean. He pulled her in and kissed her, completely forgetting about their "secret." Around him, some soldiers laughed and cheered—so he kissed her again just to spite them.

For the first time in years, he imagined a future. A peaceful one.

But when he met Alleta's eyes across the hilltop, a hint of reality sobered him. She was watching—smiling, yes—but not without concern. He gave Jean a kiss on the forehead and let her go.

There was still work to be done.

Victory didn't mean safety. Not yet. They needed to move. Fast. He ordered half of the guard to walk ahead with the caravan, giving the rest of them time to clean the battlefield and hide the worst of it. As much as he wanted Jean near, there were things he didn't want her—or anyone—to see.

After hours of burning and burying bodies, the rest of the guard and he reached their new camp. Fires flickered across the sand, and the scent of food should have been welcome—but it only made him nauseous. Still, when he spotted Jean and Alleta in the distance, a sliver of warmth returned.

Until John found him.

"COMMANDER," JOHN SAID TIGHTLY, "THERE'S someone you need to see."

Charlie's stomach dropped. He followed John past the tents to the far edge of camp—toward the makeshift infirmary. The air changed as they neared. Blood, ointment, and the unmistakable weight of grief hung thick in the air.

John spoke quietly, words catching in his throat.

"Their armor—slashed his entire side. From his underarm to his thigh." He paused, visibly shaken. "I went back. I couldn't leave him. And—I don't know how he's still alive, Charlie. I don't know how he's enduring this. He's just a child."

Charlie couldn't speak. His voice would betray too much. He took a deep breath and stepped inside the tent.

Terry lay motionless, pale and soaked in sweat. His breathing was shallow, uneven. The slashes in his tunic exposed bandages that were growing dark. John stood over the cot, arms crossed tight over his chest, jaw locked in grief.

Charlie knelt beside the cot.

"You did good, soldier," he said softly.

Terry turned his head, his voice barely a rasp. "Fred was the hero, sir. I was just the messenger."

While John's voice remained strong, it had softened.

"You saved every one of us, Terry. Don't downplay that."

Charlie placed a hand on Terry's shoulder. It was like touching a furnace.

"Terry," he said carefully, "you told John the reisers were protected. Is that right?"

Terry winced, trying to sit up, but the movement stole his breath. He fell back, eyes brimming with tears as he stared at the tent's ceiling.

"I swear, Commander," he whispered, "they were protected. I'm not a coward... I would've fought with Fred if I thought we had a chance."

John reached for his leg and gave it a firm pat. "You're one of the bravest soldiers I know. We both saw what you did."

Terry looked at John, voice shaking but louder now.

"Fred had no chance. Their armor—it was different. It didn't dent. It didn't break. Our swords—nothing worked." He blinked, tears slipping down his temples. "I couldn't stop it. I ran... to warn you. And it felt like betrayal."

Charlie's gut twisted. He needed answers, but not at this cost. Still, this change in the reisers' armor was too important to ignore.

"You did what any of us would've done," Charlie said. "You made it back. You warned us. You saved everyone behind that hill—including the civilians."

"Even your new commander's future wife," John

145

added, his voice dull, but his words brought a faint smile to Terry's lips.

Terry's eyes fluttered closed for a moment. His breathing slowed, but he forced them open again, focusing on the two men beside him.

"Second Guard or not..." he whispered, "it was an honor to fight with you two."

Charlie leaned closer, voice rough with emotion.

"You *are* First Guard, Terry. Always were. But you know how John is without supervision—someone had to keep him in line."

Terry chuckled softly, just once. Then he turned his face toward Charlie and lifted a trembling hand.

In his open palm rested a locket—half-open, worn but intact.

"Will you give this to Chris?" he asked. "Tell my commander... tell him those are my memories. Tell him I never forgot."

Charlie gently took the locket, curling Terry's fingers back over it one last time. His voice cracked when he answered.

"I promise."

Terry exhaled—and didn't breathe in again.

The tent fell into silence.

Charlie remained kneeling beside him, the weight of the boy's sacrifice pressing down like stone. Terry had died a soldier. A messenger. A hero. And no one in that tent would ever forget it.

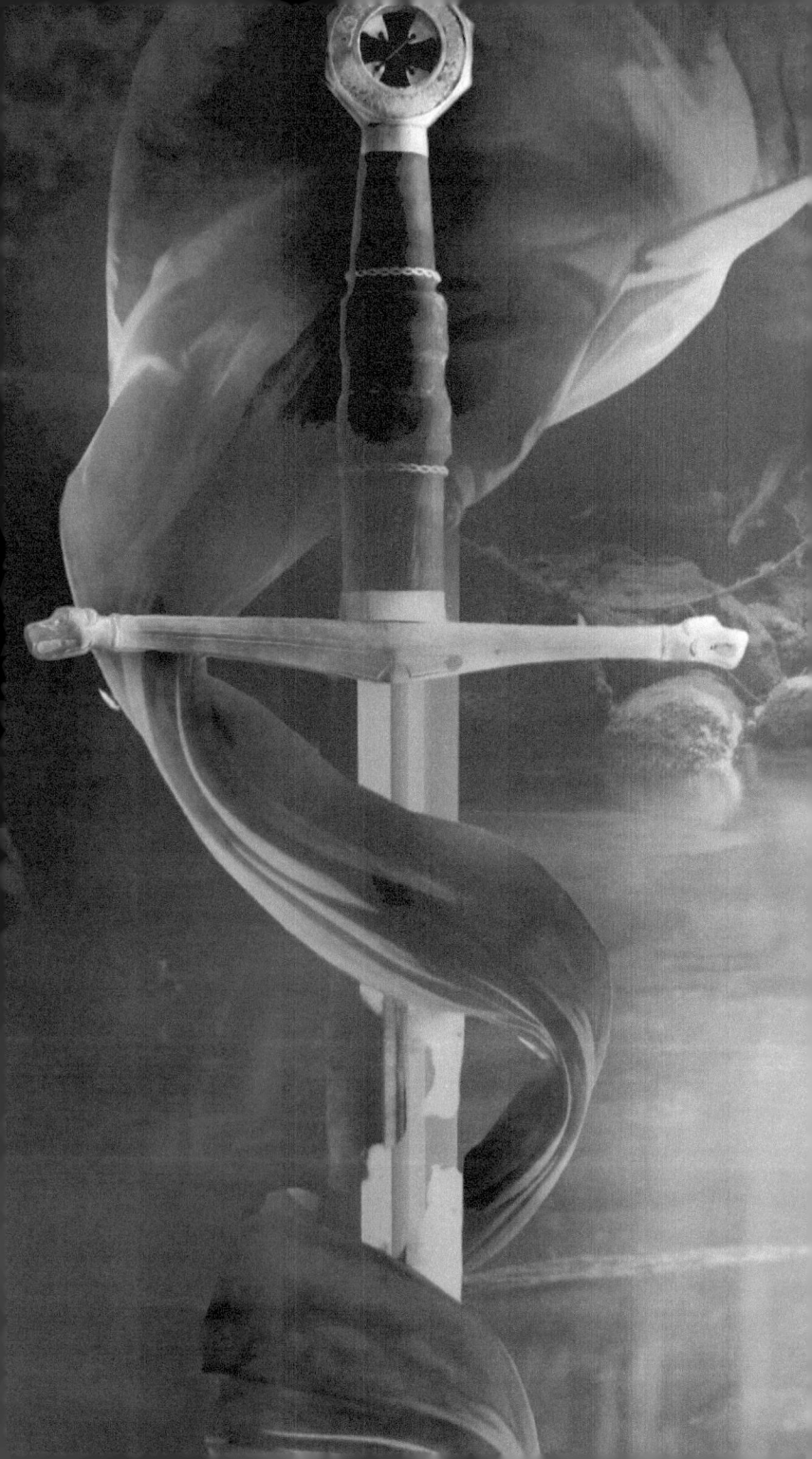

CHAPTER FIFTEEN

Morning crept in quietly, its only sign a faint warmth rising through the mist. The forest was still moving—that much was clear—but they were wasting time. Chris needed to give Donald something to do before his hysteria kicked in again.

"What are we going to do now?" Donald asked. "We don't understand where we are, we can't see the stupid mountain—how do we even go back?"

"Glad you asked," Chris said, stabbing a knife into the base of a thick root and dragging Donald to sit across from him. "You're going to tell me exactly that."

Donald blinked, confused.

"We know where we entered the Soto Forest," Chris said. "According to your own glowing description of yourself, you can calculate speed and distance, right?"

"I can, but—"

"Great! Then you can estimate the rotational speed of these freaking trees." Chris eyed his knife, already aware he'd likely never see it again. "Figure out how far we've drifted from our starting point."

Donald's pride visibly drained from his face. He stared at the forest floor.

"It won't work, Chris. Maybe there's a pattern, but too many variables. What if the trees change direction—or speed? What if they only move at night? Or randomly? It's impossible."

"I don't need perfect," Chris said. "Just a rough idea. Can you do that?"

Donald nodded, though reluctantly.

He crouched and began sketching patterns into the damp ground with a stick, grumbling under his breath and occasionally rolling his eyes at the roots. Chris wasn't surprised when, a few minutes later, Donald flung his arms up.

"This is worthless! Even if I get close, how do we stay on course? We'll end up more lost than we are now—this whole place is a giant, moving lie!"

"Hey!" Chris snapped. "I know what I'm doing. I may not be a valsing, but I've walked this world plenty too."

Donald gave him a flat look.

"Fine! For your comfort," Chris said, waving a hand, "assume the trees move at the same speed and direction, day and night. In fact, let's say I *commanded* them to do that. Happy now?"

Donald huffed a laugh, shook his head, and returned to his calculations.

Over an hour later, he presented a rough location on

the map. Based on his notes, they were farther north than expected, but not as far west—a setback, but not a disaster. It was enough for Chris to move forward.

They walked slower so Donald wouldn't collapse, giving Chris time to check his father's compass and verify they were still headed west—toward the mountain. What unsettled him most was how little he understood about the forest's movement. There was no way to track it. The only option was to keep going—and observe.

Soon the journey turned maddening. Crawling under or climbing over roots was easier than guessing their direction. The forest seemed to mock logic, shifting subtly, just enough to disorient. But every night, when they checked their map, the mountain was closer.

That was enough.

After nearly a week, the terrain changed.

The roots thinned out, giving way to an open valley wrapped in a dense, silver fog. In the distance, Chris spotted the crumbling shapes of what could only be buildings.

"So... this is the village," Donald said softly.

"Reign Mountain should be just beyond it."

The legends about the cursed village suddenly felt too real. The fog slithered along the ground, revealing more of the ruins—homes left in partial collapse, doors broken open, stone walls crumbling. Strangely, there was no moss or growth. Just rot.

Chris stepped forward—and paused. The usual sound of dry leaves crunching underfoot was gone. He knelt and touched the ground.

It wasn't dry.

It was decaying.

"Donald, wait!" he called.

"Well, look who's scared now!" Donald called back from deeper in the fog.

Chris yanked up his scarf to cover his mouth and nose and charged after him.

As soon as he entered, the fog thickened. His skin prickled with stinging cold—like being stabbed by a thousand needles. He held his breath, unwilling to risk that same pain in his lungs.

Within seconds, he stumbled into Donald, who was doubled over, clutching his side and groaning.

Chris pulled him up, trying to retreat, but the fog had shifted again. The forest was gone. Everything was gray.

His chest burned. His vision blurred.

Then, faint and flickering—a glimmer of light.

It reminded him of the blossom.

He followed it.

The village twisted like the forest, and it took him far longer than it should have to find their way back. He could barely think. His body slowed. His limbs dragged. Eventually, he dropped Donald and began pulling him.

Then, at last—the silhouettes of trees.

Chris pushed forward, lungs screaming, muscles aching. When the roots finally reappeared, he gave one final heave and hauled Donald into the cover of the forest.

He collapsed to his knees and sucked in air, ignoring

the stabbing pain in his back and the fog still clawing at the edges of his mind.

Beside him, Donald coughed violently.

"As a general rule," Chris gasped, "if I stop... you stop. You may be brilliant, but this is unfamiliar ground. Leave it to the experts."

Donald only nodded, still wheezing.

Chris sat, staring out at the fog. The village and the mountain were visible—barely—like ghosts on the horizon.

"So close," he muttered. "And still impossible."

Donald groaned. "Now what? What the hell do we do?"

Chris didn't answer. Not yet. He reached into his coat pocket and felt the soft fold of petals.

He stood, scanning the trees.

"What are you looking for?" Donald asked.

"The light that got us out."

Laughter echoed faintly through the woods.

Chris pulled out the glacier orchid.

"It came from this, idiot."

Donald blinked. "Well, aren't *you* full of surprises?"

"You know what it is?"

Donald puffed himself up, brushing dirt from his tunic and smoothing his hair.

"Of course I do. It's hope."

Chris raised an eyebrow.

Donald laughed. "You should've seen your face!"

Chris stepped forward, and Donald instantly backed up.

"Okay, okay! It's called a glacier orchid. Rare, but not

magical. Valsings use them for big events—royal weddings, coronations. Your kind mimics us, of course. I'm sure even your mother—"

Chris took another step. Donald paled.

"They're used in ceremonies," he added quickly. "They're symbolic. Not enchanted."

Chris said nothing, just slipped the flower back into his coat.

"I'm serious," Donald said, softer now. "You might be weird and human, but you clearly care about Hune. And you fight for it. That deserves respect."

Chris turned, fists tightening—but Donald wasn't mocking him.

"You're not like the others," the valsing said. "I didn't expect that."

Before Chris could reply, a new glimmer of light caught his attention. This one was larger—clearer. It wasn't the orchid. It looked more like sunlight glinting off metal.

He turned toward it just as Donald gasped.

They both grabbed their packs, and Chris began climbing.

"What the hell are you doing?" Donald called.

Chris ignored him. The reflection shimmered from high up, caught in thick roots woven into a rock face.

When he reached it, he brushed aside leaves and mushrooms to reveal a weather-worn metal plate embedded in the stone. The crest of Hune stared back at him—faded, but unmistakable. Beneath it, words were engraved: *King Leonard I*

"Donald!" Chris shouted down. "We found it!"

"Wonderful!" Donald called. "Now, what did we find?"

Chris started clearing more of the plate, but a root snapped beneath him. He tumbled through the branches, scraping against bark and moss, until he hit the ground hard.

His wrist throbbed. His face was bleeding. But he was smiling.

"For the gods above—are you okay?" Donald rushed over.

"We found it," Chris said, breathless.

"I thought you said that up there!"

"Yes. But now I know the way in."

Donald followed his gaze.

Among the roots, partially hidden by moss and shadows, stood a massive iron gate, guarding a heavy wooden door—twice as tall as any man. Behind it, the cave sloped down into the earth like the mouth of some ancient beast.

Donald paled.

"What did you expect?" Chris asked. "That the journal would be on a bookshelf? I told you—it's in the king's tomb. And that's underground."

THE SUN WAS ABOUT TO SET WHEN THE HEAVY wooden door to the king's tomb finally crashed to the ground behind them.

"Just in time!" Donald said. "We've got enough light to start a fire and make dinner. Tomorrow morning, we can explore whatever hellish place this turns out to be."

Chris didn't answer right away. His arms ached from the climb, and his wrist throbbed with a relentless pulse that made him mutter curses under his breath now and then. Still, he was ready. Ready to find the journal. Ready to leave the cursed forest—and especially that rotten village behind.

"What are you doing?" Donald asked, watching Chris gather his things.

"I'm going in," Chris said. "You can stay and start a fire. Maybe make dinner too—that'd be great."

Out of the corner of his eye, he saw Donald pick up his sack and give the ground an irritated kick.

Chris fashioned a torch from a strip of cloth and a branch. It barely held a flame until Donald silently handed him a vial of combustible liquid.

Chris wouldn't admit it out loud, but so far, he was grateful for the valsing's knowledge.

"Are you always this efficient, or is it just my lucky day?" Chris asked, inspecting the lit torch.

"It pleases me to demonstrate how *valuable* I am."

Chris chuckled. "You mean useful."

Behind him, Donald muttered something that didn't sound like a compliment, but Chris's attention shifted the moment they stepped through the entrance.

Despite the grandeur of the gate, the passage beyond was narrow and low. The air was damp and heavy, and Chris had to hunch down to move forward, using his sword to slice through the overgrown roots that twisted into the corridor.

The tunnel opened into a small chamber—no larger than his old training barracks room. Still, after the cramped crawl, it felt vast.

He stepped inside, and silence wrapped around him like a blanket.

Chris knew the story of the First King—how he died for his people during a time of famine and disease. He was revered, remembered with reverence in both lessons and lullabies. Maybe the legends embellished him, but Chris had always believed in that man. He would have followed that king into war without hesitation.

Now, standing before the stone coffin, he couldn't believe that same bloodline had led to Leonard III.

Chris knelt.

He didn't plan to. His body moved without asking.

For the first time, he felt something shift inside—a rebellion, quiet but undeniable. Not only did he no longer respect Leonard III... he wasn't sure he could follow his orders at all.

Presenting respect to a king who gave his life for his people lit something inside him: a longing for that kind of leadership. A dread of leaving his friends behind to serve a ruler who would lead them to ruin. A hunger for something better.

Maybe that's what scared him most—how *right* it felt.

He stood slowly and glanced around, trying to focus. He needed that journal. If the First King had written anything—anything at all—it might help make sense of the tangled doubts in his heart.

But something was off.

The tomb wasn't untouched.

Vases, swords, broken cups, pieces of ancient armor —all shoved aside carelessly. The valuables were missing. Someone had been here before, and they hadn't been gentle.

The crown, the scepter... and the journal. Gone.

"Gods damn it," Chris muttered, standing. "I should've known. It's been centuries since he died— someone's probably ransacked this place decades ago."

"You're kidding." Donald stepped fully into the room and began pacing, kicking objects out of his way. "All that time wasted?"

"Stop," Chris warned.

"We crossed a cursed forest for *nothing*?"

"Stop kicking things."

"We almost died in that stupid fog. You almost *died* climbing that stupid root!"

"I told you to stop!"

"And we nearly broke our arms throwing that door down and for wha—"

"I said STOP!" Chris shouted just as Donald launched a cup toward the far wall.

Then silence.

Chris paused.

There was no sound when the cup hit the wall. No bounce. No impact. It vanished.

"What the hell..." Donald whispered.

They both approached the far wall.

It looked like the others—dirt-packed, veiled in mushrooms and moss—but near the bottom, where the cup had struck, a dark hole yawned.

Chris knelt and took the torch from Donald, lowering it to the opening. The light revealed a hidden tunnel—a narrow, winding descent that twisted deeper underground. He could only see the first few feet.

"You think it'll collapse on top of me?" Chris asked.

"We're not going in there," Donald said, taking a step back. "No way!"

"Got a better idea?"

Donald said nothing.

Chris grabbed another cup and placed the torch in Donald's hand. Then he crouched and slid feet-first into the tunnel, wincing as pain jolted through his wrist.

At the first bend, he paused and set the cup down, letting it roll.

It clattered downward—never stopping.

Not exactly reassuring.

He slid back out, brushing dirt from his arms.

"Listen," he said. "I don't think you should come. You panic easily, and down there—"

"Oh, gods, will you stop trying to get rid of me?"

Donald took a breath.

"I'm not a coward. And I'm not just following orders. I care about saving Hune too—for someone I—"

Chris raised his eyebrows.

Donald stopped himself.

Chris nodded. "Let's get ready, then."

Much as he hated to admit it, his wrist wouldn't let him lead the way. Holding the torch, pushing himself forward, managing his sword and sack? It was too much.

"Just remember," Chris said, "if you see anything strange—"

"Stop and tell you. Yes, yes, I understand!" Donald knelt at the mouth of the tunnel. "Honestly, Chris, your instructions are *painfully* simple."

Chris glanced back at the stone coffin one last time.

He wasn't sure what they'd find down there.

But something had already changed inside him.

And whatever it was... he couldn't turn back now.

CHAPTER SIXTEEN

For hours, they crawled and slid through a passage that felt endless. Like the Soto Forest, the tunnel twisted, inclined, and declined—even though Chris's compass insisted they were moving in a straight line.

His hands were covered in bleeding sores, and his injured wrist pulsed with sharp, constant pain that slowed him down. Dirt and sweat soaked his uniform, turning cold the second he stopped to rest. Ahead, Donald kept taking random breaks, likely as exhausted as he was.

Chris longed for a larger space where he could sit down—or better, stretch his legs and roll onto his back. He worked hard to block the memories of the vault, but being crammed inside another narrow hole in the ground brought them back with painful clarity. Just like before, the worst part wasn't the crawl—it was not knowing when, or if, it would end.

Neither of them spoke of it, but Chris knew time was

running out. If they didn't find the tunnel's end soon, they'd be in complete darkness. All their combustibles were nearly spent. And the only thing worse than crawling back... was doing it blind.

"Chris, there's a light up ahead!"

A wave of relief surged through him when he saw the small point of light in the distance. It could've been a trick of the mind, but he let himself believe it was real. That hope gave him the strength to crawl faster behind Donald.

The light grew larger with every movement, until at last, they reached the tunnel's end.

"Donald, before you go jumping out, look first."

"Why? You think it could be worse than *this* freaking tunnel?"

Chris rested his head against the ground and just breathed for a moment.

"I don't know where we are," he said. "Do you remember the fog?"

Donald's face clouded. But curiosity won.

He crept forward, peeking through the opening. "You need to see this." Without waiting, he jumped out. "I'm not sure I like it."

Chris followed, crawling out onto the rocky ground. He let himself fall to his knees and arched his back to stretch. Beside him, Donald lay flat on the floor, arms and legs sprawled, staring upward.

When Chris followed his gaze, he understood.

Instead of open sky or the canopy of the Soto Forest, they saw a massive dome overhead. Sunlight poured in from a jagged hole at the top and reflected off shimmering crystal walls. With no point of reference, it was hard to judge the height, but Chris imagined one of the Soto Forest's massive trees could easily grow inside the cavern.

The cave was filled with crystalline formations—some low as steps, others tall and slick like glass towers.

"We must've crawled all night," Chris said. "The sun's out."

Donald just grunted and stretched again.

Chris rose, cradling his sore wrist to his chest. Standing was a relief, but this place didn't feel safe. The tunnel behind them might've been cramped and miserable, but it was an exit—and he didn't like the idea of needing it again.

As he wandered, something caught his eye—objects strewn across the floor: cups, plates, statues, tiaras, trumpets... even toys. They looked random, but Chris sensed a connection.

Then he saw it.

A gold scepter. Old and dirty, but unmistakably royal.

Beside it, a broken crown.

And just beyond that—an upside-down book.

Chris pushed his aching legs into motion, scooped up the book, and brushed the dust from its cover. His heart pounded as he flipped through the aged pages. His excitement grew with every line. When he closed it, he stared at the golden name engraved on the leather: *King Leonard I.*

It was smaller than he'd expected—meant to fit in a coat pocket—but it was real. The journal.

"Donald! We found it! The freaking journal!"

He couldn't see the valsing, but Donald's shrieks of laughter echoed through the cave.

"What kind of idiot would steal treasure and leave it on a—" Donald's voice cut off.

Chris froze. "Are you okay?"

"Chris, *stop!*"

Too late.

A hot breath curled behind him, and something massive exhaled at his back. The air trembled with each breath. The pieces fit together fast: ancient treasures... a cavern... a guardian.

"A dragon," Donald whispered.

Chris spun around—but not fast enough. Something struck him like a battering ram, sending him crashing into a crystal wall. He gasped, trying to suck air back into his lungs as a nightmare stepped into reality.

It was enormous. The dragon towered over him, at least three times his height at the shoulder. Its claws matched the size of his sword—if not its strength. Its golden scales shimmered like armor, thick and unbreakable.

It lowered its head, heat radiating off its snout.

"Hey! *You!*" Donald's voice rang out. "I'm right here!"

Chris wondered if the valsing planned to distract it or just get them both killed. Either way, he took his chance. With his good hand, he struck upward at the dragon's chin. The blow might as well have been a mosquito bite.

"Donald, *get back!*" he yelled, as the beast recoiled.

The dragon roared, shaking the cave. Shards of crystal rained from the ceiling.

Chris bolted for the tunnel—but the dragon was faster. Its heavy steps thundered behind him. The smooth floor betrayed him, making him slip. He knew he wouldn't make it in time.

Then, out of the corner of his eye, he saw Donald holding the crown.

The dragon pivoted and charged him instead.

"No! *Donald!*"

The tail whipped out. It hit Chris like a club. He crashed to the ground. Hard.

He opened his eyes and although he could hear the rumbling footsteps of the dragon, things crashing around him, and Donald yelling something, he was looking at another place and time.

A little girl ran through the Soto Forest, her laugh muffled by her small hands. She wore an oversized robe, cinched with a ribbon, and a crown of wildflowers on her head. Her smile made her bright blue eyes sparkle.

She stopped and knelt, brushing mushrooms and leaves aside. Her face lit up at the sight of a glacier orchid.

Chris knew her. She looked years younger than in his other dreams—hallucinations, but he would always recognize those eyes.

A man's voice asked her.

"What do you have there, sweetie?"

Chris couldn't see his face. He didn't like the man's tone, and a feeling of unease crept into his thoughts. Yet, the girl smiled, pleased to see him.

"That's a special piece," the man said. "Magical... and dangerous."

She looked down at her hands.

They were covered in blood.

Chris leaned forward, reaching for her—but the memory shattered.

The dragon's roar dragged him back to the present.

He opened his eyes, pulled the glacier orchid from his pocket, and yelled.

"Hey, you freaking beast!"

He balanced the blossom in his injured hand and raised his sword in the other. He was grateful, for once, for the extra hours he'd trained with both hands.

The dragon stopped. It stared at him.

And then—

A voice boomed inside his mind. A growl turned to speech, deafening and direct.

"Who do you think you are?"

Chris stumbled, his back hitting the wall.

"I'm Christopher Riddley," he said. "Commander of the First Guard of King Leonard the Third."

Donald's voice echoed from somewhere nearby. "I know who you are, moron!"

The dragon turned to him and let out a blast of fire. Donald barely dodged it.

"Wait!" Chris shouted. "He's with me!"

The voice returned, louder this time. Chris nearly dropped the orchid.

"You came to my home to steal from me. You expect mercy?"

"We're not stealing," Chris said. "We didn't know this was your—"

"Do I look like a fool?"

Chris dropped to his knees, hands over his ears.

"You and that creature took what is mine!"

Donald shouted something in return, but Chris couldn't make out the words.

The crystal wall behind him began to glow. The dragon paused and sat down.

Chris seized the chance and stood up.

"We're here on orders from the High Council of Hune. We're looking for the First King's journal—that's all."

The dragon exhaled, flames brushing past Chris.

Donald stepped closer.

"You'll need more than a valsing to survive the sorcerer who just saved you," the dragon said. *"I pity you."*

Chris blinked. "Wait—what sorcerer?"

The dragon huffed. *"The High Council didn't tell you? Typical. Only a sorcerer can read that book. And Gemli is the last one."*

Chris's stomach turned. So many pieces didn't add up.

"Dead or not, I have a mission," he said. "I'm taking the journal."

The dragon laughed, shaking his head.

"You'll do what I allow you to do, human. Gemli wants to see you. I'll take you... now."

Chris didn't hesitate. "Donald, get the bags!"

He shoved the journal in his pocket and grabbed his sword.

A massive claw closed around his waist.

He heard Donald yell beside him as the dragon took flight.

The cave was even more enormous than he'd imagined. They flew upward, then out through the hole—big enough for an entire castle. Light blinded him at first, but as his vision cleared, Chris realized they were flying above Reign Mountain.

Below, the cursed fog still crept through the village, seeping out toward the Soto Forest.

The dragon circled the cliffs and landed at the edge of a narrow, icy path.

He threw them onto the rock-strewn ledge like bags of grain.

"Be careful here," the dragon said. *"Easy to slip."*

Chris caught Donald and pushed him toward the wall.

"You can borrow the journal but," the dragon leaned close, *"it belongs to me. I'll get it back."*

Before Chris could respond, the beast flapped its wings and vanished.

Wind howled. Chris flattened himself against the cliffside until it passed. Then he slumped down, breathing hard.

He unwrapped his wrist—it was purple, swollen, and stung with every movement.

But it was the cuts on his *other* hand that held his attention.

Hundreds of tiny wounds bled where the orchid's sharp edges had dug in. He flexed his fingers, grateful the cold had numbed the pain.

Donald groaned beside him. "What the hell was that?"

"We're meeting a sorcerer," Chris said, wrapping his hand with his neckerchief. "This dumb plant lets you hear the dragon in your head, did you know?"

Donald shook his head. "No idea." After a sighed he added, "Well, even I can learn something new once in a while."

Chris didn't respond. He tied the wrap over his swollen wrist.

And that's when he noticed it.

The flower's warmth was gone.

Its essence had vanished.

He hadn't realized it before.

But now, in its absence, he missed it.

And that terrified him.

CHAPTER SEVENTEEN

Darkness, cold, and rot clung to the reiser fortress like a second skin. Hidden deep within the swamps, its black walls had remained unseen by outsiders for centuries—a secret stronghold fueled by hatred and war. So far, the illusion of protection stood still in the reisers' minds, and General Murllen couldn't smile wider.

The war had brought a change to his life that hadn't been pleasant at the beginning. However, over time, he learned to appreciate his new position—and even enjoy his new appearance. Now, the swamps were more than his prison. They had become his kingdom of torment, and he called them home.

From his window, he could see the dark streams of blood running out of the lower levels of the fortress. They filled the air with a thick, warm essence that only rotting remains could release. He no longer fought in battle, but he still had things to play with.

Humans.

The memory of the latest news from Tundra erased his smile. He knew how arrogance and pride had made the humans ignore the reiser threat until it was too late. It was a mistake he would not commit.

"General," a reiser said from the chamber's door, "the Council is ready, and Colonel Green just arrived."

Murllen didn't bother to answer. He took his time gathering his weapons. Although the reisers claimed all were equal, he did not believe that. He hadn't inherited his position. He had fought for it—and won. His superiority should be obvious to all.

Once in the yard, he addressed the arriving warriors.

"Soldiers, if you think I will overlook the losses incurred because of your incompetence, you have another thing coming. We may be ahead in the war, but it is far from over. Until then, I won't let your laziness or stupidity cost us another battle."

For a moment, the screams from the dungeon were the only sound within the fortress.

"Colonel Hayden Green!" Murllen called.

"General."

The deep, deliberate voice of his colonel came from behind him.

Unlike the human armies, the reiser command structure was vast and full of experienced officers. That specific colonel was the most dangerous of all.

For many reasons, Murllen hated him. But above all, he suspected Hayden was meant to become the next leader.

Reisers held a deep belief in collective well-being. When the time came, their leader was expected to step aside for the next generation. Murllen knew they would expect him to pass the torch to Hayden.

That would never happen.

"Colonel Green, I'm sure you've heard what happened in Tundra," he said as they began to walk.

"Is there a problem with the new training? Is the development of our army compromised?"

Hayden said nothing. Murllen growled.

"Excellent. Let's talk to our magician."

The southern tower had no windows or vents. It remained in complete darkness. The torches inside lit only for visitors—but it wasn't welcoming. Only the sorcerer found it comfortable.

"Gemli!" Murllen barked from the entrance. "Where the hell are you?"

The torches flared to life along the spiral staircase—but only downward.

"You really think I'm stupid enough to go down there?" Murllen sneered.

A pitchy laugh echoed up the tower, and flames sparked upward, lighting the path to the top instead.

At the summit, a large chamber opened before them. It was here that most war strategies were born—and sometimes died. That day was no exception. Murllen's council waited, and he relished that Hayden hadn't been given time to prepare.

"Great, we're all here," he said. "Let's begin."

A tall figure lingered in the shadows. His sickly pale skin and bony frame might convince someone he was a dying human. But whether or not Gemli was human didn't matter. The power he wielded—and the horror he embodied—made even Murllen wary.

"Like always," Gemli said, "Murllen is late. I'm sure your friends love my company, but I have things to do and places to go."

Murllen ignored the sorcerer's barbs.

"Colonel Hayden Green," he began, "you are such a great warrior and a wonderful soldier. This council appreciates your hard work for our safety."

He glanced at Gemli with a grin. "And we praise your memory. Repeat my last question to these reisers."

He took his place at the head of the table, but no one sat. All eyes were on Hayden.

"You really think I'm stupid enough to go down there?" Hayden repeated flatly.

Murllen's lips curled in amusement. He joined Gemli's laughter and began circling the room.

"Colonel, I didn't know you had such a wonderful sense of humor. A treat." He stopped beside a young soldier. "Colonel, I'm not sure if you've met Sergeant Paul Torrents."

"No, General," Hayden replied.

"Such a misfortune."

He smiled as the sergeant stiffened.

"I'm sure you could've trained him better than his now-deceased major."

Murllen drew back, about to reach for his sword—but Hayden stepped forward.

"Maybe if he and his major had been trained like real soldiers—not protected flowers—they could have won. Maybe their coddling is the reason our soldiers are soft."

Murllen narrowed his eyes. He didn't care about the insult to the sergeant—but Hayden had called him *sir.* Like the humans did. An unmistakable insult among reisers.

"Oh, Colonel," he said through gritted teeth. "I'm so glad you brought up our procedures. Why don't you share your thoughts with our beloved sorcerer?"

He got in Hayden's face and bellowed, "That's an order!"

Gemli smiled—equal parts menace and delight.

To Murllen's surprise, Hayden sat. The rest of the council followed.

Something twisted in Murllen's gut. Fear and magic were the only things maintaining his grip on leadership. The reisers respected Hayden—for all the right reasons. Gemli had warned him not to touch the colonel.

Murllen wouldn't risk his position. But Hayden had to go.

"We were born and raised as fighters," Hayden said. "We exist to protect our kind, even at the cost of our lives."

Murllen smirked. Soon, the colonel would taste his own philosophy.

"For centuries, we've endured—shortages, dead land, humans, the weather, even the rage of the gods. And we've survived. Victory comes from our will, not magic. The spell to protect us has weakened us. It's made us arrogant—like humans."

Gemli's smile vanished.

Silence fell. The sorcerer radiated danger like a beast sensing prey.

"That makes no sense," Gemli said at last. "Should we fight without armor and shields, then? Because we were 'born' fighters?"

"No," Hayden said. "That would be absurd. We *make* our weapons. There's no magic in that. Or would you rather I fight with my hands?"

"You don't have hands, beast!" Gemli snarled.

Hayden collapsed to the floor, groaning in pain. The others stepped back.

"You're just a weak animal," Gemli hissed, "always hiding behind your armor. So you want to fight with your claws? Let's see if you still have them."

Hayden's arms stretched unnaturally. He shook violently.

"That's enough, Gemli," Murllen said. "Try a normal conversation for once."

The colonel's body relaxed. Major Dunstan Miller rushed to his side, but Hayden waved him off. He stood and met Gemli's gaze without blinking.

"I understand the nobility in a fair fight," Gemli said. "But war isn't fair. Only the strong survive."

Murllen crossed his arms. In the corner, Sergeant Paul Torrents stood motionless.

"Sergeant! Let's hear your report—again."

The young soldier stepped forward, voice shaky.

"We followed orders and rode to Tundra. It was empty. Our major was furious. He sent watchers and ordered us to burn the city."

Murllen's clap rang through the room. Even hearing it again, he found the story hilarious.

"He *announced* his arrival," Murllen laughed. "Gave them time to plan! Right, Colonel?"

Hayden's dark look said enough.

"Sergeant, finish."

"We burned the city. Nothing was alive. But the watchers said the humans went toward Andromeda—"

"Not north?" Hayden asked, surprised.

"No, sir. My major split us. The second group was only meant to capture prisoners, but... they were all killed."

Voices exploded. Some wondered if the humans had removed their protections. Others feared the gods had sided with them.

Hayden glared at Gemli.

"You said the protection was lifted for one battle only!"

Murllen raised an eyebrow. The colonel was right.

A few months ago, he'd ordered the magic barrier lifted—one time—to allow King Leonard's escape.

"I thought you hated my protection," Gemli said coolly. "Who was protection Tundra?"

Paul stammered. "I—I don't know."

Gemli stared into his eyes. "How did *you* survive?"

"My major. He sent me back—to report to you."

"Isn't the human colonel's son leading them now?" Dunstan said quietly.

Agreement passed among the room until Gemli took a step forward.

"That doesn't mean he should have been there," the sorcerer said and a bad feeling set on Murllen's gut.

"So, Gemli," Murllen said, "what the hell happened?"

Gemli didn't answer, and moved closer to Paul. "I need to know who was in that battle."

In a flash, Gemli stood face-to-face with Paul.

The sergeant's eyes turned black. Blood poured from his nose and ears. His body crumpled with a gurgled scream.

When silence returned, Gemli dusted off his sleeves.

"Humans," he said. "So curious peculiar creatures. So full of wonders and futility."

He returned to his seat and waved at Murllen.

"Well, my dear Murllen, it wasn't just *any* guard. It was the First Guard."

Murllen nodded as understanding dawned on him.

Across the room, Hayden knelt beside Paul's body. The sergeant was still alive. Barely.

"Colonel," Murllen said, "there's no need for that. I'll make sure he gets attention."

He turned back to Gemli. "Didn't the High Council send the First Guard to Laconia?"

"I know they did," Gemli said sharply, "perhaps fear has jeopardized our longstanding agreement."

Murllen clapped his hands once. That wasn't something for the whole Council to hear about.

"Great! Just make sure we're not surprised next time."

He turned to Hayden, his smile returned.

"Colonel Hayden Green, you're now in charge of capturing that bastard king and his guard. Bring them back—alive. The rest of you, back to your duties."

One by one, the reisers left. Now it was Murllen and Gemli alone.

"I thought we had them," Murllen muttered. "Didn't you send them to Laconia?"

"No one can predict the future," Gemli said. "But here's some advice, Murllen. Take what we know and *use* it. Loyalty is fragile."

Murllen swallowed his pride and stood.

"Time to make sure our allies are following the plan —not coming up with their own."

Gemli's eyes gleamed.

"That will be my pleasure."

HAYDEN MADE SURE PAUL LEFT THE TOWER before he walked away. He knew Murllen would punish the reiser, but with some luck, he'd be far from the fortress by then. Murllen was his leader, and Hayden didn't question his orders—but that didn't mean he liked his cruel techniques.

"Could he have abandoned his position?" Dunstan asked. "I just can't see that reiser escaping the human scouts."

"I doubt he came here to hide," Hayden said. "But I agree. That reiser couldn't have evaded the First Guard."

He had seen Colonel Alexander Riddley fight during the last battle. Hayden hadn't taken part in his slaughter —and what they did to the man's body disgusted him. The viciousness of it echoed too closely the ancient, bloody legends of his own people.

In that same battle, Hayden had nearly faced off against the colonel's son, Christopher Riddley. But to Hayden's surprise, the young man had been tasked with protecting the king—and, as part of their strategy, had let his guard escape.

Hayden had seen enough to be cautious. Riddley's son was driven—and humans were predictable when it came to vengeance.

Still, the soldier's reputation extended beyond the battlefield. His strategies were sharp, disciplined, and efficient—much like Hayden's own. Neither of them liked leaving survivors, unless it was by design.

There was no tactical reason to let Paul live. The fact that he'd made it back to the fortress at all was a miracle. The only plausible explanation was that Christopher Riddley wasn't leading the First Guard anymore.

And that raised an even bigger question—why?

"We need to find out what happened to their new leader," Hayden said. "I have a bad feeling about this."

"That's an excellent idea!" Murllen said from behind them, Paul at his side. "If my best colonel has a bad feeling, we must investigate it."

Hayden kept his expression flat, shoving any emotion behind a soldier's mask as he turned to face his general.

"General."

"My dear colonel," Murllen said, his smile too smooth. "I just realized how *unthoughtful* I was to send you out again."

His grin brightened, but it only made Hayden uneasy.

"But you *are* my best reiser," he continued. "And this time, I expect proper results."

"Of course, General," Hayden said.

Murllen clapped a heavy hand on his shoulder. "Before that, though... I want to reward you."

Beside him, Dunstan tensed. Paul flinched under Murllen's arm.

A reward from Murllen was never what it sounded like.

The general stepped forward and studied Hayden like prey.

He was taller and broader—but Hayden doubted he was the better warrior. A dangerous curiosity flickered inside him, wondering what would happen if they fought.

"Colonel," Murllen asked casually, "when was the last time you visited the Asylum?"

Hayden wasn't sure whether it was the question—or the traitorous thoughts in his own mind—that unsettled him more. Murllen noticed it, of course, and smiled wider.

"I'm not sure, General," Hayden answered.

The Asylum was the reiser race's darkest tradition. Only the strongest and most intelligent were allowed to breed. It was an honor—one meant to preserve their kind —but the method disturbed Hayden.

He hated walking out of that place with no memory. He hated that he'd never seen a young reiser—not once. Children were raised in seclusion, guarded fiercely until they were ready to train. The only time a soldier entered the Asylum was to contribute to the next generation.

Murllen somehow knew his discomfort—and twisted a supposed honor into something shameful.

The hatred Hayden felt was more dangerous than his unease. It pulled his thoughts toward mutiny. Toward rebellion. Toward murder.

Dunstan had to nudge him forward to keep him moving.

"But don't worry, Colonel," Murllen said cheerfully. "I'm sure your loyal major won't mind waiting outside. After all—who knows what happens in there?"

They reached a thick metal door. It opened without a sound.

Hayden had been here before—but he had forgotten the darkness. The utter silence. Now, everything made sense.

It was a trap. A smart one.

He couldn't refuse a direct order, and he knew someone would try to kill him the second he stepped inside. But preparing for it would be treason, and he would not stand a chance against the Asylum's guards.

Those who lived inside were the fiercest warriors of their kind, trained to protect the unborn at all costs.

He had no choice.

Hayden stepped inside. The door slammed shut behind him, leaving him in total darkness.

MURLLEN SMILED TO HIMSELF.

The hesitation in Hayden's eyes had been delicious.

He *had* expected a deadly trap—but Murllen had other plans.

Hayden still had one last use.

"Major Dunstan," Murllen said. "I've heard wonderful things about your development. No wonder Colonel Green keeps you close."

"I'm just doing my job, General," Dunstan said carefully.

"Such a *humble* answer!" Murllen said with a grin. "Which is why I'm giving you a personal mission."

Dunstan stiffened.

"Sergeant!" Murllen called.

Paul nearly tripped over himself rushing forward.

"You," Murllen said, containing his desire to smash his useless head off, "always so ready for action."

"General," Paul mumbled, trembling.

"You two are going with Colonel Green to capture the humans—and their pathetic king. After that, it is my *deepest* desire to give our dear colonel a true rest."

He paused and let the weight of his words hang between them.

"He's been fighting for so long. Surely, he deserves a... *permanent retirement.*"

Paul took a step back. He looked more terrified than he had in Gemli's tower. Dunstan's face froze, unreadable—but he understood the message.

The only way a reiser stopped fighting was by dying.

"You two will make sure Colonel Hayden Green never returns to my fortress," Murllen said. "I'm giving you the *chance* to be merciful."

He pretended to adjust his armor as he turned away.

"Of course, if it pleases you, you can always bring back his *remains*. I'd never deny him a proper funeral. He *is* a legendary warrior, after all."

He stepped closer to Dunstan, voice low and cold.

"But if he returns alive... I promise, *you'll* watch me kill him myself. Slowly."

Murllen had considered doing the job personally. But Hayden would see that coming.

Now, it would be his own second-in-command—and the trembling fool he tried to protect—who delivered the betrayal.

A wound deeper than any blade.

CHAPTER EIGHTEEN

Once night fell, the cliff became an unpleasant place. It was too cold, and the wind was bitter—almost painful. Chris knew that lighting a fire would be impossible, and walking in the dark seemed suicidal. It wasn't the beginning he had hoped for, but at least his hand was getting better, and the tiny cuts had stopped bleeding.

"You should have asked it where to go," Donald said.

"Well, Donald, I'm sorry to disappoint you. Next time, I'll get all the directions you need."

"I have no doubt I would have done a better job." Donald crossed his arms and lifted his chin. "I am a diplomat. I can follow through a difficult argument."

Chris laughed out loud, remembering who he was talking to.

"You know what? I have no problem with that petition. Next time we have to talk to a dragon, you can do it!"

A burst of freezing wind hit them, slamming Chris's back against the mountain wall.

"Help!" Donald shouted, hanging from the edge. "Help me!"

The wind, snow, and frozen rain made it hard to move, but Chris reached for Donald's arm. His own wounds reopened, and a sharp pain shot up through his arm, making it difficult to pull Donald up.

"Donald, try to reach—"

Something grasped his ankle and yanked him down. His shoulder slammed against the ground, and he lost his grip on Donald. He looked back, but there was nothing there—only the tightening pressure around his ankle, dragging him backward along the icy path with terrifying ease.

He tried to grab hold of anything, but the ground was slick with ice.

The grip slid up to his throat and lifted him several feet off the ground. It tightened until the lack of air burned his lungs. A tall, dark figure approached through the storm.

"Let him go!"

Donald's voice sounded far away. Chris couldn't tell if he was too distant or if the storm was drowning them out.

"Run!" he tried to shout, but it came out a whisper. No one would hear him.

The figure stopped and smiled. It was hard to believe he was human. His pale skin looked long dead—like it had starved for years. But the worst part was the darkness in his eyes.

"Who do you think you are?" he said. Donald's scream echoed off the mountainside.

Chris struggled, but the grip only grew stronger. His vision dimmed.

"I haven't had visitors in so many years. I'm afraid it's not a good time. Otherwise, I'd enjoy myself with you two."

The man stepped in front of Chris and stared into his eyes. "So, tell me. Who are you?"

Chris's world collapsed into darkness and pain. It started at his throat and hands, then surged through his body until it was unbearable. Every wound and injury from the war returned all at once. Pain flooded his brain, tearing through memories, dreams, and knowledge—as if ripping them from his soul.

Fear narrowed his focus.

He wasn't afraid to die. But there were things he knew—things no one else should know—and he had to protect them.

So he clung to what was real. The pain. The airless burn in his chest. The ache in his hand from the fall. The stinging cuts on his palms.

His vision sharpened again. He focused on the man's eyes and noticed a small dot in the middle of each pupil. It changed color—dark gray, then brown, then orange—until it burst into a bright red flame.

The grip vanished. Chris collapsed to the ground and gasped for breath, clutching his neck. Scratches marked his skin, likely from claws. He didn't need to look at his hands to know they were covered in blood.

Beside him, the man took a step back. Chris wasn't

strong enough to lift his head, but he had a feeling the surprise was mutual.

"Well, well. You are something," the man said, crouching. "Commander Christopher Riddley."

"Am I correct to assume... you are Gemli, the sorcerer?"

Deep down, Chris hoped he was wrong.

"At your service, Commander," Gemli said. "Well—not really."

Gemli turned toward Donald, who was lying on the ground, wide-eyed.

"Let me see."

He extended a hand.

Even from this distance, Donald's hesitation was obvious. Chris wanted to help him, but he couldn't move.

"Come on," Gemli said. "We don't have all day."

Donald reached up slowly.

The moment their hands touched, Gemli yanked him to his feet with unnatural ease.

"I've always wanted to test how smart the valsings are."

He ran his hand through Donald's hair. "But you're lucky, Donald. I have important business with your friend."

The color drained from Donald's face.

"Chris's business is the same as mine—"

Gemli laughed.

"You're adorable. So eager to prove yourself. I'll give you the chance."

Donald dropped to the ground as something dragged him toward the cliff.

"Smart valsing," Gemli called, "try to survive my mountain."

Donald screamed as he vanished into the dark.

Chris struggled to crawl forward.

"Commander."

Ignoring his closer hand, the left one, Gemli kicked him in the stomach and grabbed his right hand. He slammed it against the ground and stepped on it.

"I believe you have something for me."

The pressure on his fingers grew until his bones cracked. Chris growled in pain. Somehow, he was relieved. Had Gemli read his mind, he'd have known about his ambidexterity. He could fight equally well with either hand.

"I need your help," Chris mumbled.

Gemli lifted his foot.

Chris sat up, cradling his hand.

"But of course you do. Everyone does. Let's go somewhere more suitable. The weather here is... unpredictable."

Fog rose from the base of the mountain, surrounding Chris. This time, he couldn't escape. The poison burned in his lungs.

Darkness claimed him again.

DONALD KNEW HE WOULD DIE.

Something pulled him toward the cliff. Gravel tore at his fingers. He screamed as his legs dangled over the edge.

But instead of falling, the force dragged him down the hillside. Rocks and branches tore into his skin and clothes. He tried to hold onto anything—but nothing held.

The slope changed. The ground turned smooth.

Crystal.

The vault.

Panic rose. He imagined himself falling through.

He grabbed a jagged piece of crystal and kicked wildly to break free from whatever held him.

A dark laugh echoed in the night.

"As I suspected," Gemli said, "you aren't that smart."

But when Donald turned, no one was there.

The crystal beneath him cracked. One piece broke free, and his legs slipped through the opening again.

He pulled himself up with a yell. The crystal fractured under his weight.

With a final push, he rolled onto the vault's roof and crawled away from the weak spot.

Then—a loud crash.

Their bags fell from the mountain above and slammed onto the vault. The weight shattered the already weakened surface.

It started to collapse.

Donald turned just in time to see a dragon soaring toward the mountain. He'd never forget the sound of its wings. Or the fear it brought.

The vault groaned as he tied the bag straps together. He slung one over his shoulder and got ready to throw the other. His aim was terrible—but it was his only chance. He didn't have wings.

The bag hit the dragon's abdomen. One strap snagged on its rear claw.

It was enough.

The beast lifted—and Donald was yanked into the air.

The cliff spun below him. He clutched the straps harder.

The dragon growled and tried to shake him off. When that failed, it twisted midair and flew toward the Soto Forest.

Donald's eyes lit up. If he could just reach the trees—

But the dragon had the same idea.

Branches smashed into him. He shielded his face with his arms. Within seconds, the strap tore.

He fell.

Branches snapped as he plunged, slicing into him. He managed to grab a thick limb and clung to it.

The second bag fell past him, ripping free of his shoulders.

He looked down. The bag got stuck nearby.

He hugged the tree and let his head rest on the damp bark.

Fire scorched the air above him.

Donald scrambled down the tree and didn't stop until his feet touched solid ground.

It was filthy. Wet.

He kissed it anyway.

Later, he sat in a makeshift shelter, blood dripping from his forehead, his fingers raw and nail-less. Deep scratches covered his arms and face. His clothes were in tatters. His hair—a lost cause.

He needed to find his way back.

He remembered the compass and opened Chris's sack, smiling faintly.

Everything inside was a mess. He dumped it out.

What he found shocked him. Maybe one change of clothes. Some ropes, knives, and small weapons. The Map of Hune. A few papers.

Nothing personal. Nothing that said "Chris."

Donald found the compass and began to repack the bag.

Then he saw the envelope.

No seal. But Chris's handwriting was clear:

"In case I am dead, please open."

Until that moment, he hadn't truly believed Chris could die.

He realized how stupid he'd been. He'd believed Chris would escape, like he always did.

He put the envelope back, hiding it at the bottom.

Then, with a deep breath, he opened the compass.

Losing Chris wasn't an option.

He would find him.

He *had* to.

CHAPTER NINETEEN

Chris woke up gasping for air, a burning pressure in his chest and the taste of blood in his mouth. He had a vague memory of being surrounded by the peaceful sound of the ocean. A sense of longing gripped him—as if he were missing someone or something important—but he couldn't force his mind to remember.

A sudden force slammed into his side, rolling him over. He came face-to-face with a smiling Gemli.

"Commander!" the sorcerer said, kicking him in the ribs.

Blood filled Chris's mouth as a groan escaped his lips.

Gemli crouched down. "Welcome back."

Chris forced himself upright, leaning against a cold wall behind him. Just that small movement drained him, and he closed his eyes.

Vividly, he saw Laconia's waterfalls and heard their enchanting sound. The vision shocked him. He had never been to that city. Was he losing his mind? He focused on his surroundings instead.

He wasn't sure how he'd gotten here. The last thing he remembered was the fog climbing the cliff. Now he was in a crystal cave—similar to the dragon's vault— which meant he was likely still inside Reign Mountain. This chamber was smaller but deeper. Then again, it was hard to tell if he struggled to breathe because of the dense air or his injuries.

It was also darker. The only light came from candles and their reflections on the glassy walls. He was thankful for that. The place was a grim workshop, with books and parchments crammed into ancient shelves, and grotesque specimens—flesh, organs, and skin—suspended in jars or dangling from wires. The rotting stench was unbearable.

Again, his mind wandered. He saw sunlight reflecting off ships in the Laconia harbor. John Monder stood before him, arms crossed, wearing the old Laconia army uniform.

"Longing, Commander?" Gemli said, yanking him up by his injured hand.

Chris didn't scream—he had lost his sense of reality.

Now, John shoved him, and all his belongings scattered down the cobbled street. Chris braced for a fight that never came. A kind voice interrupted, and a girl offered him his father's compass with a gentle smile.

"Oh, Commander," Gemli whispered.

Chris blinked. He was now seated in a stiff chair.

"You've got the look... longing for a better place in more peaceful times."

Chris met Gemli's eyes, using the hate rising in him as fuel.

"So that's your trick? Besides kicking unconscious people, you make them hallucinate?"

Gemli shook his head and touched his chest. "Hallucinations? No, no, no, Commander. Why would I waste my power on something so mundane?"

Chris scoffed. "Maybe if you show someone what they'll never have, you can break their will to keep going?"

Gemli laughed, nodding. "My dear Commander, you may have a future in the art of torture. There's still hope for you."

Chris held his stare. He had to remember: he needed this man's help.

"But the problem with all that," Gemli went on, "is boredom. Humans—like you—are predictable. Your minds are weak and easy to read. And your dreams? Always the same, with slight variations."

He leaned over a nearby desk, closer to Chris.

"Your better days are always peaceful ones. No war. No bloodshed. Everyone smiling. Your loved ones—especially the dead—are alive and well, laughing around a table. Food, wine, love..." He smiled, teeth sharp. "I might not be exact, but I'm close enough. Wasn't she beautiful?"

A blurry memory surfaced—the girl with the compass. Chris hated that he had to agree. But she wasn't real. She never had been. She'd been his defense against madness inside the vault.

"Oh, she isn't around?" Gemli's voice turned mocking. "Sad and pathetic."

Chris took a deep breath, fighting the urge to strike. Rage wouldn't help him here. He needed to observe Gemli. The man was arrogant and overconfident— dangerous weaknesses.

"Regardless of your little fantasy," Gemli continued, crossing his fingers, "this journal is... interesting."

He gestured to the open book on the desk.

Chris leaned forward despite the pain searing through his ribs. "Will you tell—" His throat was raw. He had to pause. "Tell me what it says?"

Gemli tilted his head. "And why would I do that? And, for that matter, why are you even here, asking for my help?"

The pounding in Chris's skull made it hard to focus. He didn't trust Gemli, so he wouldn't share everything. He took his time, letting his exhaustion show, then offered a sharper version of the truth.

"We got lost in the Soto Forest. Found a dragon. It was the dragon who said you—"

Gemli's eyes lit up. "Ah! My faithful dragon."

He walked around the desk, stopping to look Chris dead in the eyes. "And what were you doing in the Soto Forest?"

Chris met his gaze. "The king sent me."

"To do...?"

Gemli's confidence wavered slightly.

"To protect Saint Peter's Abbey."

"Interesting," Gemli muttered, stepping back. "The king has funny ideas... sometimes."

"It isn't funny," Chris said, straightening. "The reisers will destroy everything. The only way to stop them led me to you."

Gemli turned, face unreadable.

"I know you don't care," Chris went on. "But you're part of Hune—and it's dying. Maybe you're just like the zhortas. Ready to give up."

In a flash, Gemli was in his face. Chris gripped the chair to stay upright.

"I am nothing like a zhorta." His eyes glowed red, and his hands trembled. "Don't compare me to that filth."

He sat back down, though the disgust lingered.

"Why would I care if Hune dies?" he asked.

Chris didn't flinch.

"I find it hard to believe the reisers will destroy their own home. Maybe your race and the valsings, in time—but not Hune." He folded his arms. "And even if they did, why should I care? You have to be alive to die."

"So... you're dead?" Chris asked.

"No, Commander. I'm neither dead nor alive. It's quite simple."

Although the statement was anything but simple, Chris said nothing.

The sorcerer turned back to the journal. Chris was forced to wait—wounded, uncertain if Gemli had answers... or if he'd even share them.

Chris glanced at his hand. It was so swollen the skin looked ready to split. The orchid's tiny cuts still bled. When he tried to close his fist, pain forced his eyes shut.

And there she was again.

Tears streaked her cheeks as she held his face. Unlike his previous hallucinations when he was a young soldier in the vault, this one showed she had grown up, just like him—a fact that puzzled him, since hallucinations shouldn't age.

"You need to remember," she said. "Otherwise, you'll die... Please. Just try."

He opened his eyes quickly, checking to see if Gemli noticed. But the sorcerer was still absorbed in the journal.

Her voice had shaken him, and he truly feared for her. He wondered, for the first time, if she was a real person.

"Let's talk about more interesting things," Gemli finally said. "This journal is fascinating. I don't understand why you care. I love the absurdity of your first ruler's decisions, but I fail to see the relevance."

Chris didn't hesitate. "I believe it holds the key to defeating the reisers."

Gemli exhaled. "Well, it says something about that."

Chris's heart skipped. He leaned forward, ignoring his pain.

"Will you tell me?"

"Absolutely," Gemli said with glee, and fear crashed back into Chris's chest. "But I must warn you—it's ridiculous. Hopeless, really."

Chris glanced at the symbols on the journal page. They resembled those on the Map of Hune, and he couldn't read them. Trusting Gemli's word was maddening.

"Tell me anyway."

"Of course! Who am I to break our brave comman-der's heart?"

He pointed to a page. Chris saw a crude symbol for Hune and the High Council's stamp.

"There are steps—or rather, ingredients—you'll need to gather. And, naturally, a specific weapon. A sword blessed by the gods. If that's even real!"

"Does it say where to find it?"

Gemli waved a hand. "That's the least of your prob-lems. It's who can use it that's the real challenge."

Chris exhaled. His body throbbed, but his mind sharpened.

"Don't despair... yet," Gemli said. "It's a very special saber. An antique cursed weapon. It can only be wielded by a righteous and wise man. An impossible task. There is no such man. Humans are fools, and justice is their favorite myth. The strong decide the fate of the weak. That's not justice."

Chris forced himself to stand, leaning on the desk.

"You don't understand justice. But we—"

Pain shot through his abdomen. He collapsed, breath knocked out of him.

"So quick to judge."

Gemli knelt beside him.

"It's cute—you believing you're fighting for what's right. But you couldn't be more wrong." He lifted Chris's head. "There's more in this book. To free the saber from its curse, you'll need a magic touch."

He let go, and Chris's head thudded to the floor.

He saw her again. The compass in her hands spun, pointing toward the ocean of Laconia.

"Don't look so sad, Commander."

Gemli kicked him, rolling him onto his back.

"It isn't me you need."

Relief stirred in Chris.

"Would you tell me who I do need?"

"That's the thing." Gemli tossed the journal onto his chest. "You need a wizard. Only they are born with a fragment of Hune's original magic. But they're all gone. And worse, this one needs to be alive."

Chris raised an eyebrow.

"So ignorant," Gemli sighed. "A sorcerer can be anyone smart enough to pay magic's price. Some call our state a sacrifice. Others call it power. Wizards are born with magic, but to unlock their full strength, they must make the same sacrifice. No wizard can be alive and powerful at the same time."

The room spun. Chris rested his head on the floor, trying not to vomit.

In a blink, the cold crystal turned into the wet forest floor. The Soto Forest stretched around him.

The poisoned village lay far away.

"Before you go, Commander," Gemli whispered behind him, "you are... different. And I can't figure out why. Let me make you an offer."

Chris tried to stand but collapsed again.

"I've fought this war longer than you've been alive," Gemli said, bending close. "I choose the winning side. You should too. Join me, and I'll tell you everything. The reisers' plans. Hune's fate. Maybe even how to find the blue eyes you keep dreaming of."

Chris met his gaze. He didn't need to answer.

His fury said it all.

"So predictable." Gemli shrugged. "In that case..."

He twirled his hands. Chris's sword appeared, floating midair. Then it dropped—hard—grazing his cheek.

"We can't let the brave commander wander around without daddy's sword. How else will you save the world?"

As Gemli vanished, his voice lingered.

"Longing, Commander, is just another torment... for the survivors."

CHRIS RESTED HIS FOREHEAD AGAINST THE sword's handle and exhaled.

In that, Gemli was right. The sword was a piece of his past—his father, his friends, and the hope he'd just lost.

He sank to his knees, his battered body a living reminder of the encounter. Gemli hadn't given him a solution, but he had revealed a powerful enemy—one Chris hadn't even known existed. One he had no idea how to defeat.

Beyond that—and as foolish as it seemed—he couldn't shake the fear that something terrible might happen to her. He had spent countless days wishing she were real. Now, his only hope was that she wasn't— because if she was, he had no way to find her, no way to protect her. Worst of all, he couldn't even remember what she had asked of him. And the fact that Gemli knew anything about her filled him with a deeper dread than he wanted to admit.

That fear turned into anger. He opened his eyes.

In front of him, the sharp steel reflected everything he had lost—and everything he still had left to fight for.

Gemli was wrong.

He wasn't done.

The deaths of his friends and father would *not* be in vain.

He would find an answer.

CHAPTER TWENTY

Mustering his remaining strength, Chris stood and sheathed his sword. He needed to find Donald—no small task when every breath sent sharp pain through his chest.

He had barely taken three steps when he saw the journal lying on the ground. A hunch tugged at him. He picked it up and flipped it open.

Every page was blank.

All the strange symbols were gone. The entire book was nothing but empty parchment.

Hate rose like bile in his throat. Gemli had erased it. He must have—because something important had been written in it. If he didn't destroy the journal completely, it was either because he couldn't... or because he wanted to torture Chris with the knowledge of how close he'd come to a real answer.

"Chris! Chris!"

He turned. Donald ran toward him.

"For the gods above! Where have you been?"

The valsing wrapped him in a tight hug, nearly knocking him over.

"I've been looking for you for days!"

Chris blinked. "Wait. What do you mean *days*?"

Donald pulled back and grimaced. "In the gods' name—he tortured you, didn't he?"

Chris knew better. Gemli hadn't truly tortured him—not in the traditional sense. The sorcerer likely had more brutal methods for that. Still, being kicked and starved and left in near-darkness for *days* explained the bone-deep fatigue and the pounding in his head. No wonder he'd hallucinated.

"Wait," Chris said, frowning. "*You've* been out here alone? For days? Are you all right?"

Donald huffed. "What's that supposed to mean? That I can't survive without someone babysitting me?"

Chris raised a brow. "Well, I would be impressed but—" he gestured with a grin, "one of your hairs moved out of place."

"Hey! I got a *severe injury*, thank you very much." Donald pointed to a faint scar on his forehead. "But this isn't the place. We need to get out of here."

He grabbed Chris's coat and pulled him toward the trees.

"Wait—Donald, slow down. I can't—"

Donald stopped so abruptly that Chris nearly ran into him.

A familiar silhouette took shape in the forest ahead, followed by a deep growl. The creature stood in the clearing with wings extended, larger than Chris remembered. The sheer size of it struck him all over again.

Chris didn't hesitate. He reached into his pocket for the glacier orchid.

He shoved Donald aside and stepped forward, channeling all his rage and loathing into his voice.

The dragon bared its teeth, shooting a stream of fire in warning.

Chris ignored it. He drew his sword and advanced.

"You *freaking animal*!"

The dragon thundered forward, roaring in reply.

"Chris, what the hell are you doing—?" Donald tried to pull him back, but Chris shoved him away again.

"You can't scare me!" he snarled. "You're just Gemli's little cuddly pet!"

Flames tore through the air. Donald dove to escape the heat.

"*Is that all?*" Chris shouted.

The dragon lowered its massive head, blocking Chris's path. A voice echoed in his mind—deep and ancient.

"Are you trying to get killed? You're so broken you want me to end your fight? I came for what's mine."

Chris held up the journal. "This belongs to me now."

A growl vibrated inside his skull. It nearly knocked him over.

"It is mine! You stole it!"

Chris took another step forward. "You, *stupid beast*, stole it first."

Donald inched forward, voice shaking. "You are out of your *freaking* mind. You're arguing with a *dragon*."

"This journal belonged to one of my kings," Chris

said. "Who told you to take it? Was it your master, Gemli?"

"I've killed better and wiser men than you. This little stick means nothing to me."

The dragon's snout nudged Chris's sword.

"I am the only reason you still breathe."

"And why is that?" Chris said, jaw tight. "Because Gemli won't let you kill me?"

Pain exploded in his skull. His hand dropped the sword. His knees buckled.

Suddenly, he was standing in Laconia—only it wasn't the peaceful dream he remembered.

The city was in ruins. Weeds choked the streets. The waterfall was dry, and the ocean had vanished. There were no people. No reisers. Only silence and decay.

Then everything moved in reverse. Flames reformed. Water surged backward up the rivers and falls. The people ran—not away from danger, but *toward* it.

Chris didn't want to see more. He feared seeing *her* —feared what that would mean.

But the vision accelerated again, rushing through time.

A small white house appeared, quiet and still. Then a dark alley near the ports. Three caped men stood around a woman and her child, both lying on the wet cobblestones.

Chris tried to move but couldn't. He strained forward, fists clenched.

"I couldn't do anything," said the dragon's voice. *"I gave my word to the Great Wizard to protect her and the baby. But I wasn't fast enough."*

The scene vanished. Chris was back in the forest. The dragon stood before him, towering, menacing—but its eyes were wounded, haunted by the same sorrow Chris carried.

"The reisers destroyed your city. But it was humans who killed my soul."

Chris stared. The dragon wasn't just a monster—it was something more.

"The Great Wizard left the journal in my care. He would've given you the answer. But he's dead. And Gemli... Gemli is his successor, whether I like it or not."

Hopelessness gripped Chris. Wordless, he bent and placed the journal on the ground.

The dragon seized it and launched into the sky. It vanished into the clouds.

Donald rushed to Chris's side, rambling questions Chris didn't hear.

"Let's put up camp, Donald," Chris said, voice quiet.

"Finally. You're back to your senses."

Donald led the way toward the forest.

"Where are you going?" Chris asked.

"After *days* in this cursed place, I figured it out." Donald pulled something from his pocket—the compass. "And I have some good news. We've got a campfire ready, with food and water."

Chris smiled, and this time, he didn't resist following.

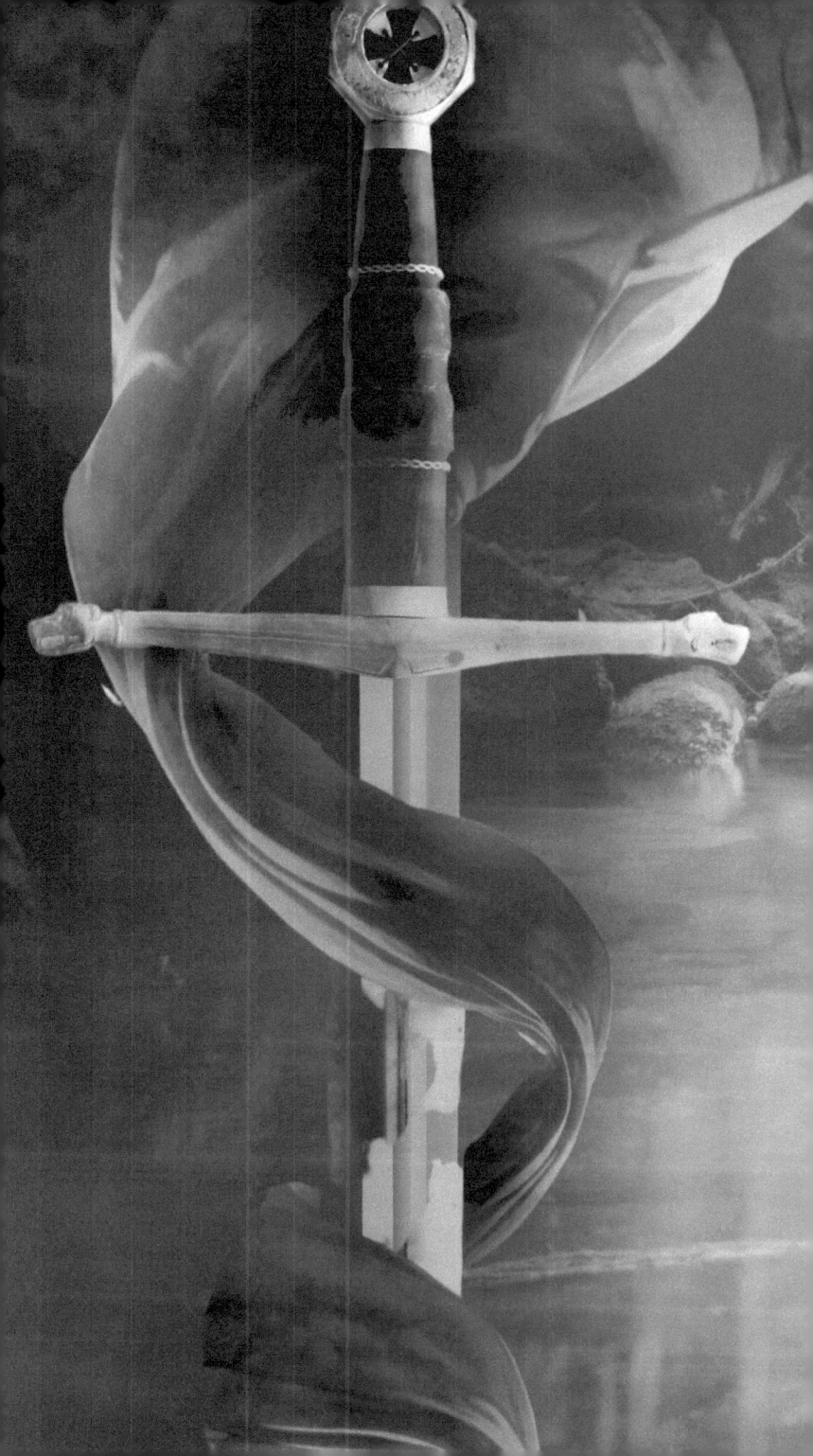

CHAPTER TWENTY-ONE

hris was too tired to sleep and in too much pain to rest. Every time he closed his eyes, memories of Gemli's twisted smile and the cruel glint in his eyes returned. His broken ribs ached with every breath, his hand throbbed, and the weight of failure sat like stone in his chest. But the wound that hurt the most wasn't physical.

The dragon's final words haunted him.

"The reisers destroyed your city, but it was the humans that killed my soul."

The vision the dragon forced into his mind, the ruined streets of Laconia, the silent port, the lifeless waterfall—it hadn't been just another manipulation. It was history. Memory. Truth.

And in that truth, he'd seen her.

The woman with the compass. The one who had appeared years ago in what he thought were dreams and delusions, who had lived in his mind as a ghost of comfort. Now, it was clear—she hadn't been a comforting lie. She had been real. *She had been there.*

The ache in his chest wasn't confusion or fantasy—it was grief. She had grown up, changed. She had cried. She had begged him to remember.

And he hadn't.

Because he had been too stubborn. Too broken. Too unwilling to believe that something—someone—good could survive his world.

Now, it was too late. He was certain she had died— because all those years of silence, when he believed he had mastered his mind, had only meant one thing: she was already gone. And he hadn't saved her. He hadn't even tried. He had failed her.

When Donald's snores grew steady in the silence, Chris reached for the compass and turned it over in his hands. The cool metal felt oddly warm against his skin, familiar, almost like a heartbeat. As a distraction, he opened the lid and watched the needle spin—until it stopped, pointing north.

His thoughts drifted to Laconia—not the burned ruins, but the city as it had appeared while he was Gemli's prisoner: vibrant, full of life and sun, with laughter echoing through its narrow streets and flowers blooming from every windowsill. A port full of color and noise. He could see the swing on the porch, the ships in the harbor. Now free of the sorcerer, he let himself be consumed by the dream.

She stood in front of him. Her touch lingered in his hand.

"This is amazing," she had said in that dream,

brushing her fingers over the engraved compass. "I haven't seen one of those in years. May I?"

Chris had handed it to her, remembering the warmth of her skin and the trace of freckles across her nose. Her dark hair curled at the ends, framing eyes as blue as the sea, and when she smiled—gods, when she smiled—it had stopped the world from spinning.

"Do you know how to use it?" he'd asked.

"The basics," she had replied, laughing gently. "But it's almost useless in my hands. For it to work, you need three things—where you are, where you're going, and which way to turn. I'm usually missing one of those."

That moment had always made him smile, but tonight, her words pierced deeper.

The wind shifted. Firelight flickered across the camp, and the scent of flowers—real ones—drifted through the clearing. He exhaled, pressing his palm to his forehead. "Please, just... just try to remember." Her voice echoed again. Desperate. Real.

Chris blinked. His eyes widened.

He saw her again—not like in his dream, but as she was now. Grown. Strong. Blue eyes shining with urgency and tears. Her lips trembled. "You have to find the way. I know you think you can't... but you must get up. Now."

He had been so wrong. No figment of a broken mind could grow older with him, could cry, could ache like that. And dead people didn't get older.

Chris sat up fast, heart pounding. He stared at the compass again—the needle pointed north. But in his dream, it had pointed south, toward the ocean beyond Laconia.

He fumbled for his bag and pulled out the Map of Hune, spreading it open with shaking hands. His eyes traced the southern line: Laconia, the ocean... but if he followed beyond the water, to the Soto Forest—

There it was. Saint Peter's Abbey.

The zhortas' home.

A thrill of hope—fragile and fierce—lit inside him.

Chris leaned back, laughter escaping him, low and broken and real. Somehow, some way, she had shown him the truth. The direction. She hadn't given up on him, even if he had.

He looked back at the compass. The needle remained steady.

A soulmate. A bond that transcended dreams and time. She had found a way to reach him through magic, memory, and longing. Not just a message—but a call.

And this time, he would answer.

An owl called from the woods. The wind rustled the trees, sending the scent of flowers through the air like a promise. Chris closed his eyes one more time and whispered, not to himself—but to her:

"I remember."

IT WAS PAST MIDNIGHT, AND THOUGH SARA WAS tired, she felt oddly relieved to delay falling asleep. For once, she had an excuse to avoid the vivid dreams that had become her nightly torment.

The zhortas had taught her that dreams were more than visions—they were a way to understand the land. A language of the soul, if you knew how to listen. And she had learned. For years, Sara had moved through dreams as if they were real: tasting the desert wind of Tundra, feeling the spray of Laconia's waterfalls as they thundered from impossible heights.

But a few days ago, her dreams had turned into something else.

A nightmare had taken hold—recurring, relentless. It made her dread the moment her eyes closed.

It always began the same way: a crushing darkness all around her, heat searing her skin as she lay on a smooth, cold floor. Footsteps echoed closer. She scrambled backward, ignoring the pain tearing through her limbs.

Then she collided with someone—and realized she wasn't alone.

A man lay facedown beside her. Shivering. Bleeding. His breathing was shallow, ragged. When she touched his arm, his clothes were soaked with blood. Terror seized her heart—not just for herself, but for him.

The air thickened, turning heavy and hard to breathe. A pale light flickered on them, revealing the full agony of the scene. He was sprawled in a pool of his own blood, his body covered in gashes and bruises. She didn't dare move him.

Then a voice whispered, cold and cruel, right in her ear.

"You were his perdition."

Some nights, she woke up then—gasping, drenched in sweat. On worse nights, she turned and found a pale face with black eyes staring back at her.

"He is dead. And your life is mine."

It wasn't true. She could still hear the man breathing—uneven and weak. But the voice shook her. The sorrow in her chest convinced her that he wasn't a stranger.

When she looked back, the figure with black eyes stepped into the light, his stare blazing into flame. His smile was twisted. Familiar.

She didn't wait to understand—she had to escape.

Crawling back to the man, she knelt beside him again. Her hands trembled as she gripped his arm. Tears welled in her eyes.

"Please, wake up... please."

He didn't stir.

"You have to find the way," she whispered, her voice cracking. "I know you think you can't, but you need to get up now. You need to *remember*. Otherwise, you'll die. Please, just... just try to remember."

A hand yanked her hair. She screamed and fell back.

"You couldn't save her either!"

Sara stared up at her attacker, and something in her snapped into place.

She knew him.

He wasn't just a nightmare. He was real—and he had killed someone she loved.

Her heartbeat thundered in her ears as panic flooded her. She scrambled away, but it was too late. A sword slashed across her chest.

She recognized the old blade. Every time. It belonged to a man she trusted, a colonel who'd protected her people despite everyone's hatred. The one she admired. The one she imagined her father might have been like.

The pain in her body blurred beneath the weight in her soul.

That used to be the end of the dream.

But not last night.

This time, a strong but gentle hand touched her shoulder—and all the pain vanished.

She turned in disbelief.

The wounded man stood in front of her. His presence radiated kindness, even as his body bore the same sword that had wounded her. His uniform was torn and bloodied. Bruises marred his face, open wounds across his hands.

Though his face was unfamiliar, a profound sadness filled her heart. Despite her fear, she reached out to him, her hands trembling.

"You're hurt," she whispered.

And then she woke.

All day, she couldn't stop thinking about him.

The nightmare should have terrified her, but it wasn't fear that lingered—it was concern. The soldier wasn't just a figment.

The sword that wounded in all those dreams, had been in his wielded by his hands, and yet, she needed him safe.

CHAPTER TWENTY-TWO

"Sara!" Lily called, hurrying down the slope toward the creek.

Sara stood still, memories crashing over her. The last time she saw Lily, she'd been heartbroken—grieving a forbidden love. Now, nothing seemed to have changed. As soon as Lily was close enough, she wrapped her arms around Sara and began to cry.

From a distance, it would've been hard to guess one of them was a valsing. Both were about the same height, with similar features. Sara wasn't tall, but Lily was considered tall among her people.

"What happened, Lily?"

"They're monsters." Lily collapsed to the ground, buried her face in her knees, and sobbed. "I'm never going back."

Sara sat beside her in silence, gently rubbing her back.

"Sara, I just—"

"Did you talk to the king?"

"I couldn't." Lily looked up.

Even in the dim lantern light, Sara saw the bruises. She slid Lily's hood down—and recoiled.

Where once there were golden curls, there was now short, uneven hair. Her porcelain skin was mottled with bruises; one eye barely opened. A deep cut marked her cheek—one that would scar.

"I'm so sorry," Sara whispered, hugging her. "If it wasn't for my stupid idea—"

"This isn't your fault," Lily said. "It was a good idea. I should've gone to the king sooner."

She hugged her knees. "He was expecting me. The king agreed to meet—but when I arrived, Gale was there. The whole congress was. I couldn't even speak for myself. The king asked if I'd found what he sent me for, but never let me answer."

She stared into the shadows.

"He said...atrocious things. Things I never imagined a king would say aloud. He called me a whore. He ordered Gale to punish me for forgetting my duty."

Sara's heart twisted.

"Gale pulled me to my knees and yanked my hair so hard I screamed. Then—he cut my curls. One by one. I watched them fall onto my lap, felt the blade scrape against my scalp. The king laughed. They all did."

Lily touched the cut on her cheek.

"I didn't see it coming. What he was doing was cruel enough. But then he hit me. Hard. He stared at me with such delight... and then he pushed the knife into my face."

Sara's fists clenched. She'd met Gale before—a cruel valsing who had always grated on her nerves when their communities lived near the Abbey. Now, after what he'd done to Lily, she didn't just dislike him. She wanted to see him bleed.

"He kept kicking me. Hitting me. I think I passed out. But I remember Orson's breath in my face. He told me I would marry Gale. That this was just the beginning."

To Sara's surprise, Lily's face cracked into a strange smile.

"Remember when you tried to teach me how to dig up those stupid mushrooms? I never got why you wanted them—but you kept yelling that I had to kick harder." She laughed through tears. "I heard your voice, Sara. I stood up. Somehow. Orson was crouched in front of me. So I kicked."

She let the tears fall. "I thought I killed him."

"They should've known how strong you are," Sara said, holding her tighter.

But her mind was racing. Where could she take Lily? The zhortas wouldn't send her away, but they weren't soldiers. They couldn't stop the valsings. She had no one to turn to. Her hands began to tremble.

"We have to get out of here."

But Lily grabbed her wrist. "I have an idea."

She looked into Sara's eyes. "You can't tell Rafael. Or Stuart. Or anyone. Not about this."

"All right."

Lily nodded. "The king sent me to learn whether Queen Vanessa was planning to join the war. He thinks she's considering it."

"You told me this before... last time you were here.

You even know who she sent to negotiate." Sara's stomach twisted. "Is the king aware? Did you tell him?"

"No, I didn't," Lily whispered.

"Good. Then he's not going to—"

"No!" Lily stood and threw her arms up. "We *have* to stop this, Sara. I saw them fighting. Your people and the reisers. It's a slaughter."

Sara rose too. "You *what*?"

"I had nowhere else to go. I wasn't going to lead them to the zhortas, so I tried to reach Tundra."

Sara's jaw tightened. "You went *into* a battlefield?"

"Tundra is gone."

The words hit like a slap.

Sara sank down, her knees weakening under her. "How do you know?"

"I saw the smoke. From miles away. Then I saw the soldiers running. I hid. I heard the fighting. It was...horrendous."

SARA TRIED TO PROCESS WHAT SHE'D JUST heard.

The reisers had taken Tundra. Humans were running and fighting somewhere in the desert. The valsings—once the only race untouched by war—had abused her best friend and were now considering entering the war. Her nightmare was beginning to feel safer than reality.

Lily gently touched Sara's arm, her voice softer. "I

learned a lot. Both armies are different—but their weapons? They're too similar."

Sara blinked. "Too similar? They all use swords and daggers. How different could they be?"

Lily rolled her eyes. "Have you ever *seen* a reiser?"

"No! And I'm not planning to."

"Well, I have. Their armor is unlike anything your soldiers wear. Potent. Intimidating. It doesn't make sense that they'd use plain steel swords. The kind your people make would never match that armor. And it's inconceivable to me that the reisers designed that armor, unless..."

Sara stared at her. "Are you saying... your people designed it?"

Lily looked down, quiet.

Sara's stomach turned. "Why hasn't anyone noticed this before?"

"Because your soldiers burn everything before studying it. They think they're better than the reisers, so they don't even try to understand them."

Sara knelt in front of her. "Lily, what did you do?"

"Nothing. Just... wait here."

Lily stood and disappeared into the roots of the trees. A few moments later, she returned with a heavy cloth sack. She dropped it between them with a muffled *thud*.

"No one saw me take it," she said. "Your people could have learned so much... It's such a waste."

Sara leaned forward—and recoiled.

A dark, twisted object peeked out from the sack. It looked like part of an arm—part of *someone's* arm—blackened and fused with metal, like skin peeled over iron.

"What the— Lily, what were you doing?!"

"I'm a researcher. You know that."

"Lily, this *belongs to someone!*"

The odor hit her, and Sara stumbled back.

Unfazed, Lily explained, "The skin is just a covering —ashes, really. Most of it was already burned. What matters is what's underneath."

She knelt beside the sack and lifted the piece. "This armor... it *grows*, Sara. Like a tree, it shows layers—stages. It's not alive, but it evolves with its wearer."

Sara stared, still repulsed. "You think it's more than protection?"

"I *know* it is. No one makes armor like this just to scare people. It's meant to survive... something greater."

Sara's thoughts drifted to old books she'd read in the abbey. "The environment," she said slowly. "It's not just for battle. It's to survive *Hune* itself."

Lily's eyes lit up. "Exactly! That's it! I don't know why I didn't see it before."

"You want to find out if your people made it? Why does that matter now?"

"Because if they did, I might know how to break it. If I can figure out its weaknesses—your army might actually have a chance."

Sara hesitated. "Then why is this... thing empty?"

Lily glanced away. "I may have... cleaned it up?"

Sara buried her face in her hands.

"I know it sounds awful," Lily said. "But most of it was already gone—burned. This was the only piece left with structural layers intact."

She moved closer, gently pulling Sara's hands away.

"Do you realize what this means? If this armor is valsing-made, I might be able to dismantle it. *Stop* the war. *Save* lives."

Sara studied her, then looked again at the armor. "Lily... what do you want me to do?"

"I need to study more. I need to see if this design matches any of ours."

Sara raised an eyebrow. "See what? In the abbey's library?"

Lily nodded quickly.

Sara's heart sank. "And after that? What's your plan?"

Lily's eyes darkened.

"If I'm right... I'll go to your king. I'll give your people what they need to win."

Sara stepped closer, alarmed. "My king will kill you before you open your mouth. You know that."

"Then I'll find another way."

"You could tell the queen. If she's really on our side—"

"There's no *time*, Sara!" Lily's voice cracked. "If my king gets involved before we act, if he joins the reisers... do you *know* what kind of weapons my people could build for them?"

The first rays of morning crept through the trees. Birds began to stir.

Sara looked around the creek, imagining it trampled, burned, destroyed. This cursed land was still her home. The idea of losing it made her throat close.

"I care," Sara whispered. "I want to help. But I'll do it with one condition."

Lily tilted her head. "What is it?"

"Answer honestly. Why do you care so much?"

"Isn't it obvious? I want to save your people. And Hune."

Sara stared at her.

"My people?" she said. "You've told me—*more than once*—how much you hate humans. How stupid we are. How ugly we are. How—"

"Fine!" Lily cut in. "Fine. What happened to me... changed my mind. What I *saw* changed my heart."

She took a breath, eyes wet.

"Donald is helping a human. If they lose this war, he'll die. I can't let that happen. I *won't*."

Sara didn't speak. She just opened her arms and pulled Lily into a hug.

She closed her eyes, and the wounded soldier returned to her thoughts. His image wasn't as overwhelming as the fierce desire to help him. For a fleeting moment, she wondered if they had met before—but Lily's sob against her shoulder shattered the thought, pulling her back to the present.

Sara opened her eyes and whispered, "Come with me. We have a lot to read."

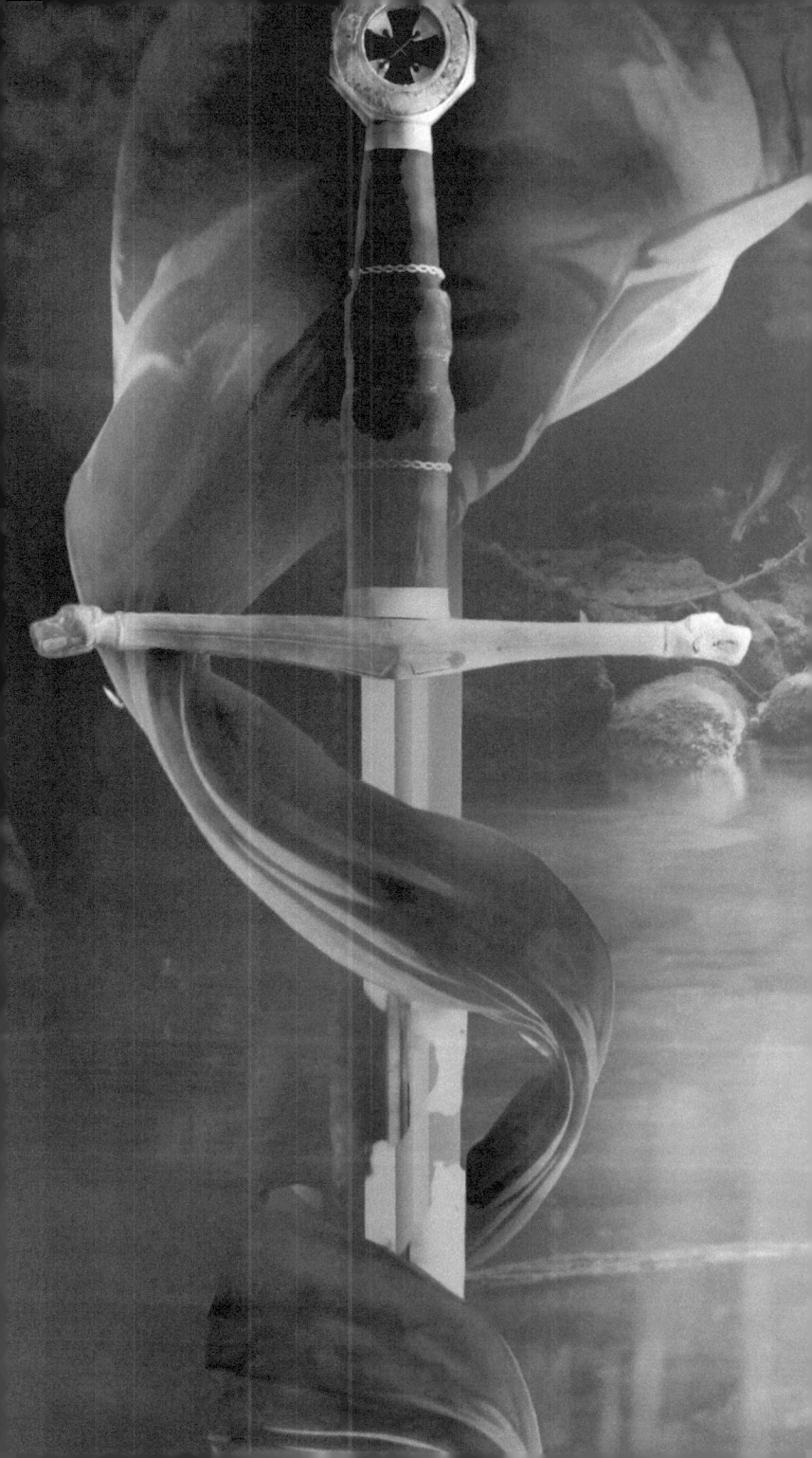

CHAPTER TWENTY-THREE

The emptiness and silence around the canyons at the edge of the desert unsettled John. Charlie avoided talking about it, but it clearly bothered him too.

They had left Andromeda not only to stay hidden, but also to find other human settlements. Their guard could use the extra soldiers. At this point, it didn't matter if the reinforcements were too old or too injured to fight. The problem was—they couldn't find anyone.

Maybe it was because the south of Hune used to be an ocean. No one wanted to get trapped between a body of water and the reisers. Or maybe it was just the desert— no easy place to live. So they pushed farther south. As far as John was concerned, the Soto Forest might be sheltering some survivors.

But none of those felt as likely as their last option:

The reisers had already taken over this side of Hune. And they were walking right into enemy territory.

John shook his head and grabbed a cup of water

before sitting near the firepit. He didn't need any more excuses to be angry—Charlie had done enough damage to his day when he forced him to stay at the main camp.

As the days passed, word of the desert battle spread through the caravan. Everyone buzzed with excitement— celebrating the victory, celebrating their "new commander." The people from Tundra couldn't stop praising the soldiers and crediting their survival to Charlie's leadership. John and the others didn't believe it.

They didn't understand the difference between the attack on Terry's group and their own. In John's opinion, that was the key—*the* key—to finding the reisers' weakness. He had led a small scouting group back to the site of Terry and Fred's ambush, but came back empty-handed. He'd asked Charlie to let him go again, even alone, but his friend refused.

Charlie also dismissed Chris's post-battle protocol. John knew how much that mattered. Chris had always emphasized: **never leave anyone behind, and never let an enemy escape.** Loose ends gave enemies room to grow.

He understood that Charlie now had to prioritize the civilians' safety. But ignoring protocol would come back to haunt them.

"We should go back to Tundra and take it," someone said, walking by him.

"Yes!" a younger girl chimed in. "We can beat them now! Our commander will destroy them!"

John clenched his jaw. *They just got lucky.*

"Chris wasn't even a good soldier," the girl added. "It was because of his father—"

"Or maybe his father wasn't—"

John didn't hear the end of that sentence. He didn't need to.

Charlie had tried to explain, but the people only seemed more drawn to his humility and loyalty. Maybe that's why he'd made John stay in camp—to give him a break from the nonsense.

"Do you mind if I sit with you, Lieutenant?"

Chris's mother approached quietly.

"Of course, ma'am."

He stood with a chivalrous smile, which earned a softer one from her.

"I hope I'm not intruding," she said. "Some days are harder. All the whispering..."

"It's always a pleasure to talk to you," he said, offering her a cup of water. "Although I'd prefer if you called me John."

"Well, John, thank you. How's your day going?"

John exhaled. "I've had enough of it. People irritate me lately."

She smiled gently, but her expression darkened.

"I'm his mother. I'm not a fair judge." She took a breath and looked him in the eyes. "Is there any truth to all this gossip?"

John reached for her hand and squeezed it.

"None at all, ma'am. All the soldiers—**your son's** soldiers, including Charlie—know that."

She nodded, but the sadness didn't leave her face.

"It's not just to comfort you," John added. "I wasn't always part of Chris's guard. I started in Laconia's army. That's where I was born—and where I fought."

"Well," Alleta said, "I guess nobody's perfect."

John chuckled.

"It was a beautiful city," she added. "Not my Tundra, but still."

They were quiet for a moment. John allowed himself a glimpse of memory—the view from Laconia's walls, the wind, the bustle. But only for a second. Some thoughts were better left alone.

"When I joined this guard, Chris was already in charge," John said. "He welcomed me like a person, a friend. Not just another soldier. Sure, he teased me for being from Laconia, but he never mocked our army. He never belittled our losses. I can't share much about the battles—we all swore—but you should know this: your son is a great warrior, and an even better leader."

Tears welled in Alleta's eyes. She smiled through them.

"I'll speak to him about mocking Laconia," she said. "That's not how I raised him."

John grinned, but then Charlie stormed up to them.

"Mrs. Riddley," he said with a nod. Then, to John: "Lieutenant. I thought I gave you things to do."

"Well..." John stretched. "Your order was to stay in camp. So I did."

Charlie wasn't in the mood.

"And you thought I meant 'sit by the fire all day'?"

John exhaled. "Oh, come on. You're the great commander now. You can do everything with your amazing talent."

Charlie stepped in, bristling.

"That how you greet your superior?"

John got to his feet, nose to nose. "Is *this* better, Commander?"

"This is *unacceptable* for any soldier of Hune," Alleta snapped. "What's next? A fistfight to prove who's the most stupid?"

Charlie backed off and apologized immediately.

John took a breath, then sat down again.

"What's really going on, John?" Charlie asked. "Still about the reisers' shield issue? You know we tried. I can't afford to send you back alone."

"It's not just that," John said. "There's more going on, but you're ignoring the real questions."

Charlie narrowed his eyes.

"You mean where everyone is?"

"We already know what happened to them, Charlie. I'm just worried you'll let it happen to *us* too."

"Chris is—"

"Chris is doing everything he can. But *you're* the one here now. It's your job to protect us. Not his."

Before Charlie could reply, a scout ran up.

"Commander! Horses!"

Charlie took off with the scout. "Lieutenant, what are you waiting for?"

John stood up and gave Alleta a half-smile. "Ma'am, I have to go."

"John," she said softly, "Charlie's never been without Chris before. He's trying. And he needs a friend too."

John nodded.

Alleta's words echoed in John's mind as they walked toward the scout's point. He didn't notice the dust cloud rising on the horizon until they reached it.

Hundreds of horses galloped across the sands.

Only the king traveled like that.

"What the hell..." John muttered, his stomach dropping.

"Look at that," Charlie said grimly. "A visit from the king—and his freaking armament. Any chance the king's not with them?"

John shook his head, eyes locked on the storm of hooves and banners rolling toward them.

The armament's presence rubbed most of the soldiers the wrong way. Once, the king's escort was formed by gatekeepers and companions. But once the war began, he replaced them with elite soldiers—the armament.

They never joined battles. Their job was to keep the king unscathed. And they did that...by running.

They had the best armor, weapons, food, and rest. Each had a horse. All of it meant nothing to John—he didn't envy them. He *wanted* them protected. He *wanted* them safe enough to run. That was their job.

Almost without thinking, he reached into his pocket and touched the worn leather bracelet inside. His only treasure—because it reminded him of the best part of his life.

He'd joined Laconia's army the moment he was old enough to hold a sword. He fought until the bitter end, through fire and poison, through the cries of the dying and the silence of the fallen. When the reisers descended on the city, they tore through every defense. John's unit had held the line outside the final shelters—not to win, but to buy time. Their sacrifice gave the last survivors a chance to flee.

A few made it. He was among them—barely breathing, broken, and carried north to an infirmary buried deep within the woods. For weeks, he teetered between life and death.

The memory of the poison stayed with him. Not just the pain—but the way it seared through his veins like fire stitched with blades. It had eaten him alive from the inside. He'd survived, but he still remembered how it felt to wake up and see the living around him, not corpses. That was his first mercy.

His second was Amanda Belk.

Her voice had been the balm. Her hands, his anchor. Her presence, the light he didn't know he needed. Even now, he could still see her—the way her hazel eyes shimmered when she laughed, the sunlight in her light brown hair, the soft freckles scattered across her nose.

She was a Tundra's soldier recovering from her own wounds. He was a soldier on the edge of despair. Somehow, between shared silences and unspoken hopes, they found something real. Love came quietly, but when it bloomed, it changed everything.

The small infirmary became their home, and when they married, it turned into a place of joy. For a moment in time, they reminded others—reminded themselves—that life could still be beautiful.

But it didn't last.

Tundra's army called him back to the front lines. And the king—damned, heartless king—recruited Amanda for the armament.

Their last conversation still echoed in his chest.

"John, this is my last chance to protect Hune," she said, her eyes wet with tears. "I can't be in a guard anymore. My leg—I can't move fast enough."

"Then don't fight!"

"That's not an option! I swore an oath to serve. To protect the people."

"What about your oath to me?" he snapped. "Or was that easy to forget?"

"You're the one leaving!" she cried. "Why can't you support me in this?"

He hadn't answered—not really. He was too furious, too afraid. Afraid of losing her, of the idea that she would willingly serve the man whose negligence had led to Laconia's fall. The man who sent help only when there were refugees left to gather. A king who cared more about his own image than the lives he ruled over.

Amanda had tried to joke, tried to soften the moment.

"You serve him too, John. You're a soldier. Just like me."

But he'd shouted over her.

"I didn't write him a letter and promise to be his servant."

And then he said the words that hollowed him out.

"Being with the king doesn't make you a princess. It makes you a concubine."

That night, Amanda left. She didn't wake him. She didn't say goodbye. She just left behind the leather bracelet he had made for her—a vow he'd tied around her wrist with trembling fingers and a heart full of hope.

He never spoke of her after that. Not to his guard. Not to Chris. Not to anyone.

And still... on quiet nights, or in the chaos before a battle, he thought of her. Wondered where she was. Wondered if she'd survived.

They had crossed paths—almost. The armament was with them during the battle when they lost their colonel, but he never had the chance to look for her. Before he even thought about it, the coward king was gone and the armament with him.

Now, as the thunder of hooves shook the ground beneath him and the dust of hundreds of horses filled the air, John's heart pounded like war drums in his chest.

He needed to see her.

Not because he deserved it. Not because he hoped she'd still love him.

But because if she wasn't here—if he didn't find her among the living—he would never stop wondering if she'd died on that battlefield... while he stood too far away to reach her.

CHAPTER TWENTY-FOUR

The armament's horses stopped in perfect formation, their black armor gleaming under the harsh sun. Each rider wore a full helmet with a faceplate—faceless shadows guarding the crown. It wasn't a massive unit, but those few could've turned the tide of battle long ago if they'd chosen to fight.

From the rear, a white horse emerged. On it rode the man who had let kingdoms fall. He wore no armor, only silk and a ridiculous golden crown that caught the light like a beacon of arrogance. King Leonard III, Regent of Hune.

John didn't flinch. The king was just an old man of average height and features, dressed up in importance and disdain. Nothing more.

"His Excellency, King Leonard the Third, regent of Hune, graces your presence," one of the king's soldiers barked. "Present your respects!"

John muttered under his breath but bowed like the rest of the soldiers. He kept his head down and eyes averted, refusing to look at the armament. Dreading not to find her.

"Your Highness," Charlie said, stepping forward, "I'm Charles Abbott, Commander of Hune's First Guard, at your service."

"You mean *my* First Guard," the king snapped. "I don't remember naming you commander. Is Riddley dead?"

John clenched his jaw. Was that *pleasure* in the king's voice?

"Sir—Your Highness," Charlie corrected, "he's fulfilling your command. He received a letter signed by you and the High Council."

"The High Council? *My* command? What the hell is going on here?" The king turned in his saddle. "Major! Explain to this *supposed* commander what happened to our real council."

From the back, the highest-ranking soldier dismounted. One by one, the others followed.

John's heart skipped when he noticed the slight, familiar limp in the leader's step. She removed her helmet, and the world tilted.

Amanda.

More beautiful than he remembered—older, yes, but stronger too. The lines around her eyes told stories of grit and sorrow. His lips curled into a smile he didn't try to hide.

"Yes, Your Highness," she said, her voice steady. "Commander, I'm afraid to inform you the reisers murdered the Council of Hune years ago."

"I'm aware," Charlie said. "I didn't say it was our council who signed the letter. It was the High—"

"Nonsense!" the king snapped. "There *is* no High Council. And I signed nothing. You've been played. Riddley's a deserter."

John stepped forward, unable to hold back. "That's *bullshit*. Commander Christopher Riddley is one of the most loyal defenders of Hune. He would never—"

"Lieutenant!" Charlie shoved him back. "Your Excellency, please forgive my lieutenant. The heat has gotten to him."

The king dismounted and marched straight to John.

"I'm declaring Christopher Riddley not only a deserter, but a *traitor*," the king said. "He no longer holds rank in this army and will be punished accordingly."

John curled his hands into fists until his nails bit into skin. He didn't care about titles or politics. The king ruled dust and shadows—and John wanted to show him just how little that meant.

"Your Highness," Amanda said smoothly, "if the goal is to see him punished to the highest degree, I recommend keeping his military status intact. Strip him of it, and a civilian court may only exile him. But as a soldier still under your command, you alone hold the right to determine his fate."

The king brightened, as if he'd come up with the idea himself. "Excellent point! I'll take care of Riddley personally."

He turned and mounted his horse again. "I want my camp set up. Far from these fools."

"Your Highness," Charlie said quickly, "the caravan from Tundra is encamped near the canyon. I'm sure they'd be thrilled to see their king—"

"No. Major, keep my camp away from their whining and questions. But not too far—I don't want any compromise to my safety. Understood?"

Amanda nodded once, crisp and cool, and mounted her horse. The rest of the armament followed her, their formation never breaking.

FROM THE MAIN CAMP, THE KING'S TENT STOOD out like a slap in the face—big, white, and surrounded by horses and soldiers. A monument to excess in a time of famine and fear. John almost laughed. He'd expected the king to demand fanfare, worship, even applause. But the man seemed more interested in isolation.

"I hope you're not planning anything stupid," Charlie said, stepping up beside him with Jean. "You've been staring at his tent since we got back. Just remember, John—he's still our king, whether we like it or not."

"Funny. Isn't that what *Chris* told *you* not too long ago?" John said. "Do you remember what the letter said?"

"Not exactly," Charlie muttered. "But I have a bad feeling about—"

"A *bad feeling*?" Jean asked. "What happened?"

John used the interruption to step away. He wasn't in the mood to explain. He just wanted to see Amanda again.

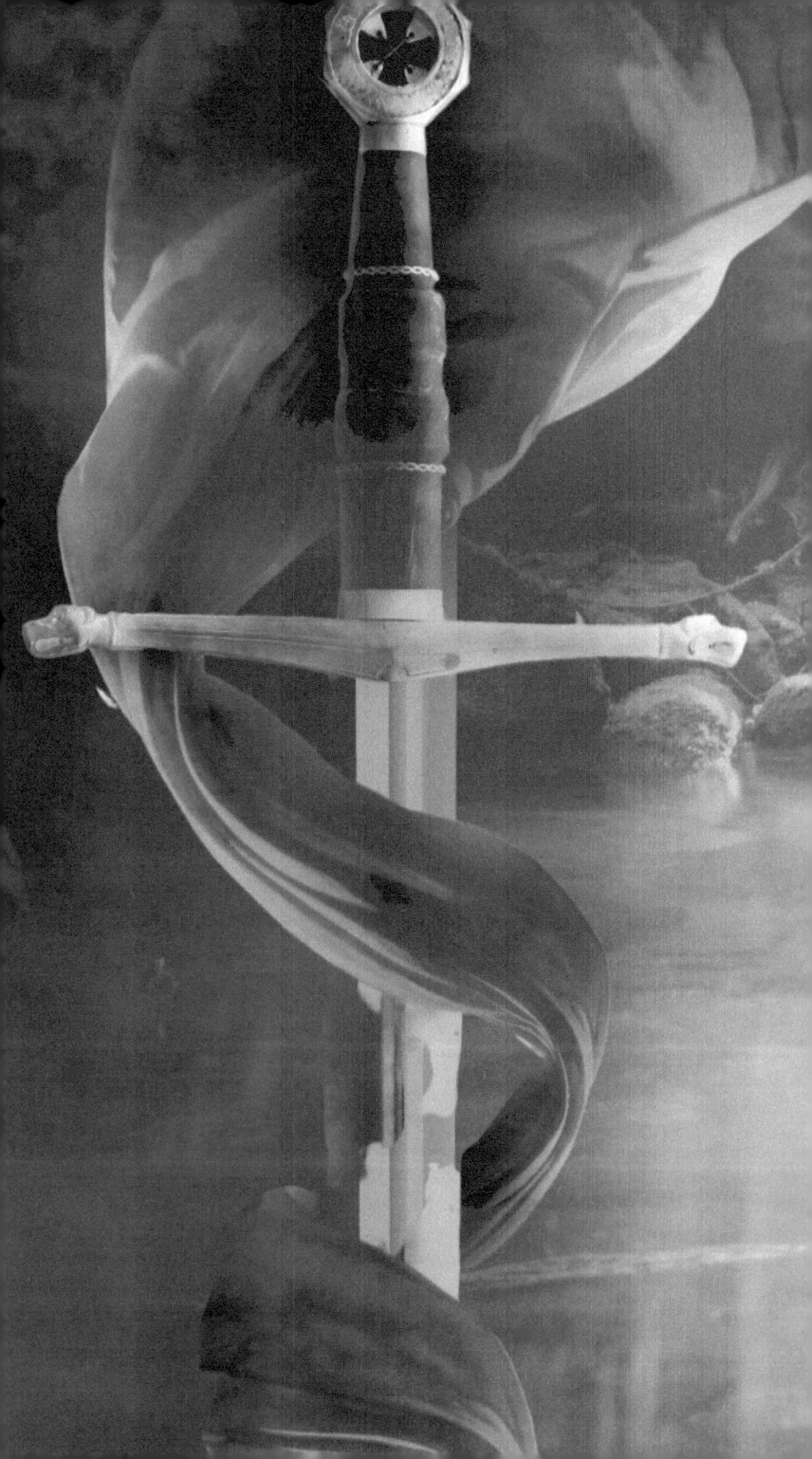

CHAPTER TWENTY-FIVE

Amanda was having a hard time getting anything done. Her mind wouldn't stop circling back to John. For once, she was grateful for the suffocating anonymity of the armament's helmet. It kept her from falling apart.

One glance at him had shaken her entire world. The years hadn't changed her feelings—not even dulled them.

She'd tried to avoid his gaze, but the few times their eyes met, he seemed... distant. Colder. His hatred for the king was obvious, and he probably lumped the armament into the same contempt. She couldn't blame him. And her most recent action—defending the king's right to punish Chris—hadn't helped. But she'd done it to protect *John*, to keep *Chris* in the army. She hadn't wanted to betray anyone. Only keep Hune from crumbling completely.

Since she joined the armament, she'd seen too much —especially from the king. His comments, his actions... they weren't just ignorant. They were wrong. And before their last battle, she'd confided in Colonel Riddley. He had agreed something was off. They'd planned to investigate.

But then he died.

Amanda had hoped to find his son, the commander she had never met but whose name carried honor. She wanted to warn him. Ask for his help.

"This is wrong," said George, the armament captain.

"I'd call it... less than ideal," Amanda replied.

"Our major, the eternal optimist," Lucy, her lieutenant, muttered. "Something's coming. Hopefully not worse than the last—"

"Listen," Amanda cut in, "that letter surprised the king. He didn't send Commander Riddley anywhere. That's our chance."

George raised a skeptical brow. "The Council is dead. He probably *did* desert. Smart man."

"I doubt it," Lucy said, and Amanda nodded.

"I do too. Do you remember when the Queen of the Valsings met with the king?"

"Hard to forget," George said. "He insulted her offer and stormed off."

Amanda's doubts ended that day. The Valsings weren't warriors, but they were brilliant. Their offer could've turned the tide. The king *knew* that.

"The queen told him she had higher supporters," Amanda said.

"That's nonsense," George said. "There is no one higher. The Council is gone. Leonard rules alone."

"No," she said firmly. "The *High* Council still exists."

Lucy froze. George actually laughed.

"Come on, Major. With all due respect... that's a fairy tale."

"So were the prophecies," Amanda said. "Until they weren't."

The silence afterward was louder than the wind. Neither Lucy nor George could argue that. No one doubted the prophecy's curse anymore. And if that was real—what else might be?

"What do we do?" George finally asked.

"I'll speak with the army," Amanda said.

"You *can't*," Lucy snapped. "If the king finds out—"

"I know the risk. But the king didn't expect Riddley to be gone. The timing is too clean. This might be the only chance that isn't a trap."

"Or worse," George said. "It might be someone else's trap."

Amanda nodded grimly. But John's words echoed in her thoughts: *That letter made one of the most loyal men in Hune abandon his guard and civilians.* Whoever sent it, they weren't working with the king.

Then Lucy paled, staring at the horizon.

A thin line moved along the hills. A low rumble followed it.

Reisers.

The soldiers stiffened around her, silent. Amanda recognized the formation. She'd learned more than she liked by *watching* battles instead of fighting them.

"This isn't over," she said. "Listen up. Protect the king—cover him from the enemy."

Then, quietly to George and Lucy: "If I disappear, say you didn't know."

George grimaced. "Amanda—"

"I have to at least try," she said. "If the reisers catch us this time, we fight. If the king betrays us, we go down swinging. Understood?"

"Yes, Major!" the armament responded.

AMANDA WALKED TOWARD THE SCOUTING point. As she expected, they didn't recognize the coming attack. She couldn't blame them. That wasn't a standard formation for the reisers.

"Do you see that line?" she asked the scout. "Those are the reisers. Light the warning fires. Now."

The soldier hesitated.

"That's an *order*," she shouted. "Light all the fires. This was a real emergency."

Only a few minutes later, Charlie arrived with the rest of the guard.

"Major?" he asked. "What's going on?"

"They're here. Commander, look."

The black line was closer now.

"I know you don't trust us," Amanda said, "and you might be right. We haven't fought. But we've *observed*."

She spotted John approaching in the corner of her eye. Her heart leapt, but she looked away to keep her focus.

"You've never seen the reisers move like this," she said. "They're advancing slowly. That means they want *prisoners*."

That got murmurs from the ranks.

"It's true," she said. "You've noticed the missing settlements. The silence. They've changed tactics."

She stepped toward Charlie. "Their leader is likely Colonel Hayden Green. I'm sorry, Commander. You won't win against him."

Charlie issued quick orders. Then turned on her.

"What the hell are you even doing here?" he asked. "Aren't you supposed to be protecting the king?"

She took a breath. "I believe the reisers are here *because of* the king."

Charlie's eyes widened.

"That's a massive accusation, Major," he said. "Hard to believe."

"I doubted it too. Until Colonel Riddley died." Her voice shook. "Commander Christopher Riddley isn't here...but Hune is."

"Are you trying to tell me you were hoping to see Chris?" Charlie narrowed his eyes. "Funny. Because hours ago, you made sure the king had the right to punish Chris himself."

"I was buying time. For Riddley. Think about it— the reisers came *after* the king did. After we were gathered in one place. The king was more than glad to see our colonel dead, and he would love the same fate for the colonel's son."

Charlie stared at the distance. The reisers were there, now so close enough to make out their formation. John leaned in, whispering so she couldn't hear. Whether he hated her or not didn't matter. It was her last chance and with a shaky voice asked.

"Do you trust Christopher?" she asked softly. "Is he like his father?"

Charlie opened his mouth, but she cut him off.

"I wasn't talking to you." She turned to John. "Do *you* trust him?"

His amazing eyes widened as he looked down at her, but he didn't hesitate to respond. "If he's alive, he'll save Hune. Or die trying."

She nodded. "Good. Then tell him. Tell him the king is a traitor. And...I believe he's behind Colonel Riddley's death."

John stepped forward, but she backed away.

"More importantly—whoever *sent* Chris away isn't with the king. That might be the only chance we have."

She looked at Charlie and the other soldiers; they believed her now. She bent, picked up her helmet. Her voice trembled.

"John... you need to tell him."

"This is my place, Amanda," he said. "There is no way I'm leaving all—there is no way I'm leaving you here. I won't—"

"You *have* to." Her tears fell freely now. "Don't you get it? I'm done here."

He searched her face, moved closer.

"It's the reisers or the king," she whispered. "Who would've thought *I* would be the one to commit treason?"

"I've missed you so much," she said.

Then the hum of the reisers came closer. And Amanda, with a broken heart, struck John's head with her helmet.

"What the hell?" Charlie ran to him.

Amanda wiped John's brow gently. Then sliced his forehead and crushed her helmet with her sword.

"We need them to think he died in battle."

Charlie helped her arrange John's body.

"Did you meet Fred?" he asked.

"Who?"

She kissed John's forehead. "That's how John survived Laconia."

"How do you know him?"

Amanda shrugged, even as pain twisted inside her. "He knows where Chris is, doesn't he?"

Charlie nodded. "You could've asked before knocking John out."

"No. This is better. The king will torture me. Let him believe it was *me* who betrayed him."

"You don't have to go back," Charlie said. "Stay. Help us fight."

Amanda smiled. Her heart thundered in her chest.

"No. I'm going to give John time. I'm going to buy us all a chance."

JOHN WOKE TO THE SOFT RUSTLE OF SAND.

His head throbbed. Blood clung to his temple, and his thoughts swam. For a moment, he couldn't explain the sand under him instead of the forest. He remembered having talked to Amanda, and the infirmary was the last place they were together.

Then all came back.

Amanda.

Her last words. Her tears. Her goodbye.

She'd saved his life. Again.

He sat up, stomach lurching as he processed the silence. The scent of blood and death crept into his lungs.

He searched frantically, hoping—praying—not to find Amanda among the dead.

But the king's armament lay scattered like broken dolls, their black armor shredded. None had their helmets. None had their heads.

The king's signature execution: a blade through the heart crest.

John staggered back, choking.

Amanda wasn't among them. Nor were her soldiers. The reisers had taken them.

He wanted to run after them. Wanted to track them through the sands and tear them apart until he found her.

But it would be suicide.

He just witnessed what the king was capable of, and the last thing he wanted was Amanda's life in that bastard's hands.

He reached inside his pocket, and when he took her bracelet out, Terry's locket fell onto the ground.

John didn't wait another second.

He tied the bracelet to his wrist and put the locket back inside his pocket. Amanda told him she missed him, so he would do whatever it took to save his wife.

The Soto Forest wasn't far away. It was time to change the path of the war.

CHAPTER TWENTY-SIX

Even though they hadn't found the abbey, Chris's optimism about their new direction didn't fade. He hadn't told Donald about the dream or what he'd realized because he wanted to hold on to the fragile hope he'd gained. He wasn't ready for Donald's logical explanations to snuff it out. So instead, he listened to Donald's theories about the zhortas—for the fourth or fifth time. That morning wasn't an exception.

"You don't want to hear it, but fear is a strong motivator, Chris."

Chris shook his head and continued packing for the day's hike. Arguing had proved useless and only added to his frustration.

"It's understandable, Chris. Not many have faced an evil sorcerer and a dragon."

Chris started walking without waiting for him. Donald wouldn't get lost this time.

A few days earlier, they'd stumbled across an almost invisible trail winding through the trees. Though overgrown, it was clear that the roots didn't twist as wildly along this path. Curiosity first drove Chris to follow it, but when he realized it was heading south—toward the abbey—his pace quickened.

He could only imagine how different things might've been if they'd come this way from the beginning. As far as he was concerned, meeting Gemli had been pointless, and the journal now left behind in the dragon's cave even more so.

"Hey!" Donald called as he caught up. "I'm still talking."

"Oh really? I thought you'd finally made your last comment. I'm scared. There. Happy now?"

"I would understand if that were true, Chris," Donald replied. "There's no shame in fear."

Chris stopped walking. "Let's get one thing straight. You've called me reckless and suicidal before. But wouldn't it be even more dangerous to throw myself into battle without fear? You think being a soldier means I'm brave? Let me tell you, I would *never* let a fearless soldier fight. Every one of mine fears the war. Bravery isn't being fearless."

Donald looked like Terry used to when Chris gave the same lecture—wide-eyed and trying to puzzle out the logic. Chris chuckled.

"What's so funny?" Donald asked.

"Nothing important. Do you have another theory? Or did that last one blow the others out of the water?"

Donald didn't answer. Instead, he marched ahead until Chris caught up.

"I was serious, Chris. Do you think...someone like

me could help in the war? Could I actually fight for Hune?"

Chris considered his answer carefully. Donald had no training, had never held a weapon, and didn't understand battle. He was smaller than most men, though that could be an advantage if used wisely.

"At this point, we need all the help we can get. But remember—fighting in a war is more than swinging a sword."

Donald frowned. "But not in battle, right?"

"Why not?"

Donald threw up his hands. "Let's see—no combat skills, no military training. I'd just get in everyone's way!"

Chris smirked. "So you'll need a guard to explain everything to you in the middle of battle?"

"If I'm joining the fight, I won't be part of the armament," Donald huffed.

Chris raised a brow. "The king's guard? What do you know about them?"

"I know enough. They get the best treatment and never lift a finger to fight. Every soldier despises them."

Donald straightened his posture. "Come on, Chris. You didn't think my queen would throw her lot in with Hune without researching who she was aligning with, did you?"

Chris tensed.

"What about the reisers?" Chris asked. "Did she send you to learn about them too?"

Donald looked pained. "I'll tell you everything. Though I suspect you already know most of it."

Chris walked ahead.

"I am not expecting protection, Chris," Donald said. "I have never done that and won't start now."

"Sounds fair. I'm serious too. We need as much help as possible. If you want to join the army, I don't see why not."

Donald grabbed his arm. "You're not joking? I can really join the army?"

Chris nodded again.

Donald did a little victory dance, then caught himself. "Apologies for the... inappropriate display. Thank you, truly. I'll give everything I've got to protect Hune."

Chris tilted his head. "All of Hune?"

Donald hesitated. "I mean... I don't want the reisers destroying everything. It's our home. You don't seem all that eager to protect *my* people, but—"

"Stop right there," Chris said. "If you are serious about this, whoever you are calling 'all of Hune', meaning that valsing you are not naming, she is your reason. Your real reason. You need to keep in mind. Anything else is a bunch of nonsense that I don't care about. Get it?"

Chris didn't wait for a reply.

His father had taught him that every soldier needed a personal reason to fight. It was the only thing that would get them through the war. Over the years, Chris had made sure all his soldiers had one—but somewhere along the way, he'd lost his own.

He wanted his soldiers to live full lives. He wanted peace. But peace had always been a theory to him—

something people talked about but never saw. He didn't know what it looked like, not really.

His family used to be his reason. But once his father sent him off to make sure his mother didn't suffer under the reisers methods, everything changed. That act justified his reason for not having a personal life. He'd met kind women, shared stolen moments, but never let anyone close. It was too dangerous.

And now, even after realizing his dreams were real—she was real—falling in love still felt like the stupidest idea.

THE TRAIL TILTED UPWARD, BECOMING A steady climb. At the top of the ridge, the trees thinned, revealing glimpses of the bright blue sky. Flowers filled the air with their scent.

"What is that?" Donald said. "It smells like a greenhouse."

"It does." Chris smiled. "Look over there."

At the far end of the valley stood the crumbling remains of Saint Peter's Abbey.

Plants grew between the stones. Most of the towers were collapsed. The wooden structures were rotting from humidity.

Chris began to walk toward Saint Peter's Abbey, a place he had hated for so many years.

"Well, that's interesting," Donald said.

"Amazing, really. It's a miracle it's still standing."

"No, idiot. The gardens!"

Chris followed his gaze to the roots at the edge of the ruins. Flimsy scaffolding clung to them, supporting garden boxes.

"My mother would have a hard time calling *that* a garden," he shouted a few steps ahead from Donald.

"With all due respect," Donald yelled back, while he stood admiring the view. "she's never tried gardening in *this* place."

Chris laughed, but before he could reply, something slammed into him from the side.

He reacted instantly, grabbing the attacker's arm. They tumbled down the hill. He pinned them, ready to strike—then hesitated.

A root snapped above. Chris rolled them both into a ditch just before it crashed.

The attacker's head was against his chest. He reached for his sword but froze when he heard her voice.

"No, please—I'm sorry—I didn't mean—"

She pushed off him, fumbling with her hood. "Please don't hurt me. I just didn't want the root to fall on you."

Chris sat up, heart racing.

The face he'd seen in dreams for years stared back at him—real and terrified.

"It's all right," he said softly.

"Dear gods above!"

A man, who could only be a zhorta, appeared behind her and hugged her tightly.

"You're okay, my child?"

Without making a noise, more zhortas appeared. None looked friendly.

She reached down and offered her trembling hand.

Chris took it like it was made of glass, but before he could get up, she stopped.

"You're hurt," she said the last word from his dream while she kneeled by him.

She removed the ribbon from her hair, letting dark waves spill to her shoulders, and wrapped his hand.

"Let me see," she said, taking his other hand.

Chris's mind flooded with memories of all the times he'd been with her—holding her hand without hesitation, brushing the hair from her face, and losing himself in her beautiful eyes. But now, her hands trembled in his, uncertain and wary. She didn't trust him—and he hated that.

He held her hand a little tighter, and when she looked at him, he smiled. It was strange to see her awake, and he wouldn't change it for anything.

For years, she had only lived in the quiet corners of his mind—glimpses in dreams, a voice in the dark, a feeling just beyond his reach. Now, she was here. Real. Breathing. Scared.

And yet, even with fear in her eyes, she was the most extraordinary thing he had ever seen.

"These are serious injuries," she said. "You need to have them cured as soon as possible."

"For the gods above, Sara! What the hell happened?" a new zhorta said.

She stood up and cleaned her hands on her skirt. "I was trying to—"

"Chris, are you still alive?" Donald said. "Why are you sitting there? Did you break your legs?"

He shook his head and brushed his shirt and pants as he got up.

Around him, most of the zhortas moved back while a surprised gasp escaped the new arrival.

"For the gods above!" the zhorta said. "Why you didn't tell me the soldiers have arrived?"

His enthusiasm was clear but belonged only to him. The others looked concerned and serious.

"Please forgive this poor girl; she sometimes does—"

"Forgive her?" Donald said. "She just saved his life! You should take better care of this place. It is a shame, the state of this poor people. As their leader, this speaks poorly of you."

"Donald!" Chris said.

Such an accusation would not improve their welcome.

"For the gods above," said the zhorta who hugged Sara. "Rafael, can you believe it? Valsings and their opinions! You can't expect less of them."

Donald's mouth opened as Chris's aversion of the situation grew.

"Please forgive me," Rafael said. "I'm not sure what happened, but believe me, I am so glad you arrived. Are the others arriving later today?"

The extra second that took Chris to understand the question was enough for Donald to answer it.

"This is Commander Christopher Riddley and...and me. We are all you get, zhorta."

Rafael exhaled. "Oh well! We'll manage," he turned to the others. "Back to work, everyone! You two, come with me. We'll get you all—"

Sara stepped between them. "He needs medical attention."

"He looks fine to me," Rafael said.

"His hands—"

"Later," he said firmly.

Sara started to argue, but the zhorta Stuart, pulled her aside.

Chris didn't like that. Not one bit.

"What was that all about?" Donald said.

Chris lifted his hand to show his new blue bandage.

"Oh! Why immediate attention? Did you do something else?"

Chris shook his head, still looking for her in the crowd.

All his hope from before dimmed.

He wasn't sure what hurt more—that she didn't recognize him, or that she might have been scared because she did.

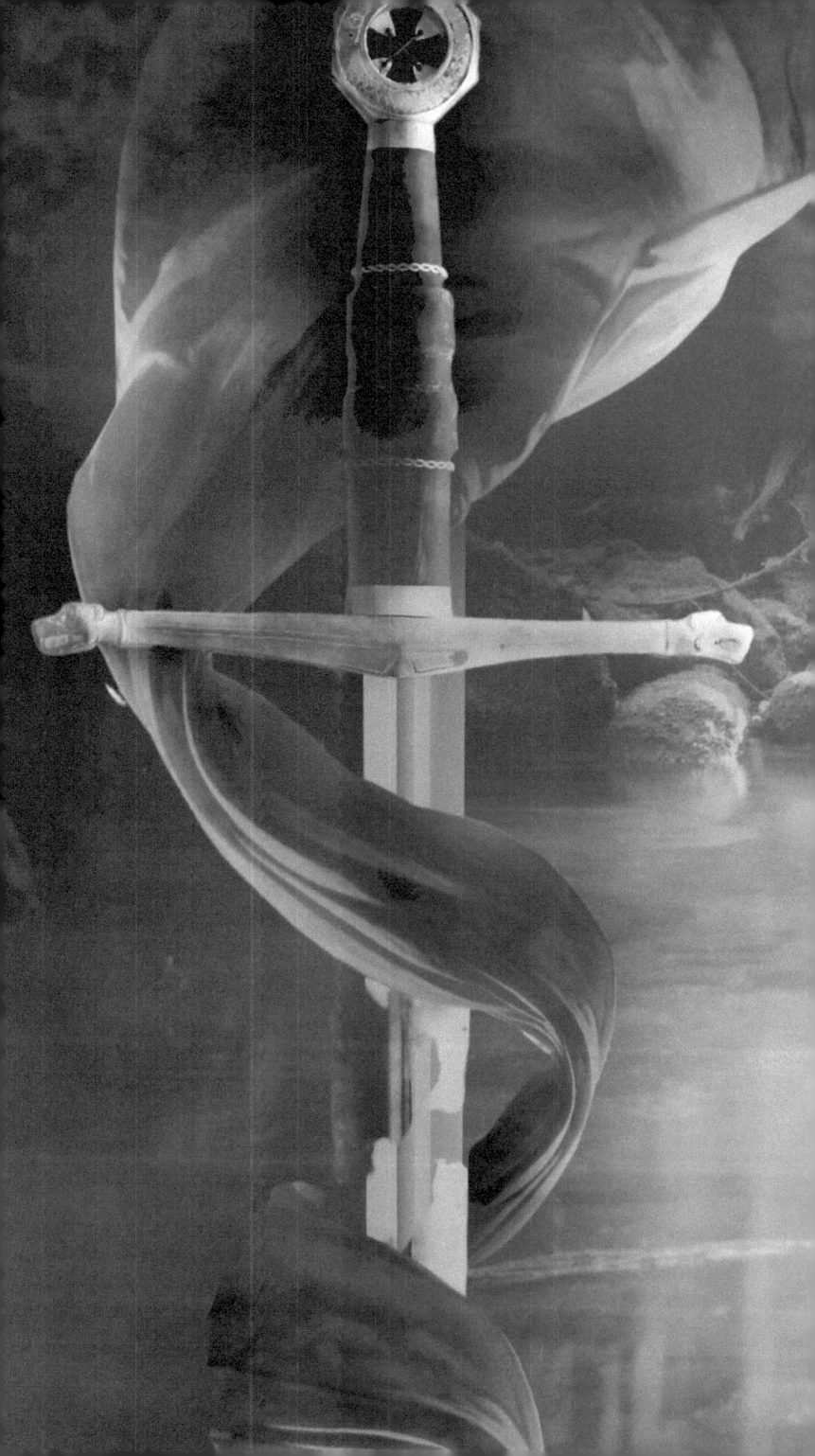

CHAPTER TWENTY-SEVEN

Rafael realized the castle was just as bad inside as it was outside—but he hoped the warmth would help. All zhortas, including himself, liked a cozy home. The fireplaces blazed with healthy flames, and the abbey's walls were crowded with memories—portraits, hand-carved symbols, and relics too old to name. It might not impress a soldier, but it might soften a heart.

"This is marvelous!" Donald said, wide-eyed, and Rafael couldn't help the smirk tugging at his lips.

The valsing's curiosity and reverence for history would win him over easily. The real challenge was the commander. His jaw remained tight, his boots striking the floor like each step was a warning. Rafael noticed the alarmed expressions of the other zhortas as they passed, and he wasn't surprised—Christopher Riddley carried the war with him, and it made everyone nervous.

Upstairs, Rafael led them to his office. His doubts

had grown heavy over the past weeks, and this meeting might finally tip the scale. Everything now depended on what the commander would say—and what he would believe.

"Zhorta Rafael, do you need help outside?" Zhorta Wilson, one if his scholars asked, stepping into the hallway.

"No, no," Rafael said. "But I was wondering if you'd mind giving this young valsing a tour? I'm sure there's much he'd love to see."

As expected, Donald lit up and practically bolted after Wilson, who didn't look particularly pleased to be assigned the task. Rafael wasn't sure if Wilson was annoyed or just wary of Christopher, but the soldier didn't notice either way.

"After you," Rafael said, opening the door to his office.

It was a small, lived-in space, warm and lined with books. The fire crackled pleasantly. Rafael settled into his favorite chair without waiting.

"Please, Commander. Sit. I'm too old to run these hills anymore."

Chris approached but didn't sit. His stance was rigid, watchful. A soldier who had learned never to let his guard down—not even beside a hearth.

"First, I want to offer my condolences for the loss of your father," Rafael said gently.

Chris's face flickered. Just for a moment. Then the emotion was gone.

"I had the pleasure of meeting him, many years ago.

It's a loss not just for the army, but for those of us who had the honor of knowing him."

"Thank you," Chris said. "But I doubt we're here to talk about my father." His eyes sharpened. "Why are your people afraid?"

Rafael nodded. So the commander noticed. It wasn't fear of *him*, then—it was fear of *what* he represented.

"Oh, son. That's been a problem for weeks now. I tried to explain that if the king were sending his soldiers, it wouldn't be to hurt us. But some memories... they leave scars that never fade."

Chris's brows knit. "Excuse me?"

This was Rafael's opening. His one chance to explain the truth.

"When the army began losing the war, blame turned toward us. We zhortas were accused of everything—from harboring secrets to weakening defenses. Soldiers and civilians alike came after us. Many of my brothers never made it to the abbey. I don't say that to accuse. What's done is done. But I couldn't let my people die for nothing. We ran."

Chris finally sat. He looked younger in that moment, more human. The weight on his shoulders was almost visible.

"Commander, I have to ask," Rafael continued. "I was told the king sent the First Guard. Did something happen to them?"

Chris's eyes hardened again. His voice became careful. Calculated.

"The king's letter left room for interpretation. In my

experience, that means the one in charge makes the final call. My soldiers were the last of the human army, and Tundra our last safe city. I couldn't leave those people unprotected."

Rafael let out a breath of relief. *So his suspicious were true. He defied the king to protect his people.*

"Good," Rafael said. "It's the hard decisions—the ones that cost us—that end up bringing the most hope."

Chris leaned forward. "Why are we here, Rafael? What did the king order you to do?"

So that was it. The soldier wasn't just looking for sanctuary. He was trying to untangle the king's plan.

Rafael stood and moved to the window. From there, he could see the grounds—and the familiar silhouette of Sara moving across them.

The girl he'd raised. The one he'd promised to protect. Now, the war was knocking on her door.

"Zhorta Rafael?" Chris asked from behind.

"May I call you Christopher?" Rafael said. "And please—sit properly. This may be the first honest conversation you've had in weeks."

Chris adjusted his seat, and Rafael took a moment to gather his thoughts.

"You remember the prophecy that's cost us all so much? We keep it here. Along with every historical document of Hune that might help us understand it."

Chris tensed, and Rafael pressed on.

"We've searched for ways to break it. But no matter what we do, one truth keeps rising to the surface: there was no way to avoid this war."

Chris sat back, lips tight. "So... there's no hope."

"That's not what I said." Rafael raised a brow. "There *is* hope. But it rests on someone very specific."

He waited for the moment the commander would push back, and right on cue—

"Who?"

Rafael exhaled. The hardest part was still ahead—he would have to convince Chris of the half-truth he'd been telling everyone else. A far more difficult task, considering his listener had the trained eye of a soldier, sharpened to detect lies.

"I was in Laconia the day the reisers breached the city. As the last ships were evacuating, I heard a woman singing by the docks. She was cradling a little girl, barely two years old. The mother was dying. I offered to help—but by the time I reached her, she only had the strength to whisper her daughter's name: Sara."

Chris leaned in, motionless.

"Three reisers appeared. I thought it was the end. One of them reached for Sara—but before it could touch her, a light exploded from her tiny body. A silence so complete it erased the world. When I opened my eyes, the reisers were gone, and the child was crying in my arms."

He looked over at Chris. "It's unbelievable, I know. But it happened."

"And you didn't tell anyone?"

"I told the king. *He* is the one who said she should stay hidden. He feared what others would do if they found out."

Chris's silence was heavy.

"After years of study," Rafael continued, "we believe

Sara is the only one who can wield the weapon that will end this war."

Chris stood and paced, angry and uncertain.

"What weapon?"

"We're not entirely sure," Rafael admitted. "The texts speak of an incarnation of a sword—metaphor or magic, I can't say. But she's the key. I'm certain of it."

Chris looked skeptical. "So you've been training her? Teaching her to fight?"

Rafael didn't flinch. "No. We raised her in peace. Because if the prophecy is right, she doesn't need a blade —she *is* the weapon."

Chris scoffed, but he didn't leave. That was something.

"We've kept much from the world, I know," Rafael said. "But the prophecy also says that salvation will come when the races unite. The humans can't do this alone. Neither can we."

Chris didn't speak, so Rafael moved to the window again.

"I'm not asking you to believe everything today. I'm asking you to listen. You came here for answers—well, now you have one. What will you do with it?"

Chris followed his gaze and found Sara again, working in the distance.

"I can't..." he whispered. "I don't even understand what this means."

"Then talk to her," Rafael said gently. "Start there."

Chris turned toward the door, but hesitated. "And the weapon? How will we find it?"

Rafael chuckled. "*We?* Oh no, that's on *you and Donald.*"

Chris blinked at him.

Rafael laughed and waved him toward the hall. "Go on now, Commander. You'll want to get some rest. You're about to set the future in motion."

CHAPTER TWENTY-EIGHT

Chris had a lot of questions—and even more doubts—when he walked out of Rafael's office. He didn't trust the zhorta and was certain he knew more than he'd said. It seemed encouraging that Rafael, like him, hadn't followed the king's orders. But now, Chris wasn't sure what to do next.

He slowed down, taking in his surroundings.

The hallway leading to the stairs brought him to a balcony. Pieces of wood covered the broken windows around the vestibule. High ceilings bore stains from moisture and moss, though hints of golden paint peeked through. Each archway was marked with a chipped emblem of Hune, engraved on columns identical to those in Tundra's castle.

If the reisers had already reached the city, then his hometown was likely in worse shape than this place. Too many weeks had passed. He could only hope Charlie had understood his message and left in time.

He heard Donald's voice coming from a room on the

main floor and moved toward it—until he spotted Zhorta Wilson showing a vase to a wide-eyed valsing. Chris kept walking.

As soon as he opened the door, he missed the warmth of the fireplace, but the fresh air was what he needed. The soft scent of flowers drifting through the forest helped, too.

"Captain—I mean, Commander," said a familiar voice behind him.

Chris turned—and froze.

"Commander Madeck?" he said. "I would've never expected to find you here. Or wearing that."

"Ha! Commander," the man laughed. "As you well know, I'm not in the army anymore. You can call me Daniel now."

His rich laugh echoed through the woods as he stepped closer. "Though I'll admit, I miss the title sometimes."

In the past, they'd butted heads often—both too proud, too stubborn. But that changed during their final mission together. Back then, Chris had still been a captain, recovering from a harsh punishment. And Daniel had just left the army.

"Did you come here to find—" Chris began.

"An unorthodox way to end this war?" he interrupted Chris. "No. But you did, didn't you?"

Chris frowned.

"Rafael must've told us a hundred times the king's First Guard was coming."

Daniel grinned and gave him a once-over. "You were

a good soldier, Riddley—but not that good to be the entire guard."

Chris smirked and rubbed the back of his neck.

"You just never let me shine enough."

They moved to a rusty old bench and sat down.

"Riddley, I'm not surprised you're commander now. But I never imagined I'd see you with a valsing. How did that happen?"

Chris burst out laughing. "Even better—he's the former fiancé of the princess."

Daniel blinked. "Former, because of your inappropriate interlude with her?"

"No." Chris shook his head and chuckled.

He explained the king's orders, how he'd left the guard in Tundra, and how he'd met the valsings. Daniel laughed as Chris recounted his travels with Donald—but turned serious when Chris talked about Gemli and the dragon. Then, to his own surprise, Chris shared his connection with Sara.

As he repeated Rafael's words, it all sounded hazier, more inconsistent—despite the strange alignment with what Gemli had revealed. Too much was missing. Or maybe he was being misled.

Chris trusted Daniel, though. As commander, Daniel had been tough, but his soldiers knew he cared. He'd even kept Chris's true reason for meeting King Orson a secret—something Chris deeply appreciated and had been grateful for ever since.

After a long silence, Daniel stretched out his legs and crossed his arms. Chris knew the gesture well.

"That's more interesting than anything I've learned around here, Riddley."

Chris sighed and let his head fall into his hands.

"I just don't trust any of it. There are too many coincidences. I don't—I can't—believe."

"Coincidences?" Daniel patted his back. "Some call that good timing. But I get it. Still... I never thought I'd see the day Christopher Riddley feared a girl."

"What?" Chris looked up. "I'm not afraid of her. I'm afraid of what could happen to her. You weren't in that damn cave. You didn't see what Gemli can do."

"True. But didn't he say he didn't believe a human could be righteous or wise? Maybe he doesn't see Sara as a threat."

"Or maybe he lied."

Chris turned toward the forest—and the ache to find Sara returned, sharper than ever.

"I don't know about the cave," Daniel said, "but I've lived here for years, and I know Sara. Trust me—she's special. Sweet. Kind. You know what? You're right. You should stay far away from her. I've seen you around pretty girls before."

The teasing grin on Daniel's face made Chris laugh.

"No, Ex-Commander."

"What? You don't think she's pretty?"

"No—I mean yes—but that's not the point. I'm not planning to ask her out. I'm supposed to ask her to fight the leader of the reisers. That's not her job—it's mine."

Daniel nodded, then pointed toward a distant scaffold.

Chris turned and saw Sara collecting something in a basket. Even from afar, she looked delicate—small.

"So you know her," Chris said. "Do you think she could do it? Gods, I doubt she's even held a sword."

"I don't think so either," Daniel said. "But she's strong in her own way. She's lived in this cursed forest her whole life—that says something. And she cares for Hune just as much as you and I do. She's kind to it."

"Kind? This is a war!"

"You, of all people, should know not every battle is won with a sword."

Chris looked down, dragging his boot through the dirt. Daniel was right.

"She's not fragile, Riddley." He nodded toward her. "Just... different."

Chris stared at her again. "So what now? I just talk to her?"

"Ha! Once again. Never thought I'd live to see the day you'd ask me for girl advice."

Chris shook his head and started walking toward her.

"Wait, Riddley. There's something you should know."

Chris stopped. Those were never the words he wanted to hear.

"Sara is kind. Sweet. Caring."

"Don't worry, I'll behave like I should."

"No, that's not it. I'm pretty sure she won't even consider you as a date." Daniel exhaled. "She's not fond of soldiers. In fact, they terrify her."

Chris closed his eyes. He remembered how close he'd come to hurting her during their first encounter.

"Great. Because we really needed this to be harder."

"Well," Daniel said, "isn't it a coincidence you've got some charming skills to help her work through that?"

AFTER SWEARING AT DANIEL, CHRIS COULD only laugh at the absurdity of his situation. The irony wasn't lost on him—she might distrusted him more than he distrusted Gemli.

He slowed his pace as he neared her. Daniel had called her kind, and that was the word that clung to Chris's memories too.

The vault had been merciless—physically, mentally, utterly brutal. Staying still turned his skin into burning wire, stretching brought the ache of blood back into desiccated veins. Breathing hurt once his lungs dried out, and every scratch became a flame when dirt lodged into his wounds. But the torment dimmed when he lost his grip on reality. Because that's when she appeared—smiling, soft-spoken, and constant. Sara.

For years, he'd pushed those memories away. He convinced himself she wasn't real—just a comforting illusion conjured by a fractured mind. He had loved listening to her talk about Hune's forests, its rivers, and the stars overhead. It had made him feel like a person again, not just a soldier. But that couldn't be real... could it?

He'd promised himself he wouldn't let her become a weakness. She had been a figment, a coping mechanism. Nothing more.

Until the cave.

Until now.

As he stepped into view, he found her standing quietly beneath a tree, holding something delicately in her hands, her gaze tipped toward the sky. He didn't want to startle her. Still, she was the one who broke the silence.

"Noisy," she said gently, without turning around.

Chris blinked. "I've been called a lot of things, but noisy is a first."

She turned—and stepped back.

It stung, more than he wanted to admit.

"I didn't mean you," she said quickly, shaking her head and glancing toward the sword at his side. "Your shoes. Your boots. They're too loud for these trees."

Chris looked down at the leather-wrapped soles.

"They don't like it. The trees, I mean," she continued. "Being so close to the abbey, they've become... sensitive. Sound bothers them. Too much of it and things fall." She gave a small smile, almost shy, but looked away too fast for him to hold onto it.

"I'm sure Zhorta Rafael can give you quieter boots."

She was just as he remembered—gentle but perceptive, and unexpectedly funny. Chris followed her gaze and finally saw what she'd been holding: a bird's nest, fragile and full of hope.

"He told you," she murmured, her smile disappearing as she turned away. "Of course he did. Less than an hour, and he's already started preparing you."

She took a breath and straightened her spine. She was

trying to sound sure of herself. Brave. But Chris could see the tremble beneath her words.

"I can't help you, Sergeant. I understand how important it is, and I'm sorry, but I don't remember. You're wasting your time."

He didn't correct her on the rank. "Has anyone else asked for your help?"

She hesitated, then shook her head. "Not exactly. Just a lot of questions. Too many. I still can't remember."

Something dark flickered behind her eyes.

"It was also the night you lost your mother," Chris said quietly. "No one should be asked to relive that."

Sara stared at him. Slowly, she sank to the ground. "No one's ever said that before."

Chris crouched across from her, careful to keep his distance.

"I'm sorry for your loss," he said.

Sara's voice wavered. "Colonel Riddley was a good man. It isn't fair that he's gone."

Chris blinked. He hadn't expected that. She had known his father?

He swallowed the ache in his chest. "Thanks," he said, gently shifting the subject. "Why the nest?"

Sara's face softened as she looked at the twigs and leaves in her lap. "It's a bluebird's. I found it when the root fell earlier. I'm trying to put it back. If it's not up before sunset, the mother won't return. They'll leave it behind."

She looked up at the tree. "These trees are the only ones they'll nest in."

Chris stood and studied the trunk. "I'll climb up and—"

"No!" Sara reached out and pulled his hand away. "That root is poisonous."

"What?"

A sharp burn hit his skin. "Gods above, of course it is."

Without hesitation, she pulled off the wrap on his hand and pressed cool moss to his palm. The pain ebbed, turning to a gentle throb.

"I can't believe Rafael didn't ask anyone to help you." She looked at his other hand, still wrapped with her blue ribbon. "Unbelievable! He should know better. Come on, I'll clean them up."

Although the offer was tempting, Chris had an idea that could win at least part of her trust. He got a hold of her hand as she was trying to wrap it.

"I didn't hurt you, did I?"

"Not at all," Chris said, and he couldn't stop looking at her bright blue eyes. "It is almost sunset. What about your nest?"

She shrugged her shoulders and looked back at the ground where she left it.

"It's all right. I'll come back later. This is more important."

"You mean my old wounds or the new poison on them?" He didn't let her answer. "Whatever you put on it is already better, and if you want to know, I got these other cuts weeks ago."

"Weeks?"

"They won't get worse this evening, but those little eggs won't make it. Is there a rope around here?"

He turned and walked to one scaffolding.

Sara ran to catch up with him.

Chris climbed the scaffold and grabbed a long rope. He bet those roots were more stable than that wooden structure.

"Does it have to be that root?"

"Yes." She looked down. "It is the only tree the blue-birds use for nesting."

"Of course. Who doesn't want to live in a poisonous tree?" Chris said while he climbed down. A shy smile illuminated Sara's face.

"Your choice," he said. "I lift you, or you lift me."

Sara looked at the nest, then at him. Her eyes sparkled. "You think I could lift you?"

Chris laughed. "There's a better chance of that than me getting it right up there."

She smiled. "Well, in that case, Captain."

"My lady," he said, bowing slightly.

Her cheeks turned pink, and Chris committed the sight to memory.

She looped the rope, one arm around it, nest balanced in her other hand. He lifted her gently, guiding her as she placed it in the crook of the tree.

He was pulling the rope down and starting to fold it when he felt her arms around him in a nervous hug. It shouldn't have surprised him since she had done it countless times in his memories.

"I'm sorry," she exhaled and moved a few steps away.

"Sorry, I didn't mean to. Thank you so much for your help."

"It was all my pleasure, Sara," he said, giving her a small bow that made her grin.

He finished gathering the rope and walked to the platform. This time, he gave it to Sara. The new injury on his hand was bothering him more, and he wasn't sure he could hold onto the wobbling structure.

"You should make a wish," she said. "Bluebirds are known for luck and gratitude. You just saved their babies. I'm sure they will grant you anything."

"I don't know, Sara. It was more you than me."

She shook her head. "It was you who figured out how to save them, and—"

Sara turned, but whatever she was going to say never reached her lips. Instead, she stared at his eyes for a long moment that Chris didn't want to interrupt. He was sure she recognized something in them, especially when her face paled.

She cleared her throat. "What do you have to lose?"

Without waiting for him, she walked toward the abbey.

Chris wanted to ask, but he knew better. He looked back at the nest and found himself wishing that those birds could pay back the favor to Sara. That they could protect her from that prophecy, and from what Gemli and Rafael had told him.

When he realized what he had done, he shook his head and laughed at himself.

As he followed Sara back to the abbey, the atmosphere grew warmer, and the silence wasn't as profound as it was in the middle of the woods. The little bit of sunlight gave a peaceful sensation.

"What is it?" Sara said, and only then Chris realized he was grinning.

"Well, I lived in a desert for so long that I hated the heat and couldn't wait for the sun to set."

"The sun is a blessing here, Admiral."

Chris laughed aloud. "I'm flattered, but I'd make a terrible admiral. We don't even have an ocean. I have to give it to you though, as a child I always wanted to become an admiral."

Sara gasped and covered her mouth. "Oh no! That's not your rank?"

"Let's just say you haven't hit it yet."

She looked so mortified that he softened. "It's all right, Sara. Really."

"I didn't mean to offend—"

"Offend me? I haven't laughed this much in years. You're fine."

She paused, brows furrowed, and then murmured, "Christopher. Your name is Christopher. And I know you're not a colonel..."

Chris raised an eyebrow.

"Commander?" she said, peeking up.

"That's the one," he replied. "But I prefer *Chris*." He wondered if he should mention that it was what she used to call him, but he lost his chance.

Sara smiled. "Chris. I like that."

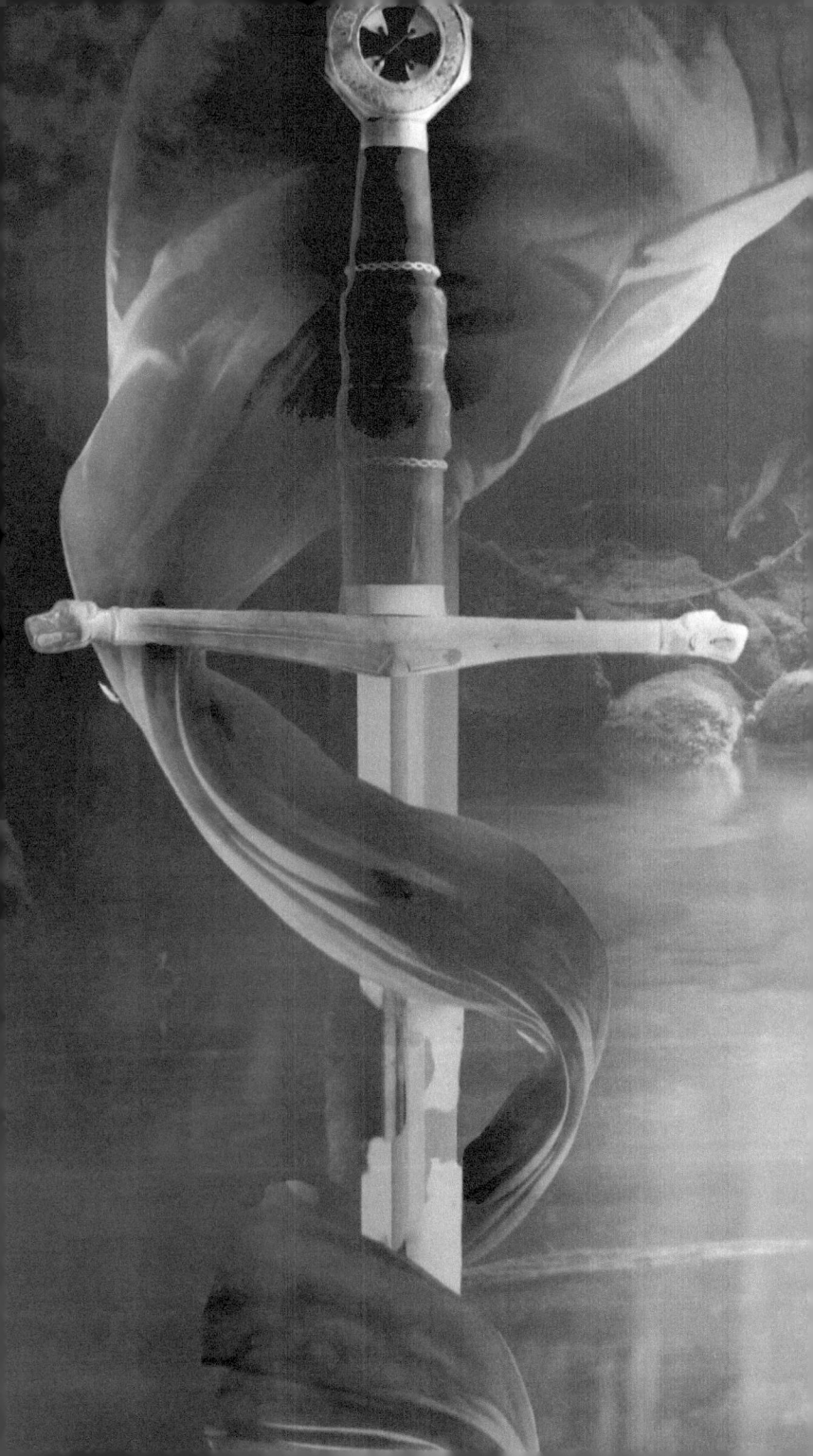

CHAPTER TWENTY-NINE

The door they used passed by the kitchen, and the rich, earthy scent of food reminded Chris just how long it had been since he'd had a real meal—something warm, something that wasn't rationed or rushed. Still, Sara didn't stop. She walked on, steady and silent, through the long hallway.

They passed tall glass doors that seemed too refined for the abbey's rustic tone.

"That's the library," she said, barely glancing at it. "Everything we know about Hune is in there. You can visit it later."

Chris lingered for a heartbeat, tempted by the thought of old maps and forgotten truths, but Sara didn't wait. He followed.

Not much farther, she opened a plain wooden door, revealing a long infirmary lined with empty beds. All of them were covered in dust—except one. Clean white sheets gave it away as the only bed used regularly. Cabinets were still stocked, though time had clearly slowed this room's purpose.

Sara motioned for him to sit while she gathered supplies—bottles, gauze, and utensils arranged carefully on a tray.

"Are you some kind of doctor?" he asked, placing his sword beside him and easing down onto the bed.

"Nope," she replied over her shoulder. "I just live with a lot of old people in a very humid place... full of poisonous things."

Chris smiled softly.

But when she turned and saw the sword beside him, she froze.

Her breath caught. Her eyes locked on the weapon as if it were alive. Her fingers trembled before she pressed them flat against her thighs.

"I'm sorry," he said, already reaching for it. "Let me put it somewhere."

"No," she said quickly, blinking away the shine in her eyes. "It's all right. I should've guessed you'd carry it."

She lowered her gaze, but her voice stayed calm—almost too calm. "Your father's sword and I share some history."

Chris's heart stuttered.

"You knew my father?"

Sara nodded without looking up. "He used to visit the edge of the Soto Forest to check on us. We brought supplies—food, medicine. He didn't hate us. He never blamed the zhortas. I was just a little girl then, and he... he let me ride the horses. Told me stories."

Her voice grew quicker, like she was trying to outrun the emotion building inside her.

"He stopped coming a few years ago. The war changed things. He couldn't come anymore."

Chris stayed quiet. There were too many feelings tangled in her words—and in his mind.

She cleared her throat and added, "But I'm sure the story behind your wounds is far more interesting."

Chris understood she was closing that door, and he wouldn't force it open. Just like he wasn't going to tell her how he really got injured.

"Right," he said. "Another great war story."

Sara gave a faint smile and moved toward him. "Since you've had these cuts for weeks... this won't be easy. It's going to hurt."

Chris chuckled, trying to shake off the lingering thoughts of his father. "Believe me, I've had worse."

She reached for his hand, unwinding the blue ribbon slowly, her fingertips careful not to graze his skin.

"I know your life's not safe," she said softly. "You fight to protect us... well, not us here. Hune."

He stared at her. "Sara, you *are* Hune."

But she only smiled faintly and continued unwrapping his hand.

"You recently broke these fingers," she murmured, more to herself than to him, "and held a glacier orchid far too long."

Chris raised an eyebrow. "How do you know that?"

Sara glanced up, eyes twinkling. "Those blossoms are pretty enough that a little girl might try to pluck one."

The image from the dragon sliced through him unexpectedly—Sara as a child, reaching for something. The idea of the dragon—Gemli's dragon watching her turned his stomach.

He shook the thought and asked instead.

"When did you realize I was a soldier?" he asked, though part of him regretted it.

She flinched. Her hands paused. She turned to rinse a cloth, and after a moment, answered without facing him.

"Pretty much when you almost broke my arm."

Chris exhaled, guilt wrapping around him like barbed wire.

"Sara, I'm so—"

"It was my fault," she interrupted. "I was rushing. I didn't think. You don't just jump on people like that... especially not dangerous ones."

Dangerous. He didn't mind being seen that way by his enemies. But from her—it pierced something deeper.

"Sara, I—"

He leaned down until she looked up. And when their eyes met, the hurt in hers stole the air from his lungs.

"I know you didn't mean it," she said. "You were just doing your job. I just... knew you could've killed me if you wanted."

She tried to smile, but it didn't reach her eyes.

Chris hated that look. Hated that it was there because of him.

Rafael had warned him. Daniel too. But hearing it... seeing it...

He reached for her hand. Held it carefully between both of his.

"Sara," he said, his voice low, "I will *never* hurt you.

I'm sorry for the confusion. And for frightening you. I should've known. There was no way you were an enemy."

She looked down at their hands, then back at him. Her fingers relaxed. Her lips curved—just a little.

"And," Chris added, "thank you... for saving my head back there."

Her cheeks flushed, and she glanced away. He ached to lift her chin, to see that smile again—but didn't.

"Did you get hurt?" he asked.

She shook her head. "Nope."

"Good," he said. "You shouldn't have to fear me. Not ever."

Her eyes sparkled when she met his gaze again, and Chris realized he had a favorite smile now—the one she gave him right then.

"I wish I could say the same to you," she said, "but we're out of sedatives."

Chris blinked. "Wait, what—?"

The second the towel touched his palm, pain exploded across his hand like fire laced with glass.

"Holy crap," he muttered, biting back a string of curses.

Healing wasn't pleasant. At times it felt like someone was driving splinters under his skin. Other moments it echoed the sensation of Gemli crushing his fingers beneath his boot. Not the worst pain Chris had ever felt —but it was constant, and it dragged on forever.

"You've gone through this?" he asked through clenched teeth.

"Not as bad," she replied. "Need a break?"

Chris shook his head just as footsteps approached.

Sara's eyebrows lifted. "I told you—it's noisy."

The door flew open.

"What the hell?" Donald marched in like he owned the place. "Where've you been? And what's all this?"

Sara ignored him. Chris didn't.

"Ah, Wilson finally got rid of you," he said.

Donald scoffed. "Ha-ha. Still not funny." He stepped up beside Sara and watched her for a beat before declaring, "It's pointless, girl. I already tried. Those cuts don't heal."

"That's why you don't mess with a glacier orchid," she replied.

Donald frowned. "You told her?"

"She figured it out," Chris said.

Donald blinked, then turned to Sara. "How?"

"They're distinct. Anyone who's ever had one remembers."

Donald climbed onto the bed beside Chris and gave Sara a look of practiced arrogance.

"I am the royal medic of the Valsing queen," he said smugly.

Sara's eyes widened, as if she had recognized his title.

"And," Donald continued. "I already told Chris he needs to get used to the scars."

"That must've been hard to hear," she replied, "but lucky for Chris... you're wrong."

Donald huffed. "I'm a Valsing. We're barely ever wrong."

"'Barely' leaves room for error," she said, calm and unbothered. "If you were sure, you'd have said 'never.'"

Chris smirked. He was proud of her.

Donald grumbled. "Fine. Let's see what you can do."

Sara poured something cool onto his palm. A wash of relief spread through his hand, soothing even the bruises on his fingers. When she finished, she gently wrapped it.

"I'll check them again tomorrow if you'd like," she said softly.

Chris didn't wait for her to ask and offer her his other hand. "All yours."

Donald stared at the finished bandage, dumbfounded. "No scars?"

"Not at all." Sara lifted her palm and although she didn't have tiny cuts, a single scar cut across it—deep and old.

Chris's stomach twisted. Only a sword could have caused that.

"Who knew a flower could be so dangerous?" Donald mused. "We use them in ceremonies. I almost gifted one once!"

"They're fine unless you hold them too long."

As she cleaned up, her voice shifted.

"Some say they have powers."

Donald rolled his eyes. "Like what?"

"Visions. Premonitions."

Chris held his breath.

"Premonitions?" Donald scoffed. "Is that how the zhortas see prophecy?"

"Some are born with that ability. Others are here to learn. The orchid isn't needed—but it's believed to help."

"So, it's just a rumor."

Sara shrugged. "They say it lets you talk to dragons, too."

Donald looked back at Chris, but he couldn't say anything.

A zhorta burst in. No footsteps anticipated his arrival. Something Chris didn't like at all.

"Sara! Dear gods, there you are."

He noticed Chris and Donald and forced a smile. "Dinner is ready. Follow the hallway. Your things are in your rooms."

He hooked his arm around Sara's and whispered urgently as they left.

"We need to talk, Sara. We need to tell her..."

Chris stood, gripping the hilt of his sword. He didn't like the way the zhorta looked at her.

"That was odd," Donald muttered.

They headed toward the dining hall. The scent of roasted vegetables and bread made Chris's stomach growl.

"Chris?" Sara's voice stopped him.

He turned—and nearly bumped into her. Her blue eyes searched his face.

"I forgot about our silent shoes," she said with a soft smile. "You'll get used to it. I assume this is yours?"

She held out a small brass compass—his father's.

His heart clenched as he took it, brushing her fingers just like in the dream.

Sara studied his face. For a second, he thought —*hoped*—that she recognized him.

"I have to go," she said, stepping away.

Chris nodded.

But then she turned back.

And smiled.

That smile.

The one he'd missed for years.

The one that made it hurt more that she didn't remember.

Because deep down... he knew it was his fault.

CHAPTER THIRTY

Only ruins and ashes remained from the once-great city that had symbolized human dominion and pride. Fire had consumed everything within its ancient stone walls. Even the royal castle—where Murllen, King Leonard III, and Gemli had once schemed—now lay in blackened rubble.

Murllen couldn't be more pleased.

Pockets of survivors still hid in scattered shelters, but in his mind, he had already won the war. All that remained was to claim Hune as his.

"A beautiful view," he muttered, watching from his camp as Gemli and several reisers departed. His city. His victory.

For a moment, unease curled in his gut. Gemli wasn't supposed to be there. But the message he'd delivered from Reign Mountain had been too important to ignore.

Weeks ago, Murllen and the sorcerer had suspected King Leonard III was planning a betrayal. Gemli had confirmed it. The king had hoped his First Guard would reach the zhortas, probably the only hope for humans—a naïve move that backfired when the young commander disobeyed and ordered the guard to stay behind to defend Tundra's civilians.

Murllen had considered traveling to the forest himself. But fortunately, Gemli's hatred of the zhortas made that unnecessary.

Just days ago, another report arrived—this time from Colonel Hayden Green. His reisers had successfully captured the cowardly First Guard, the remnants of Tundra's army, and the king himself. They were on their way to the fortress now.

Chris Riddley had unwittingly proven useful. Gemli loathed him, which only made Murllen more confident the sorcerer would tie up the loose end himself.

Reign Mountain had been the site of Murllen's transformation into a full reiser. Gemli had performed the ritual. According to the sorcerer, to preserve the balance of Hune, he needed to leave an option to destroy his work. Balance was primordial in a land founded in magic.

Murllen saw it as a safety net, a way for Gemli to eliminate him, but he remained unconcerned. A cursed saber hidden somewhere in Hune that only a specific person could use wasn't an easy condition to meet. Also, the identity and location of that person weren't a mystery to him.

Thinking of her always returned him to thoughts of his brother—Landford White, colonel of Laconia. The only person Murllen had ever loved.

It was Landford who'd first brought him into the

army, who taught him to fight for what he believed in. But they never believed in the same things.

Landford had tolerated Murllen's brutal methods. He even used them when it suited his needs. But once Gemli entered the picture, Landford had tried to stop them.

That betrayal had hurt. And Landford paid for it in blood.

The only lingering regret Murllen had was that one —his brother's death, but his brother had given him no choice.

Then came the final insult: the Great Wizard choosing Landford's infant daughter as the saber's destined wielder.

For years, Murllen listened to Gemli's advice and let her live. He didn't want the Great Wizard choosing someone else. But now, he had finally tricked the sorcerer that night and convinced him there was no danger anymore. They were the new rulers of Hune, and no one could stop them. Her life was a liability they didn't need. His niece would die, and knowing Gemli, he felt sorry for her.

When the valsings arrived near midnight, Murllen's reisers stood back as ordered—armed and holding their strikes.

Colonel Green had barely left the fortress when word came from the north: the valsing king requested an audience. Murllen had expected more resistance from their people, not an offer of alliance.

Then the valsings parted, and King Orson emerged.

"General Murllen," the little man said with grandeur.

"An honor to meet the reiser who conquered the human race."

Murllen almost laughed. "King Orson, I presume?"

"Yes, indeed!" Orson grinned wide, his jewels gleaming in the firelight.

The valsing king was half Murllen's height but twice as dramatic, with silver-threaded robes and finely styled graying hair. Behind him, a nervous attendant stepped forward, holding two packages.

"My gifts to mark the occasion," Orson said, waving a hand. "A meeting of such consequence must be honored."

The packages were opened. The first revealed a black sword—sleek, perfectly balanced, engraved with elegant patterns.

"My own design," Orson said proudly. "The etchings keep it sharp, absorb shock, and prevent light reflection —perfect for night strikes. I call it *Nocturne*."

Murllen tested the blade. It moved like smoke in his hands. Deadly and beautiful.

"I'm almost moved," Murllen said, handing it off to a reiser. "Almost."

The second gift was a bottle of deep red wine.

"A vintage worthy of kings and conquerors alike. You do drink, I hope?"

"Absolutely," Murllen replied, gesturing Orson into the nearest structure—one of the few shelters standing.

"Apologies for the setting," Murllen said. "My soldiers burned the city to the ground."

"I never liked the architecture anyway," Orson replied with a shrug.

Once seated, Orson finally dropped the small talk. "Some in my community are making foolish choices," he said. "Including my ex-wife."

Murllen raised a brow. "This is about a divorce?"

"No, no. Well... partly." Orson chuckled, and took a long sip of his wine. "Forgive me. Talking about my ex-wife is a good reason to drink...heavily."

Murllen chuckled and toasted for that. He didn't have or care for a relationship. Another reason he liked the reiser's ways more. Still, he could drink in the name of the futility of others.

"Our community got divided into two sections. Vanessa rules one, or pretends to."

Murllen knew that already, but he nodded.

"As things go, and by several arrangements, she ended up with our best space designers. The ones that can build amazing shelters or tents, which is very important in our lifestyle, but not as relevant as my artefact designers."

Murllen raised his eyebrows. "Don't you want to live in a comfortable place?"

"I do!" Orson said. "But I am not picky. A dry and warm tent is enough. On the other hand, better and more advanced personal items surround me, like cups, bags, swords, weapons. You figure!"

Murllen's interest grew.

"Ex-wives! They do everything to bother you, even after you leave them." Orson took another long sip and licked his lips. "A few weeks ago, I heard that Vanessa joined the war, and not on the winning side."

That was news.

"Listen, Murllen, she is a problem. That is the reason I am here. To be by your side."

Murllen smiled and shook his head. "Orson, I don't want to get in the middle of any marital issues. I'm sure you notice, I'm very busy with a war here."

For the first time, Orson's expression turned serious, and he sat up straight, leaving his cup on the table.

"I know you are already winning. Help must appear pointless at this stage. And I am certain you wonder how someone like me, compared to someone like you, could serve as support. But I am sure you have allies...now."

Murllen stopped smiling and set down his cup. "I don't have a problem with my allies, Orson. I have everything where it needs to be."

"Of course! But like in any other powerful arrangement, things change once you achieve your goal, and with these changes, most of your allies may...let's just say they may gain other motivations."

Orson brought a good point. Leonard had already tried to betray him, and he didn't trust either of his other two allies that much.

"Orson," he said, "if you want to be part of this, a nice sword and a good wine help, but it's not enough."

"Absolutely!" Orson said. "In fact, let me start with history. Centuries ago, when every race started their own way and Hune was not at all what it is now, we valsings helped you reisers to survive the curse that the High Council and the gods put upon you."

Murllen sat back and looked at Orson. He had no way to corroborate his story since he hadn't been born as a reiser, but it was worth a listen.

"The reisers made some bad choices that irritated those superior bastards. They condemned your race to live in the worst part of Hune and made you weak against the land. The valsings felt empathy for your race and helped. We designed the amazing armor that you are wearing right now. The High Council stopped us before we could give you tools and weapons to survive."

"Let me guess," Murllen said, "they thought the reisers could become dangerous?"

"Yes!" Orson said. "But it was pointless. You have the instincts anyway."

The black sword came to Murllen's mind. It was a magnificent weapon. If he ended up at odds with Gemli, it would be wise to have the best defense.

"All of this is interesting," Murllen said. "Rather, motivating. But, how far will you go in this war? Treason is something I don't take lightly."

Orson nodded.

"In this moment, half of my people are committing treason. It hurts me, Murllen, and I will do anything to correct that."

"Good. You need to make sure they get what they deserve."

Orson smiled, but this time the dreadful and sinister craving in his eyes allowed Murllen to see another side of the valsing.

"The valsing punishment for treason involves a fair trial, where we listen to the other—"

"Orson, you are missing out on this one." Murllen took a sip of wine. "Tell me, is there anything that your moronic ex-wife could say that will change your mind?"

The king shook his head and raised his cup, pleased. "Then, death to all of our traitors."

"Now my question," Murllen said. "What do you want from the reisers?"

Orson choked on his drink.

"Well, I was hoping your reisers could help us in that quest," Orson said. "My valsings are not warriors."

"Consider it done."

"Good," Orson said. "I need to make sure Vanessa gets what she deserves very slowly. I would also like your pardon for the other half of my community, so we can work together for the best future of Hune."

Murllen knew Orson's type. They liked to take advantage of the weak under the strong's protection. In a word, he was a coward, but a smart coward.

"Then let's drink to our new agreement and make sure we leave with some good company in the morning."

Orson's skin turned pale. "Are you coming?"

"Well, of course! I wouldn't miss the opportunity to use my new sword!"

EPILOGUE

Gemli stared at the distance, satisfied with the view in front of him. The high trees of the Soto Forest were a sight that marked the beginning of the new era in Hune. Everything was proceeding as he'd foreseen.

The reisers were good soldiers, but the humans had a formal army for a longer time. Without Gemli's help, his current ally would have never gotten that far. They wouldn't have even secured Laconia, and the humans would have found their fortress. He didn't need credit for it though. In time, it would all be worth it.

Like he predicted, his alliance would not survive the war.

King Leonard the III made the first mistake. He had never been the smartest, and his attempt at treachery was careless and ridiculous. It didn't take more than a minute of consideration to be certain that Christopher Riddley would have never left Tundra unprotected. The guard reaching the zhortas to protect them was as impossible as it was to defeat him.

He was glad to have met Christopher though. He would help him achieve the real goal of the war, why he created Murllen, and the way he balanced his existence.

The gods' saber was his deepest desire. With it, he could create his own world, under his own conditions. The problem was the sword's curse. To solve that, Gemli created an evil dangerous enough to force Hune and the Great Wizard to use their own laws in his favor.

Only the saber had the power to destroy Murllen, and just one person could free its curse. He knew the Great Wizard and his favoritism for Colonel Landford White. It was just natural he used the colonel's daughter to avenge his murder. It was a beautiful coincidence she was Murllen's niece.

Now, on his way to Saint Peter's Abbey, a place that saw him grow, he would make sure Commander Christopher Riddley and Sara White left intact, and find the saber for him. He would use her to free the sword to make it his.

A wide smile brightened his expression.

Murllen believed he tricked him into killing his niece and felt sorry for the reiser. He had always been a puppet in the show and did not understand how little he or the other two allies cared for him.

As soon as they won the war, Gemli had planned to allow the real leader of the reisers, Colonel Hayden Green, to kill Murllen with the saber. Then he would show the reisers who was in charge of Hune.

As for the third party in the alliance, Gemli had a

personal plan for him. For years the sorcerer had left him just at the edge of his plan, letting him believe he was untouchable. Now it was the time to confront him. Patience had always been one of Gemli's virtues, along with a very long memory.

I HOPE YOU ENJOY THE BOOK. IF you want to learn how everything started, you can read the Free prequel here:

BOOK 2 EXCERPT:

SHADOWS OF TOMORROW

"You need to go back," he said. "Warn the others."

"No." Her voice shook. "I'm not leaving you. If they see you—"

Another root pulled violently from the earth—and behind it, she saw them.

Dark silhouettes emerged through the undergrowth. Hundreds. Twice her height. Clad in dripping armor so thick it looked alive, like it had grown over their bodies instead of being forged. It reeked of rot. Of death. A thick ooze clung to them—flesh? Decay? She didn't know.

The dissected arm Lily had shown her rose in her mind like a scream.

Daniel saw them too—but his gaze returned to her instantly.

"We don't have much time. You know this forest better than anyone. Wilson and I will draw them off, take a different route—buy you minutes, maybe more."

"No, you can't stay here! They'll—"

"Go, Sara," Wilson said. He leaned in and kissed the side of her head. "You need to reach them. That's the only thing that matters now."

Tears stung her eyes, and her body started to tremble.

"Sara," Daniel said, firmer this time. "Only you can get there in time."

Continued here:

Acknowledgments

For your patience, support, belief in the cause, staying with me and tolerating the time that I took away from all of you to sit down and write. During these years, I learned so much from all of you. For listening to my stories, complaints, and successes. For your help and critiques, for all of these and more.

To Each one of you, who loves to read mysteries and took the time to read my take on them. My amazing coaches; Scarlett and Bryan, my mystery group friends, Mom, Gloria, Teddy, Josephine, and You up there...

Thank you.

ABOUT THE AUTHOR

Hi, I'm Monica Red, and I have a passion for forging worlds where magic collides with destiny, and adventure is never far from danger—or from the heart. From sweeping romantasy to daring steampunk adventures, my stories are filled with peril, secrets, and bonds strong enough to change the course of kingdoms.

My greatest inspiration is my daughter, whose courage and imagination remind me why stories of love and resilience matter. At home, I live with two loyal dogs, five outspoken birds, and a husband who insists that golf and sports are the only safe escapes from the battles, quests, and rebellions unfolding in my head.

When I'm not writing fantasy, I step into another realm of storytelling under the name Montie Red, where cozy mysteries bring twists, secrets, and the occasional murder to small-town life. Whether the journey is through enchanted forests, skies filled with airships, or quiet streets hiding dangerous secrets, I'm always chasing the spark of a good story.

Thank you for traveling these worlds with me—arm yourself with courage (and maybe a little tea), and let's embark on the next great adventure together.

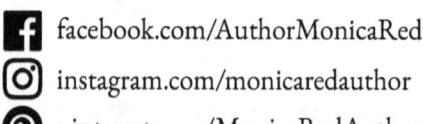

facebook.com/AuthorMonicaRed

instagram.com/monicaredauthor

pinterest.com/MonicaRedAuthor